Eric
Wilder

Night
People

Gondwana Press
Edmond, Oklahoma

Other books by Eric Wilder

French Quarter Mystery Series
Big Easy, Book 1
City of Spirits, Book 2
Primal Creatures, Book 3
Black Magic Woman, Book 4
River Road, Book 5
Sisters of the Mist, Book 6
Garden of Forbidden Secrets, Book 7
New Orleans Dangerous, Book 8
Cycles of the Moon, Book 9
Half Past Midnight, Book 10
Thief of Souls, Book 11
Krewe of Illusion, Book 12
Wild Magnolias, Book 13
Paranormal Cowboy Series
Ghost of a Chance, Book 1
Bones of Skeleton Creek, Book 2
Blink of an Eye, Book 3
Oyster Bay Mystery Series
Oyster Bay Boogie, Book 1
Oyster Bay Tango, Book 2
Oyster Bay Two Step, Book 3
Oyster Bay Limbo, Book 4
Standalone Novels
Of Love and Magic
Diamonds in the Rough
Anthologies and Cookbooks
Murder Etouffee
Over the Rainbow
Lily's Little Cajun Cookbook

© 2025 by Gary Pittenger

Gondwana Press
1802 Canyon Park Cir. Ste C
Edmond, OK 73013

Front Cover by Gondwana Graphics

ISBN: 978-1-946576-22-4

Acknowledgments

I wish to thank Donald Yaw and Linda Hartle Bergeron for beta-reading, editing, and providing valuable input on timeline and character development.

for Marilyn

The scariest monsters are the ones that lurk within our souls.

— Edgar Allan Poe

Night People

A novel by
Eric Wilder

Prologue

The torches lining the cavernous chamber cast flickering shadows on the ancient stone walls, their glow revealing the glitter of gold accents carved into the black marble floor beneath the assembled disciples. At the center of the room stood a circular altar of obsidian, etched with sinuous runes that seemed to shift under the wavering light.

Around the altar, the thirteen chosen stood, stripped to the waist, their pale skin gleaming with cold sweat in the dim light. The air was heavy with the acrid scent of burning incense and something metallic—the unmistakable tang of blood.

At the head of the altar stood Athénaïs de Montespan, her silken hair cascading over her bare shoulders. Though her cheeks were flushed with fever, her beauty remained undiminished. She swayed, clutching the altar's edge for support, her eyes darting toward Louis XIV, who sat upon a gilded throne, watching the proceedings with an expression that wavered between divine authority and human desperation.

Behind the altar loomed Etienne du Clairvaux, the Sun King's enigmatic court magician, robed in black velvet trimmed with gold thread. His long fingers clutched a chalice of dark liquid that seemed almost alive, swirling and rippling despite the chamber's stillness. His other hand held a gleaming iron needle, its tip glowing faintly with a crimson hue.

"Tonight," Etienne said, his voice deep and resonant, "you are no longer men or women of mortal consequence. You shall transcend death, cast aside frailty, and take upon yourselves the eternal covenant. Through pain, through blood, through this mark, you shall become immortal."

He stepped toward the first disciple, a burly man who flinched as the glowing needle touched his chest. The room filled with the sizzle of seared flesh, mingling with the man's stifled groan. The others watched in silence, their faces tight with anticipation and fear as the magician's hand worked unnaturally, carving an intricate sigil into the man's flesh. The symbol—an ornate drop of blood framed by scrollwork—shimmered briefly as the final stroke was completed, then sank into his skin, darkening into a permanent mark.

The disciple gasped, clutching at his chest as his body convulsed, the veins beneath his skin turning black for a heartbeat before fading. He fell to his knees, breathing hard, and looked up at Etienne with crimson-tinged eyes.

"It is done," the magician said coldly, moving to the next.

The process continued, and each chosen member received the Crimson Sigil. With every mark, the air in the chamber seemed to grow colder, the shadows deeper. Finally, Etienne reached Athénaïs. She was trembling now, her lips pale and eyes fever-bright, yet she held her ground.

"Are you ready, my lady?" Etienne asked, his voice softer now, almost reverent.

"I will endure it," she said, her voice steady despite her apparent weakness.

Louis XIV leaned forward on his throne, his knuckles white against the gilded armrests as Etienne pressed the glowing needle to her chest, just above her heart. Athénaïs inhaled sharply as the needle bit into her flesh, the scent of burning skin filling the air. The sigil glowed brighter than ever before, pulsing as though alive. As the final stroke was completed, Athénaïs cried out—not in pain, but in a voice that seemed to echo with ancient power.

Athénaïs's body convulsed, her head thrown back as the veins of her neck darkened, and her eyes turned to glowing rubies. She hovered between life and death, her beauty ethereal and terrifying. Then she collapsed against the altar, gasping for air as her transformation completed.

Etienne raised the chalice above his head. "The blood of eternity binds us. Drink and seal the covenant."

The disciples approached one by one, each drinking deeply from the chalice. When it was Athénaïs's turn, Louis XIV stepped forward, guiding the chalice to her lips. Her eyes met his as

3

she drank, her expression unreadable, a mixture of gratitude and something darker, more knowing.

As the last disciples partook, the runes etched into the obsidian altar flared to life, bathing the chamber in a crimson glow. A guttural hum emanated from the stone as if the earth acknowledged the birth of the Ordre du Sang.

Etienne lowered the chalice, his voice rising in a chant, the language arcane and guttural. The disciples joined in, their voices blending into a chilling harmony. As the final words were spoken, the sigils on their chests ignited, burning like embers before fading into their skin, leaving no trace but the mark itself.

The chamber fell silent. Louis XIV stood, his gaze sweeping over his creations with pride and unease.

"It is done," Etienne said, his voice trembling slightly. "The Ordre du Sang is born."

Outside, a wolf's distant howl echoed through the night's stillness, a harbinger of the dark legacy unleashed by the man the world knew as the Sun King.

Chapter 1

French Quarter Fest had finally ended. All the tourists had gone home, and Bertram's Bar on Chartres Street was empty of customers as I sat at the zinc-topped counter talking with the Cajun bartender.

Bertram had dark hair, eyes, and a Gallic nose. He didn't like it when his bar was empty and wasn't happy about his lack of business. His frown disappeared when someone we knew entered the front door.

"Well, look what the cat drug in," he said in his inimitable Cajun drawl.

It was our close friend, Eddie Toledo. I hadn't seen him in over a year since he'd been fired as the Assistant Federal District Attorney of New Orleans and had moved to an island south of the city. Eddie had fallen for the gorgeous daughter of the local mob boss, Frankie Castellano. The Feds fired him when he and Josie Castellano became engaged.

The wedding of the year never occurred. Eddie's aversion to commitment caused him to leave Josie standing alone at the altar. Seemingly none the worse for wear, he strolled to the bar and pumped my hand.

"Wyatt Thomas, my favorite human being," he said. "How the hell are you?"

I smiled and said, "Doing well, Eddie. And you?"

Eddie reached over the bar and shook hands with Bertram. It's been too long," he said.

Eddie was usually the picture of a successful lawyer, good-looking, with dark hair and eyes, moussed hair, an expensive pinstriped suit, and polished brogans. Today was different. He'd let his hair grow over his ears, and the sun had lightened it to brown. Instead of a suit and tie, he wore khakis, a colorful tropical shirt, and sandals.

When he saw me staring, he said, "My new persona."

"Suits you," I said. "I like it."

"I haven't been away that long, Bertram," he said. "Did you forget I'm a scotch drinker?"

Bertram was already pouring Eddie a drink from a Monkey Shoulder bottle he kept under the bar.

"I ain't forgot my best customer," he said. "What brings you back to the Big Easy?"

"Problems," Eddie said.

"What problems?" Bertram asked. "Not getting enough wild sex on Oyster Island?"

Eddie grinned and said, "Worry about your own sex life. That's not my problem."

Eddie sat on the stool beside me and sipped his scotch.

"You're looking good," I said. "Island life must be agreeing with you."

"Now that I've settled my differences with Frankie, they are," he said.

Eddie owned the Majestic, a Prohibition-era hotel on Oyster Island. He'd gotten the property from Frankie Castellano. Frankie and his wife, Adele, had hoped that giving Eddie control of the hotel would result in a reconciliation between

Eddie and Frankie's daughter, Josie. It hadn't happened.

Josie was a gorgeous, financially successful, and brilliant woman. I had always kept my distance because she strongly resembled Desire, the former love of my life.

"I hear you now own the Majestic outright," I said.

Eddie slugged his scotch and returned his glass to Bertram for a refill.

"Frankie's on board now with me owning the Majestic. That's not my problem."

"Then what is?" I asked

"We're all ears," Bertram said. "Tell us about it."

"My sister Gia called a few days ago. First time I'd talked to her in a year. Her daughter, my niece, left home a while back. Gia hasn't heard from her in a month and fears she's dead."

"What's your niece's name?" I asked.

"Eliza."

"Any idea where she went?" I asked.

"I think she's right here in the Big Easy," Eddie said.

A sudden spring rainstorm had blown up from the Gulf and began pounding the front window. When lightning flashed, all the lights flickered and then went dark.

Bertram grumbled and said, "Here we go again." He headed to his suite of rooms to start his generator. "I'll be back. Help yourself to the bottle."

"Why do you think Eliza is in New Orleans?"

Thunder shook the rafters as Eddie topped up his glass from the bottle of scotch.

"Long story," he said.

"It's raining outside, and I have no place to go. Tell me."

"Eliza was a graduate student in anthropology at Princeton. She's uber-intelligent and had a full ride."

"Damn!" I said. "She must be smart."

"Gia's phone call upset me. When I got Sis calmed down, I called Eliza's thesis advisor. He told me a few things."

"Like what?"

"He said she was researching local folklore, specifically the rumored coven of vampires who thrive in the French Quarter."

"Just because something in New Orleans interested her doesn't mean she came here," I said.

"Gia found an AMTRAK schedule in Eliza's room. She'd highlighted the route from New Jersey to New Orleans in yellow and circled New Orleans in red. Law enforcement friends confirmed she'd purchased a one-way train ticket to the Big Muddy. She's here, I know it."

"Sounds like it," I said.

"One more thing. Eliza scribbled something at the bottom of the AMTRAK schedule."

"What?" I asked.

"La Porte Mystique."

I glanced at Bertram and said, "It's French for The Mystic Gate."

"I checked it on the Internet," Eddie said. "It's a botanica on the edge of the Quarter that sells voodoo paraphernalia."

"Interesting," I said. "What other information did the Internet provide?"

"A woman named Mambo Elzora owns it. She's a practicing voodoo mambo."

"Too bad Mama Mulate isn't here to ask what she knows about her," I said.

"Where is Mama?"

"She and her beau, Jake Huntington, left earlier today for a few weeks in Tulsa. I'll call her

later and ask what she knows about Mambo
Elzora."

"Then you'll help me?"

"You knew I would," I said. "The French
Quarter's only a single square mile. If she's here,
I'll find her for you."

"Thanks, Buddy," Eddie said. "I can always
count on you."

The rain was drumming a steady tempo on the
awning over the sidewalk. Bertram had started his
generator, and the lights flickered and popped on.
Bertram returned to the bar and topped up Eddie's
scotch.

"Thanks," he said. "I needed a drink in the
worst way."

"How long you going to be in town?" Bertram
said.

"Until I find Eliza," he said.

"Where you staying?" Bertram asked.

"Josie owns a house abutting the yacht harbor
on the West End. She's letting me stay there."

"You and Josie a number again?" Bertram
asked.

"Never going to happen," Eddie said. "She's
back with her old boyfriend, the father of her son
Jojo."

"Where did he come from?" Bertram asked.

"Florida. His name is Carlos Palacio. His dad
was Frankie's best friend until they had a falling
out. Carlos and Josie grew up together. She never
told him about Jojo."

"I'm happy for them," I said. "Are they getting
married?"

"One little problem," Eddie said. "Carlos is
already married and has kids."

"That always puts a cramp on the situation."

"I hear those houses by the yacht harbor are
high-dollar," Bertram said.

Eddie smiled and said, "I didn't ask."

"Let's get back to your niece. Do you have a picture of her?" I said.

Eddie thumbed through his wallet and produced a photo of him, Gia, and his niece. I gazed at it. Eddie's sister, Gia, was attractive. Her lightened hair, cut in a short bob, made it easy to see the family resemblance. In the picture, Eliza was standing between them.

Eliza was a striking young woman with dark hair that fell in loose waves past her shoulders. Even in the small photo, I could see her eyes were a deep brown, almost black, the freckles dusting her nose and cheeks contrasting with her olive complexion.

"She's a runner," Eddie said. "We competed in a 10-K when she was fifteen."

"And?"

"She beat my best time by two minutes."

Eliza wore jeans and a muscle shirt, and I could see how toned she was.

"She looks athletic," I said.

"Don't get any ideas," Eddie said. "She's my niece and way too young for you."

"You can trust me," I said with a grin. "Besides, you're like the pot calling the kettle black."

"And that's what's worrying me," he said.

"Your sis is hot," I said.

"Don't go there," Eddie said. "She's happily married."

"Relax," I said. "She's half a country away. Tell me about Eliza."

"Like what?"

"Anything about her that people I question might have noticed. It's important," I said.

"She has a style of her own, a mix of practicality and subtle flair. She usually wears jeans, casual tops, and leather jackets."

"Good," I said. "Give me more."

"She's religious and wears a gold crucifix necklace and a small bracelet with charms of saints given to her by her mother."

"What else?" I asked.

"Eliza is independent, curious, and bold, traits that sometimes put her at odds with her family," Eddie said.

"How so?"

"She's fiercely loyal to those she loves, especially Gia and me. She calls us her pillars of strength."

Bertram was polishing a glass, and Eddie frowned when he said, "Heaven help us!"

"She inherited Gia's good looks and charm but with an added layer of quiet determination. She's intelligent and resourceful, often finding herself in situations where her sharp mind gets her both into—and out of—trouble."

"A devout Catholic?"

"Yes," Eddie said. "She's less strict than her mom. To Gia's chagrin, Eliza often questioned the boundaries between good and evil."

"This is all helpful," I said. "Keep talking."

"She's compassionate but has a rebellious streak. While she respects her family's values, she has her own ideas about life and freedom. She's perceptive and empathetic, often picking up on emotions others try to hide."

Eddie shook his head and sipped his scotch.

"What?" I said.

"What makes her disappearance all the more unsettling—something about it feels out of character, as if she was on the cusp of uncovering something she shouldn't have."

"You're on a roll," I said. "Give me more."

"She once told me that anthropology fascinated her because of its connection to different cultures, stories, and mysteries."

"That's it," I said.

"What's it?" Eddie said.

"Maybe Eliza's curiosity led her to explore the hidden corners of New Orleans, digging into the city's underbelly and the lore of the French Quarter," I said.

"You think my description helps?" Eddie said.

"Immensely," I said. "Now, I know who I'm looking for."

Eliza's disappearance has rocked the family. Gia is heartbroken, and I'm determined to find her at any cost."

"We'll find her," I said.

The rain had intensified, buoyed by yet another hurricane in the Gulf heading for Florida. Though I felt bad for the Sunshine State, I thanked Heaven that it wasn't another Katrina we had to face.

"The house Josie is lending me has two bedrooms and a loft," Eddie said. "Shut down the bar, and you and Wyatt stay with me. There's a nearby lounge with plenty of single women. We'll have a blast."

"Not me," Bertram said. "Got customers to attend to."

Eddie glanced around the empty bar and said, "Oh yeah? Where are they?"

"They'll be back," Bertram said. "You two have fun. I'll take care of that mangy cat for you."

"Sounds inviting," I said. "I'd like to check out La Porte Mystique first thing tomorrow."

"I'll take you," Eddie said. "I want to see the place myself."

"It's raining," I said. "I was thinking of hitting the sack early."

"Get a grip," Eddie said. "This is my first night back in the Big Easy, and I need a drinking partner."

"Those days are in the rearview mirror for me," I said.

"Bullshit!" Eddie said. "Go pack an overnight bag, and let's go. We haven't terrorized the Big Easy in over a year, and I'm buying."

Someone we knew entered the front door, overhearing the last part of our conversation. It was Josie Castellano.

"If you are going partying, take me with you," she said.

Josie looked gorgeous in a light blue cocktail dress that was so short it highlighted her world-class legs. Her skirt, high heels, and black mesh stockings indicated she was ready for a night on the town. The problem was that the rain had soaked her, and she was dripping on the oiled wooden floor.

"Josie," Eddie said. "What are you doing here? Did you and Carlos break up?"

"Carlos is married," she said. "Our relationship was never meant to be."

It was easy to tell by Josie's slurred words that she'd already tipped a few. She hugged Eddie and then engaged in a sensual embrace with me, which lasted a bit too long. Eddie noticed.

Bertram climbed under the bar, grabbed Josie's shoulders, and directed her toward his living quarters in the back of the bar.

"You got to get out of those wet clothes before you catch a bad cold," he said.

Josie hugged him and said, "Bertram, I didn't know you cared."

Bertram returned alone from his living quarters.

13

"I showed her the bathroom. She's taking a warm shower," he said.

Josie smiled when she returned to the bar thirty minutes later, dressed in a terrycloth robe and drying her damp hair with a towel.

"Thanks, Bertram," she said. "I didn't realize how uncomfortable I was until I got my clothes off and stepped under the hot water in the shower."

"My guest bedroom is vacant, and Josie's staying the night. Eddie, you can sleep on my couch. It's too nasty out there. We can all drink here, and I'll even fix a midnight snack for us."

I could tell by Eddie's sour expression that he wasn't happy with the idea. Even with wet hair, Josie looked enticing.

She grabbed his arm and said, "Please, Eddie, it'll be like a slumber party."

"Okay," he said. "Are you still lending me your lake house?"

"If you let me come with you," Josie said. "I love the place and stay there every time I'm in town, though it's not nearly often enough."

"I'm not so sure that's a good idea," he said.

"Nonsense," she said. "Wyatt can come too. We'll have a blast."

"What are you drinking, pretty lady?" Bertram asked.

Josie smiled and said, "Cuba libre."

Bertram was already reaching for a bottle of rum. "You got it," he said.

"How did you know I was here?" Eddie asked.

Eddie gave me another dirty look when she said, "I didn't."

Chapter 2

I rented my little apartment from Bertram at the top of the stairs. When I returned to the bar the following morning, the sunlight filtered through the front windows, bouncing off the rows of liquor bottles and casting golden streaks on the dark wood.

I leaned against the counter as Bertram served up a plate of bacon, eggs, and grits, the scent of butter and spices filling the air. Josie sat across from me, her damp curls tucked behind her ears.

She wore one of Bertram's faded bar tee shirts, a size too big, with the sleeves rolled up to reveal her slender arms. She paired it with his old cargo shorts, which hung loosely on her hips, and flip-flops, which slapped against her feet as she fidgeted, looking at ease as if she owned the place.

Despite the casual clothes, Josie still had an allure. The morning light kissed her face, and her skin glowed even without a trace of makeup. Her eyes, a bit tired and still rimmed with the remnants of last night's mascara, locked onto mine for a moment.

"How did you get so wet last night?" I asked.

"I had a business meeting over dinner at Antoine's. Since I was so close to Bertram's, I decided to see who was there. The cabbie dropped me off on the wrong street."

"Bummer," I said.

She smiled and said, "It turned out all right."

Josie shook her head when I said, "You didn't know Eddie was here?"

I watched as she took a bite of the grits, her eyes fluttering in satisfaction.

"Best breakfast in the Quarter. Bertram, I swear I don't know how you do it."

Bertram chuckled from behind the bar, flipping another piece of bacon. "Trade secret, darling. But if I told you, I'd have to marry you."

Josie laughed, glanced sideways at me, and said, "Don't tempt me. My cooking skills aren't exactly keeping me out of trouble."

"So many of your family and friends are great cooks. It's a skill you don't need to have," I said.

"Eddie's passed out on Bertram's couch," she said. "What kind of trouble has he got himself into?"

"No trouble," I said. "His New Jersey niece is missing. He asked me to help him find her."

I nodded when she said, "His niece is lost somewhere in New Orleans?"

"The French Quarter, we think. Eliza arrived here by train on a one-way ticket. We have a single clue to check out. I'm going there after breakfast."

"Where?" she asked.

"A botanica on the edge of the French Quarter called La Porte Mystique."

I nodded again when she said, "The Mystic Gate."

"A voodoo woman named Madam Elzora runs the place. I need to speak with her."

"I want to go," Josie said.

"Hoping for some excitement?" I said.

"I'd love to come along."

"It'll probably be boring as hell."

Josie leaned back in her chair. "Oh, come on, Wyatt. You're going to some spooky voodoo shop in the Quarter. You know how much I love that kind of stuff."

Her enthusiasm lit up the room. "It's not exactly a tourist trip."

Josie batted her eyelashes. "You might need some help."

Bertram cut in, setting another plate down for me. "Or trouble? I think Wyatt's got enough of both already."

Josie crossed her arms and smiled. "I'm always trouble, you know that."

"Eddie wanted to come along. He might be jealous if you go with me?"

Josie scoffed. "Eddie has no right to be jealous. He forfeited it long ago."

"Right now, he's sleeping like a baby," Bertram said. "Take Josie with you and let Eddie sleep off whatever demons are bothering him."

"Listen to Bertram, and let me come with you. What could go wrong?"

"You name it," Bertram said, wiping his hands on a towel. "Cowboy doesn't deal in thunderstorms. Every time he gets involved in something, it turns into a full-blown hurricane."

"Good," Josie said. "I don't mind getting wet."

Last night's thunderstorm had blown over, replaced by dark clouds casting damp shadows over the French Quarter as Josie and I left Bertram's.

"Where is La Porte Mystique located?" she asked.

"On St. Louis, not far from N. Rampart," I said.

"Good place for a voodoo shop, near the St. Louis No. 1 Cemetery."

"Same thing I was thinking," I said.

17

Though it wasn't raining, the sky looked dark and threatening. Few tourists braved the humidity as we hurried to our destination, hoping not to get wet.

"There it is," Josie said.

La Porte Mystique sat inconspicuously at the edge of the French Quarter, half-hidden beneath the drooping branches of an ancient oak. When we entered its creaky wooden door, a tarnished brass bell chimed. The air inside was thick with incense, herbs, and something more arcane—a blend of earthiness and the metallic tang of ritual.

Candles of varying sizes and colors flickered on every available surface, casting dancing shadows across the shelves. The botanica was crammed with curiosities: jars of dried herbs, vials of mysterious powders, and shelves lined with carved wooden figures of spirits, saints, and loa.

A large counter at the back was covered with more paraphernalia—tarot decks, bones, and bundles of sage. Behind the counter hung a black curtain leading to a back room. A faint drumming sound emanated from beyond the curtain as though an unseen ceremony was perpetually underway.

Josie whirled around when someone or something said, "Hello."

A cage in the corner of the shop contained a raven watching us. Someone appeared from behind the black curtain and spoke to the raven in Creole.

"Kiyès li ye, bèl mwen?"

Josie glanced at me and said, "What did she say?"

"I believe it's Haitian Creole for, 'Who is it, my pretty,'" I said.

"Pwoblèm," the bird said.

I nodded when Josie asked, "Did he just reply to her in Creole?"

The woman who'd appeared from behind the curtain approached us with a smile before I could answer.

"I'm Madam Elzora," she said. "Welcome to La Porte Mystique. Calypso speaks several languages."

"Calypso?" I said.

"My regal raven."

Madam Elzora was a striking figure with a commanding presence that felt both ethereal and intimidating. She had deep ebony skin, her age difficult to determine, as her features carried a timeless quality—her eyes sharp and observant, yet framed by laugh lines that hinted at both wisdom and mischief.

Madam Elzora's long braided hair was adorned with colorful beads and small charms that rattled as she moved. She wore a flowing dress in vibrant hues—indigo, crimson, and gold—that seemed to shift in color with the flicker of candlelight.

Multiple necklaces hung around her neck: bones, amulets, and even small bottles of mysterious powders. Herbs or ash dusted her hands, and her fingernails painted a glossy black.

"I'm Wyatt, and this is Josie," I said.

"Is there something I can show you? A potion, perhaps, or maybe a special amulet?"

"We're looking for a missing person," I said.

Madam Elzora's eyes blinked, and she said, "I see. Who is it you seek?"

"A young woman named Eliza." I showed her the picture I'd gotten from Eddie. "Have you seen her?"

Madam Elzora studied the picture and said, "Many people visit my shop. Was she here for a particular reason?"

Madam Elzora smiled when I said, "Don't know." She was a student pursuing a degree in anthropology, a field that fascinated her because of its connection to different cultures, stories, and mysteries."

"Many people seek the mysteries of the French Quarter," Madam Elzora said.

"This curiosity led her to explore the hidden corners of New Orleans, digging into the city's underbelly and the lore of the Quarter. It was during one of these explorations that we believe she disappeared," I said.

"I seem to remember the young woman in the photo," Madam Elzora said. "Describe her to me; perhaps it will jog my memory."

"Eliza is slender but athletic and likely to wear fitted jeans, casual tops, and leather jackets. Her favorite jewelry is a delicate gold crucifix necklace and a small bracelet with saints' charms."

"Ah, yes," Madam Elzora said. "I remember her. She was looking for something."

"Why did she think you might know the answer?" I asked.

You know what La Porte Mystique means?" she asked.

"The Mystic Gate?" I said.

Madam Elzora didn't reply to my response. Instead, she said, "The young woman was here seeking specific information."

Madam Elzora smiled when Josie said, "What information?"

"Directions," she said.

"To where?" Josie asked.

"Depends," Madam Elzora said.

"On what?" Josie asked.

"All things have a price," Madam Elzora said.

Josie didn't miss a beat when she said, "Good, because I'm looking for something expensive. What do you have that fits the description?"

"Something as dangerous as it is beautiful. A crystal skull," Madam Elzora said.

"I like dangerous and beautiful," Josie said. "How much?"

"No money; a trade."

Madam Elzora smiled and rubbed her hands when Josie said, "May I see the skull?"

When Madam Elzora disappeared behind the black curtain, I said, "What's that all about?"

"She has valuable information for us but wants something in return," Josie said. "I'm giving it to her."

"How do you know?" I asked.

"I'm a woman. I know," she said.

Madam Elzora returned with a beautiful though grotesque crystal skull about the size of a grapefruit, flickers of light emanating from its inner veils.

"It's beautiful," Josie said.

"Carved from a single piece of vein quartz mined from an outcrop near an ancient Aztec temple," Madam Elzora said. "Not only is it beautiful and dangerous, it's also magical."

"How so?" Josie asked.

"Once you possess it, you'll find out," Madam Elzora said. "Your watch will work in exchange."

The voodoo woman smiled when Josie removed the expensive watch from her wrist and handed it to her.

"If the crystal skull is powerful and magical, why are you trading it?" I asked.

"The magical skull will eventually return to me. Until then, its power and magic is yours. Use it wisely."

21

"Now," Josie said. "Can you tell us what you know about Eliza?"

"The young woman you seek arrived at La Porte Mystique in search of something."

"What?" I asked.

"As I've already told you. Directions," Madam Elzora said.

"Where did she want to go?"

"Her desired destination requires a circuitous journey. I told her where to begin."

Josie and I shared a glance. "What destination was Eliza seeking?"

"The passage between day and night, darkness and light."

"Please explain," Josie said.

"The Quarter functions almost as two parallel worlds—one that tourists see during the day, full of musicians, colorful balconies, and lively street performers, and another at night, where the true 'Night People' emerge. Your young woman sought to visit the darkness."

"And?" I said.

"I provided a name," Madam Elzora said.

The old mambo nodded when I asked, "Can you share the name with us?"

"You will find a bar called After Midnight down a narrow alleyway cloaked by a canopy of creeping vines and gas lanterns that flicker in the shadows. True to its name, it doesn't open until midnight."

"Never heard of it," I said.

"It's near Pirate's Alley and caters to an eclectic crowd of night owls, locals, and mystics. Someone you meet on the way will tell you how to get there." Madam Elzora said.

"Who do we speak with when we reach the place?" I asked.

"Marceline, the bartender. Her dark eyes can see into your soul, and she will have answers to the questions you seek. If your questions are true, she'll direct you on the next leg of your journey."

"Will she speak with us?" I asked.

"She is a bartender. She'll talk to you."

I had more questions for Madam Elzora, but Josie grabbed my wrist and nodded toward the front door. As we exited La Porte Mystique and the door creaked shut behind us, Calypso, perched high above on the wrought iron balcony, ruffled her inky feathers and cocked her head. Her voice, low and husky, echoed through the still air.

> "Beneath the shroud of night's embrace,
> A house appears in a fleeting place.
> Its walls aglow, a beacon bright,
> A marvel born of shadow and light."

Chapter 3

When we exited La Porte Mystique, the weather was still dank and dreary. Josie had the heavy crystal skull in her arms.

"I'll carry it for you," I said.

"Thanks," she said. "I never realized how heavy a chunk of quartz could be."

"The metallic inclusions are probably lead," I said.

"They ought to be gold. The watch she took in trade cost me a cool ten grand."

"We can return and demand a refund," I said.

"No way. There's something about this monstrosity that makes me think I got the best end of the deal."

"You read the old woman better than me," I said.

"I don't believe she would have told us anything without the trade," Josie said.

"What do you make of her raven?" I asked.

Josie thought about it and said, "The bird can't be as smart as she seemed."

"Or as ominous," I said.

"What now?" Josie asked.

"Return to Bertram's. It's hours before midnight."

"What's your plan for After Midnight?" she asked.

"Check it out."

"I'm going," Josie said.

"Not a good idea."

"I won't get in the way."

"I'll let you know after gauging Eddie's pulse," I said.

"Eddie's only a friend," Josie said. "After what he pulled, that's all he'll ever be."

I didn't comment on Josie's assertion. It was raining when we reached the awning over Bertram's front door. Thunder shook the window. Despite the weather, the place was hopping. Eddie sat alone at the bar, and his frown when we joined him told us all we needed to know about his foul mood.

"You could have awakened me," he said.

"Bertram said you were sleeping like a baby. We decided not to disturb you," I said.

"You should have let me decide," he said.

"Give it up," I said. "We're back now."

Bertram saw us sitting at the bar and quickly mixed a martini for Josie and a glass of lemonade for me.

"How did it go?" he asked.

"Better than expected," I said. "We have a lead."

"Tell me," Eddie said.

Before I could answer, Mama Mulate and Jake Huntington hurried out of the rain and joined us at the bar. Mama knew Josie and Eddie, and I introduced them to Jake. Mama hadn't seen Eddie in over a year. While they were embracing and exchanging pleasantries, I quizzed Jake.

"I thought you were going to Tulsa," I said.

"Slight delay," he said. "A rotor problem on the chopper. It's at the airport being repaired."

"Uh oh," I said.

"No big deal. Colley could tell there was an imbalance and turned around before we'd gone fifty miles."

Mama squeezed Eddie's hand and said, "If not for the mechanical problem, I would have missed seeing you. What brings you to New Orleans?"

"My niece is missing," Eddie said. "What clues I had led me here."

"Oh no!" Mama said.

"Wyatt's helping me. He and Josie visited a botanica earlier today to check out our primary clue," Eddie said.

"Botanica?" Mama said.

"A place called La Porte Mystique," I said. "Are you familiar with it?"

Mama nodded and said, "It's rumored to be a gateway."

"Please explain," Josie said.

Josie and I exchanged glances when Mama said, "A door between planes of reality. The mambo who runs the place is the gatekeeper and rumored to be supernatural."

"You have to be kidding," Josie said.

"Madam Elzora is supernatural?" I asked.

"I haven't met her, though that's what I've heard," Mama said.

"La Porte Mystique sounds like a perfect episode for Cryptid Hunter," Jake said. "Why didn't you tell me about it?"

Mama smiled and said, "Sorry, my dear. It must have slipped my mind."

"You are forgiven," he said.

"What did you and Josie learn during your botanica visit?" Mama asked.

"Madam Elzora told us Eddie's niece Eliza was looking for information about 'night people.' She gave us the name of a bar near Pirate's Alley called

26

After Midnight and told us to speak with Marceline, the bartender," I said.

"Jake and I would go with you except we're leaving for Tulsa again as soon as we hear from the repair shop."

"No problem," I said. "We can handle it."

"The bar doesn't open until midnight," Josie said.

"My kind of place," Mama said. "Wish I could go with you."

"We can stay another day," Jake said.

"Not on your life," Mama said. "We're going to Tulsa as soon as the helicopter is repaired." Mama noticed the ornate box on the bar. "What's in the box?"

I opened the lid and removed the crystal skull. When Mama touched it, it began emanating a soothing shade of blue.

"Oh, my God!" she said. "Where did you get this?"

"Josie traded Madam Elzora her favorite watch for it," I said. "You know what it is?"

"Yes, though I never in a million years thought I'd ever actually see one. It's a one-of-a-kind antiquity."

"Madam Elzora told us the quartz was mined from a vein near an ancient Aztec temple. She said the skull is magical."

"You can't imagine," Mama said.

"What makes it magical?" Josie asked.

"Many things," Mama said. "It provides premonitions and warnings."

"Like the way it flashed blue when you touched it?" I asked.

"Yes," Mama said. "The person who possesses it may have visions or hallucinations."

"That's frightening," Josie said.

"For most people, it's too much to handle," Mama said.

"What else?" I asked.

"The skull can offer guidance. For instance, it could act as a magical compass, glowing brighter when you are on the right track or dimming when you veer off course."

"Madam Elzora likely meant for us to take it to After Midnight," I said. "Anything else?"

"When exposed to certain stimuli, the skull could reveal hidden things. For example, if placed under moonlight or submerged in water, it could illuminate secret symbols, words, or locations on a map."

"Damn!" Eddie said.

"That's not all," Mama said. "The skull's magical aura could have a subtle but powerful influence over others. It might cause a person to act out of character, revealing truths they would usually keep. It also glows red when someone lies."

Jake's cell phone rang. When he put it away, he said, "That was Colley. The chopper's ready, and there's a cab waiting outside."

After a round of warm hugs, Mama and Jake left Bertram's and hurried into the cab waiting on the street.

When they were gone," Eddie said. "What now?"

"Relocate to my house on Lake Pontchartrain," Josie said.

"I'll get my car and pick you up out front in about ten minutes," Eddie said.

I got an overnight bag from my room upstairs and met Josie on the sidewalk. Eddie soon pulled up to the curb in a baby blue Miata I recognized. Since the little car was only a two-seater, Josie sat in my lap.

"I knew someone who had a car like this," I said.

"It was Pancho's girlfriend's car," Josie said.

Pancho was the father of Adele, Josie's mother-in-law, and owned a pizzeria in Covington, a little town on the other side of Lake Pontchartrain.

"Freya Becht? She loved this car. Why did she sell it to you?" I asked.

"Freya's dead," Eddie said. "She was killed on Oyster Island."

"Oh, my God! You have to be kidding," I said. "What happened?"

"Long story," Eddie said. "Bottom line is she left her Miata to Pancho. Pancho didn't need another car so he traded it to me."

"What else haven't you told me?" I asked.

"Freya's daughter, Delta, is my new law partner," Eddie said.

"We have lots of catching up to do," I said. "Good thing it's raining."

Because of the rain, the top was up on the little two-seater, Josie's arms around my neck as she squirmed to fit between my lap and the car's roof. Her intelligence and good looks had always attracted me. Now, the roll of the vehicle and Josie's intoxicating perfume and warm body had propelled me into a state of sensual bliss. Eddie's attention riveted on the traffic and rainy streets, he didn't notice. I could tell by Josie's sudden stiffening that she had.

"Sorry," I said.

"It's okay," she said. "We're almost there."

Eddie drove through the rain to the West End lighthouse and yacht club. Josie's house was on a narrow strip of land between Lake Pontchartrain and the yacht basin. A single row of large houses extended to the tip of the small peninsula.

"My house is all the way to the end," Josie said. "Pull up in front. I have a garage opener."

All the houses on the narrow strip of land were identical, at least on the outside. Eddie stopped the Miata in front of the last house. When the garage door opened, he drove inside. Neither Eddie nor I was prepared for what we were about to see.

As Josie led us through her modern home, the storm outside intensified, rain drumming against the expansive windows echoing throughout the house.

"Come in," she said, her voice carrying over the distant rumble of thunder.

With a sweep of her hand, she gestured toward the living room, showcasing the open-concept space where polished wooden floors gleamed under soft lighting.

"My-oh-my!" Eddie said. "The lap of luxury."

"Indeed," I said.

Josie was smiling. "This is where I unwind. When the weather's warmer, I can slide open the doors and let the breeze from the lake fill the room."

The massive windows, stretching from floor to ceiling, gave the space an airy feel, even in the stormy gloom. Lightning flickered, briefly illuminating the view of the lake on one side and the yacht basin on the other. The house's modern design blended seamlessly with the natural elements outside. Eddie admired the sprawling kitchen, with marble countertops and state-of-the-art appliances.

"Emeril would be on cloud nine with this kitchen," he said.

"This is where I try to cook," Josie said, tapping the island. "But mostly, I just watch other people do it."

I glanced toward the wide staircase that seemed to float upwards, the steel railings reflecting the ambient light. But before we ascended, Josie guided us past the kitchen toward a spacious bedroom on the first floor.

"This is my room," she said, opening the door to reveal a bedroom that felt like its own sanctuary. The bed was framed by more floor-to-ceiling windows, offering panoramic views. The lake looked dark and wild, rain lashing against the glass. "It's something else when the sun sets or rises, but tonight—well, we've got quite a show."

Eddie nodded in appreciation. "It's stunning."

Josie turned toward the stairway, leading us to the second floor, her heels clicking on the wooden steps as we ascended. The second level opened up to a cozy den, sleek but inviting, with deep couches arranged around a glass-topped table. Another set of windows framed the storm-tossed lake, and the sound of rain was omnipresent.

"I'm blown away," Eddie said.

Josie gestured toward a door. "There's another guest bedroom here. But this space? This is where I spend most evenings when I'm not in bed." She shrugged, grinning. "I've got the best views in the city."

I caught sight of the spiral staircase leading to the third-floor loft. Josie waved us forward again, and we climbed up to the lofted space. It was more intimate, the ceiling lower, and the bedroom simple but elegant. A door led to the roof, and Josie beckoned us outside.

"This, gentlemen, is the crown jewel," she said, her voice filled with pride as she opened the door to the roof.

The wind howled as we stepped out, though the rain was lighter now. The observatory offered a

360-degree view of Lake Pontchartrain, the lights of New Orleans, and the yacht basin below. The storm swirled around us, lightning flashing over the water.

"Love it," I said.

"This vantage is even better when the sky's clear, although I think the storm adds a bit of drama, don't you?"

I nodded, impressed, and said, "Best view in New Orleans."

Eddie gazed out over the tumultuous lake. The blend of natural beauty and modern luxury impressed us both. Josie watched our expressions.

"Well, what do you think?" she asked.

Chapter 4

Eddie and I retrieved our bags from the trunk of his Miata as rolling thunder vibrated the picture windows overlooking the lake. It was still hours before midnight, and Josie directed us to our bedrooms.

"Eddie, you take the bedroom on the second floor. Wyatt, you get the loft. Since we aren't leaving here until almost midnight, I'm napping. Let's meet back here around midnight."

"Sounds like a plan," Eddie said.

Josie wasn't finished. "Oh, I suggest we all dress for the occasion."

"How so?" I asked.

"As if we're part of the scene," she said.

Eddie grinned and said, "How will we know the scene until we visit?"

"Improvise," Josie said. "We don't want to look like tourists."

I left Eddie on the second floor and climbed the steep stairs to the loft. The tiny loft bedroom was cozy, perched above the rest of the house like a crow's nest. The ceiling sloped gently, adding to its snug atmosphere. Large windows wrapped around the room, offering an almost panoramic view of the stormy waters of Lake Pontchartrain and the yacht basin below.

Dim lighting from a single bedside lamp cast soft shadows over the wood-paneled walls, giving the room a rustic feel. Rain pelted the windows, a rhythmic sound that blended with the occasional rumble of thunder in the distance. I sat on the edge of the bed, my overnight bag half-unpacked and thoughts drifting.

The bed was small but comfortable, covered in crisp white linens and a simple quilt thrown over the top. I lay on the bed, the cool air from the storm seeping in through the slightly cracked window. The scent of rain and wet earth filled the room as the storm raged beyond the glass. I watched the lightning flicker over the choppy water until my eyes grew heavy, and I fell into a vivid dream.

The scent of Josie's perfume—rich and floral with a musky undertone—overcame my senses. She stood at the edge of the room, her long hair flowing down her back like a dark river. She moved toward me, lithe and graceful, as if she was floating. Though I knew it was Josie, something about her felt like Desire—my former love. Desire's face merged with Josie's in the shadows of my mind.

Josie's hands glided over my chest, her touch warm and electric. She pressed close to me, her lips ghosting over my neck, her breath sweet and soft. Her fingers tangled in my hair, and I was suddenly overwhelmed by a burning lust, a hunger I couldn't quite explain.

As I reached for her, the scene shifted. Suddenly, it was Desire standing before me, not Josie. Desire, in her white nun's habit, was serene and untouchable. Her eyes held a quiet sadness, and she whispered my name. I tried to touch her outstretched hand, but she slipped away, her figure dissolving into the shadows.

I awoke with a start, heart pounding, tangled in the sheets, as Eddie's voice called from the stairs below.

"Wake up. We need to leave in a few minutes."

The dream lingered as I hurried downstairs, unsettled and reminded of complicated feelings, unresolved longing for Desire, and my growing attraction to Josie.

The rain continued its steady beat against the windows as I joined Eddie and Josie on the first floor.

"What were you doing?" Eddie asked.

"I fell asleep. Sorry," I said.

Josie was smiling as if she could see into my heart. "What were you dreaming about?"

I hoped they didn't see through my lie when I said, "I can't remember."

Josie had asked us to improvise and not look like tourists. A good plan, I thought. Our outfits should blend into the edgy world of After Midnight and our encounter with Marceline.

Josie wore a fitted black leather jacket over a deep red blouse, dark skinny jeans, ankle boots with a slight heel, and oversized hoop earrings.

I opted for jeans, a well-worn leather bomber jacket, and a fitted gray crew-neck tee-shirt underneath. My boots were scuffed but sturdy, so I didn't bother polishing them.

Eddie stood out with a slightly flashier ensemble: a button-up shirt—something in an eye-catching paisley—untucked, dark slacks, and a tailored blue blazer, casual but sharp. Josie smiled when she checked us out.

"Perfect," she said. "Let's go."

It was long past midnight as we followed Josie to the garage. I wondered exactly how and when she had become the boss as she unlocked her black Range Rover.

"We can take the Miata," Eddie said.

Josie glanced at me and said, "I'll drive. I need to keep my mind on business and not on other things."

Eddie had no idea what she meant, though I did.

The weather was damp and humid as we exited Josie's expensive vehicle and headed toward Pirate's Alley. A young couple, complete with smiles and tattoos, directed us to After Midnight.

The little bar felt like a place pulled straight from the shadowy edges of a dream. Hidden deep within the winding French Quarter paths, its entrance was marked by a barely noticeable sign— a tarnished talisman hanging from an iron hook above the heavy wooden door. No one stopped us when we pushed into the bar.

After Midnight was dimly lit with an amber glow emanating from old-fashioned gas lamps mounted along the walls. The little establishment felt intimate, almost claustrophobic, as if it kept secrets within its smoky corners.

Strange artifacts adorned the walls: an ancient voodoo doll in a glass case, faded tarot cards pinned like art, and shelves of old apothecary jars containing herbs, stones, and odd trinkets that seemed to hold forgotten magic. The bar was carved from dark mahogany, and countless hands had worn its surface smooth over the years. Behind it, a collection of curious bottles lined the shelves—some filled with shimmering liquids, others with cloudy potions that glowed faintly in the dim light.

The crowd was as unusual as the setting, a mix of the mysterious and eccentric. At one table, a woman with a wild mane of curly hair dyed electric blue was deep in conversation with a man wearing a vintage velvet smoking jacket, his fingers adorned with ornate rings. The woman gestured ardently, and her fingers sparkled with silver-tipped claws. A couple dressed in black leather vests and lace sat at the far end, their heavily tattooed arms linked as they sipped from oversized chalices. Their eyes flickered with mischief as they whispered to each other.

In one corner, an older man with a weathered face and silver hair sat alone, staring into his drink. His coat draped over his chair, revealing a sleeveless vest partially covering the cryptic symbols tattooed across his chest. A heavy wooden cane rested against his leg, the handle shaped like a serpent coiled around a crystal orb.

A fortune teller-type figure sat near the bar with long scarves wrapped around her waist and arms. A deck of cards was spread out on the table before her. She glanced around the room, her gaze sharp, as if she was privy to things no one else could see.

The music, a low and haunting melody, filled the air with an ethereal quality, as though it was being played just slightly out of time. The scent of incense mingled with the tang of spiced rum and the earthy smell of burning herbs, creating a rich and immersive atmosphere.

As I stepped further into the room, I felt a subtle charge in the air, as though the bar was alive, watching, waiting, its patrons part of a secret world dancing out of reach. Every glance felt loaded with meaning, every shadow concealing something more. The bar was like no place I'd ever visited—both intoxicating and dangerous, a place where the lines between reality and the occult seemed to blur.

No one sat at the bar, so Josie, Eddie, and I pulled up high-backed stools. Josie placed the crystal skull on the counter as the woman waiting bar smiled.

Our bartender was the kind of woman who commanded attention without even trying. Her presence was magnetic and mysterious, and she glided toward us with effortless grace. She was probably in her early thirties, with a youthful but ageless quality, like someone who existed slightly outside the normal passage of time.

Her long hair fell in cascading waves over her shoulders, as black as midnight. It caught the dim light and gleamed like silk. Her eyes were the first thing I noticed—deep, dark pools that seemed to draw you in, full of secrets and shadows. They flickered with something ancient, something knowing as if she'd seen more than her years suggested. Her skin was smooth and pale, almost luminous in the low lighting of the bar, enhancing her otherworldly aura.

She wore a low-cut black dress that clung to her curves in all the right places. Elegant in its minimalism, the neckline plunged just enough to reveal a glimpse of a cryptic tattoo nestled above the right breast—a delicate design, perhaps an arcane symbol or a runic sigil, something that spoke of hidden power or an ancient secret. The tattoo seemed to pulse subtly with its own life, drawing the eye though never quite revealing its meaning.

"I'm Marceline. What can I get you?" she asked.

"Martini for me," Josie said.

"Scotch. Monkey Fingers if you have it," Eddie said.

"Something non-alcoholic for me," I said.

The crystal skull began to glow a neutral yellow. Marceline didn't seem to notice. After bringing our drinks, she leaned over the bar across from Eddie.

"I haven't seen you here before," she said with a smile.

"Because it's my first time in," he said.

"What's your claim to fame?" Marceline asked.

"I was the Assistant Federal District attorney here in New Orleans."

"Was?" Marceline said.

"Now, I'm a hotel owner and live on an island about fifty miles from here," Eddie said.

"I'm impressed," she said. "You must know the dirt on everyone in the district."

Eddie nodded. "Things the average public never hears. Like I said, this is my first time to visit After Midnight."

"Don't make yourself a stranger," she said.

The skull's glow changed to red. Josie and I noticed. Eddie, who was flirting with the beautiful bartender, didn't.

Marceline had brought me a Shirley Temple. I wanted to tell her that I was an adult. I kept quiet, sipping the syrupy drink without commenting. Sensing my unease, Josie squeezed my hand.

Marceline continued putting the moves on Eddie, and It soon became apparent that he'd forgotten why we were there. After another scotch, Marceline took him in back to show him something.

I looked at Josie and said, "We made a mistake bringing Eddie."

She nodded and said, "That boy thinks more with his dick than his brain. What now?"

"Let's go sit with the man in the corner. He looks lonely."

Josie's dark eyes lit up. "Good idea."

The silver-haired older man smiled when Josie and I approached his table.

"Mind if we join you?" Josie asked.

"Please do," he said, removing his cane from the empty chair beside him.

"Love your tats," Josie said. "What do they mean?"

"Maybe a lot; maybe nothing," he said.

"I'm Josie, and this is Wyatt. Who are you?"

"Steve," he said.

"Wyatt and I have never been here before. You look like a regular."

Steve laughed. "I have no idea what these tattoos on my chest mean."

"Tats don't have to mean anything," I said.

"These tattoos mean something. My life has changed since I got them."

"Then why did you get them?" Josie asked.

Steve smirked. "I was like your friend during my first visit; naïve and horny. Marceline changed all that. Tomorrow, your friend won't know what hit him."

I pulled out the picture of Eliza and showed it to Steve. "Have you ever seen this woman?"

Steve nodded and said, "She was looking for someone."

"Who?" I asked.

"The Prince of Darkness," he said.

"Does the Prince of Darkness have a name?" I asked.

"Lucien."

"What's his last name?" I asked.

"The devil doesn't have a last name," Steve said.

Chapter 5

A new bartender had taken over, causing Josie and I to wonder what had happened to Marceline and Eddie.

We looked at Steve when he said, "Your friend has gone home with Marceline."

"Impossible," I said. "Marceline wouldn't have left this quickly."

"Tending bar isn't her only job," he said.

"What else does she do?" Josie asked.

Steve didn't directly answer her question. "I'm a software engineer. At least I was. First night I visited, Marceline asked me what I did and who I worked for. After telling her, she whisked me out of here and took me to her home."

"What are you suggesting?" I asked.

"Though the memory of my night with Marceline is hazy, I remember revealing the project my company was spending big bucks on. My discretion got me fired. Not long after that, my marriage fell apart. All I got for my experience were these tattoos."

"You think Marceline is responsible?" Josie asked. "Why would she do that?"

"Marceline and the person she works for," Steve said. "It's part of her job."

"Tending bar isn't her only job?" Josie asked.

41

"Other than After Midnight, who does she work for?" I asked.

When Steve didn't answer, Josie blinked and said, "Why do you continue coming here if Marceline and her boss ruined your life?"

"Because it was the most exciting night I've ever experienced."

"What does that have to do with our friend?" I asked.

"I overheard him tell Marceline he was the Assistant Federal D.A. of New Orleans."

"A job he hasn't held in more than two years," I said.

"Doesn't matter," Steve said. "He got Marceline's attention."

"He'll be back," Josie said. "He wouldn't have just left us here."

"Don't be too sure," Steve said.

"Eliza, the young woman we're looking for, told you she came here searching for a man named Lucien. Is he a real person or the Prince of Darkness?"

Steve glanced around to see if anyone was listening to our conversation.

"His last name is D'Arcy."

What made her think she would find him here?"

"Someone sent her. Maybe the same person who sent you," he said.

"Then maybe we came to the right place," I said. "You didn't tell us your last name."

I grinned when he said, "Vincenzio."

"Never heard that one," I said.

"Not a common name," he said.

"Who did you work for, if you don't mind me asking?" I asked.

"NeuroGenesis Systems, a startup with more tentacles than an octopus."

"Sounds intriguing. What do they do?" I asked.

"You wouldn't believe me if I told you," Steve said.

"Try me," I said. "I'm all ears."

"The company specializes in brain-wiping technology."

Josie was bored, tapping the tabletop. I gave her a dirty look and said, "Pardon me?"

"Soft tissue transfer from one host to another," Steve said.

Our new bartender gave Steve a dirty look when she brought us fresh drinks and a bloody Mary for him.

"Put Steve's drinks on our tab," Josie said.

"You got it, babe," the young woman said.

"Thank you," he said.

"My pleasure," Josie said.

"You say you don't know what your tattoos mean. Any ideas?" I asked.

"Something occult," he said.

"Can I get a picture of them?" I asked.

"Knock yourself out," he said, opening his vest to make it easier for me.

"One more thing," I said. "Eliza came here looking for Lucien D'Arcy. Was she successful?"

"Don't know," he said. "I gave her the name of someone who might know D'Arcy. It was the best I could do."

"Will you share that information with us?" I asked.

"There's an artist named Giselle who lives here in the Quarter. She's reclusive and paints disturbing images of the French Quarter at night. She has a studio on Dumaine."

He scribbled the address of Giselle's studio on a bar napkin and handed it to me.

Josie snatched it from my hand and said, "It'll be safe with me."

43

"Please don't tell her I gave you her name," he said.

"Don't worry," I said. "We're hip."

Steve finished his drink and got out of his chair. "It'll be dawn soon, and I have to go."

"Wait," I said. "Where do you work now?"

He laughed without answering and pointed to the darkness of a window.

"Duty calls," he said. "Got to go."

When we were alone at the table, Josie said, "That's one of the strangest people I've ever met. Is it as late as I think it is?"

"It's late. We got a late start," I said.

Thunder shook the roof, and lightning flashed through the window.

"Were you watching the crystalline skull as we talked with Steve?" Josie asked.

"Not really, though I glanced at it a time or two. What was it doing?"

"It never ceased to glow red. When Steve mentioned Lucien D'Arcy, I thought it would explode."

"What do you think it means?" I asked.

"That D'Arcy is an evil man, and Steve wasn't telling us all he knows," she said.

"Maybe we should get our tab and go," I said.

"What about Eddie?" she asked.

"He's a big boy and can take care of himself. Besides, it's not his first rodeo."

"That's no lie," Josie said. "Let's have one more drink and question the new bartender. Maybe she can tell us about Marceline."

"Why not? The night's pretty well shot."

The young woman behind the bar smiled when we sat the crystal skull on the counter and pulled up stools.

"I'm Nicolette. More drinks?"

"Please," Josie said.

44

Nicolette smiled when I said, "I'll have iced tea instead of the Shirley Temple."

"Marceline hates alcoholics," she said. "Sorry."

"I didn't realize she'd noticed," I said.

"Marceline doesn't miss much," she said.

Nicolette's shoulder-length raven-black hair was styled in soft waves, her green eyes glimmering with curiosity. A simple silver pendant shaped like a crescent moon adorned her neck.

"Do you know the man we were sitting with?" Josie asked.

"Steve? People around here like to say he's... different. If you're asking if he's a vampire, this is New Orleans, and people love their stories."

Josie smiled and said, "You aren't a vampire, are you?"

Nicolette glanced at the glowing crystal skull and said, "Night people fall into several categories. Some are vampires; others are werewolves or maybe just denizens of darkness. Many of us are only seeking something different in our lives."

The skull glowed blue. After glancing at it, I said, "Is that the category you fall into?"

"Yes," she said. "I came to After Midnight looking for something."

"Like Eliza?" I asked.

The skull glowed red when Nicolette said, "I don't know anyone named Eliza."

"What about Lucien D'Arcy?"

Nicolette stiffened, her gaze returning to the skull as its pale glow turned blue.

"You're playing with fire, asking about D'Arcy. He's not someone you find—he finds you."

"Does he frighten you?" I asked.

"You're crazy if he doesn't," she said.

"Do you know an artist named Giselle?"

"Me and everyone else who works the night shift in the Quarter," Nicolette said. "She's bat shit crazy, even more than most of the people I serve drinks to."

"Steve told us she may point us toward D'Arcy," Josie said.

"Did he now?" she said.

"What can you tell us about Marceline?" I asked.

"She's beautiful, though I think you can see that for yourself."

"She's almost..."

I nodded when she said, "Supernatural?"

Josie handed her a credit card and said, "Tab us out."

"You got it, babe," she said.

When Nicolette returned with our ticket, I handed her a business card with my name and number.

"Please call if you have any information you'd like to share," I said.

The young bartender's eyes flickered briefly with amusement.

"I'm not one of them," she said. "I've got both feet planted firmly in the daylight. At least for now. But I know how things work around here."

"How do they work?" I asked.

"Be careful digging around. You might not like what you dig up."

The rain had ceased, though thunder continued to rumble as we exited After Midnight.

"What did you think?" Josie asked.

"That place is hiding more secrets than the C.I.A.," I said. "I think Nicolette knows something about Eliza."

"Me too, and so did the crystal skull," Josie said.

Lightning flashed across the darkened sky as we hurried to Josie's Range Rover. In the French Quarter, the party was just getting started as the sound of music and crowd noise emanated from the direction of Bourbon Street.

"I hope Eddie's okay," I said.

"I thought you said he can take care of himself."

"With humans," I said. "I'm not so sure Marceline fits that description."

By the time we reached the West End, the rain had resumed. It mattered little as Josie used her garage door opener to drive into the gigantic garage and park. We were surprised when we reached the living room on the first floor.

Eddie was lying on the couch, a damp washcloth draped over his eyes.

"Eddie," Josie said. "What happened?"

"My head's killing me. If you have a gun, please shoot me and put me out of my misery."

"I'll get some aspirin," she said.

"I have something better," I said, handing Eddie two capsules.

Eddie didn't ask questions. "Thanks, pal," he said.

"What did you just give him?" Josie asked.

"Headache medication. Mama gave it to me. Voodoo stuff. It works," I said.

In about ten minutes, Eddie sat up, rubbed his forehead, and then drank the glass of scotch on the side table.

"I don't know what is in those pills, but if we could patent it, we'd make a fortune."

"They've always worked for me," I said.

"What happened to you?" Josie asked.

"Marceline asked me to join her behind the bar. When she showed me those big tits of hers, I was putty in her hands," Eddie said.

"You're despicable," Josie said.

"Don't worry," he said. "I got my comeuppance."

"What happened?" I asked.

"She slipped something into my drink. It was like getting kicked in the head by a horse. I woke up in Marceline's apartment."

"If she wanted to have wild sex with you, why did she drug you?"

"Marceline didn't want me. What she wanted was information. I awoke in a dark room that seemed like a cell, bright light shining on me. She was naked, her body painted in bright colors. She wasn't alone."

"Who was she with?" I asked.

"A shadowy figure of a man who never spoke. Marceline did all the talking. I was as naked as she was, and she stroked me, her actions causing me to think everything was all right."

"But it wasn't?" I asked.

"Not even close," Eddie said. "Marceline was probing for information."

"What information?" I asked.

"A case I worked on before the D.A.'s office canned me," he said.

"Marceline and the shadowy person knew about a specific case the Department of Justice was working on?" I asked. "What was it about?"

"If I told you, I'd have to kill you," he said.

"Can you tell us anything about it?"

"It's an ongoing case involving widespread corruption of some of the blueblood elites of the city. That's all I can say."

"How did Marceline know about it if it was so secret?" Josie asked.

"You tell me," Eddie said. "My head was killing me. They left me alone for a while, and I somehow managed to drag my sorry ass out of there. I hailed a cab and came here."

"Do you know where you were?" Josie asked.

"No idea," Eddie said. "I got the hell out of Dodge and came here."

Thunder shook the floor-to-ceiling windows, and the sound of rain intensified. Lightning flashed over Lake Pontchartrain.

"Have you ever heard of a man named Lucien D'Arcy?" I asked.

Eddie didn't immediately answer. "He was part of my ongoing investigation. I can't tell you any more than I already have," he said.

"Eliza went to After Midnight looking for Lucien D'Arcy," I said.

"Sweet Mother of God!" he said. "Surely she's not involved with him."

"What if she is?" Josie asked.

"Then God help her." Thunder shook the house again. "And us too," he said.

Chapter 6

I awoke the following morning to the aroma of strong coffee wafting from the first floor. I soon joined Eddie and Josie sitting at the kitchen table. Like the rest of the open house, large windows provided a panoramic view of the yacht basin. Last night's rain was gone, replaced by golden sunlight.

"We thought you were going to sleep all day," Eddie said.

"The bed is so comfortable, I could have," I said. "Hope you saved me a cup of that wonderful-smelling coffee."

Eddie was already dressed in chinos, sandals, and a sports shirt. An old terrycloth robe draped Josie's shoulders, and she looked as if she'd just woke up.

"Coffee's great, and I love the view," I said. "Your house would be the envy of everyone who loves Lake Pontchartrain."

"I've had an offer to sell it," she said.

"And?" Eddie said.

"I'm torn. I haven't stayed here often. Every time I do, I get more attached.

"Keep it," Eddie said. "You don't need the money."

"I know," Josie said. "Problem is, a large house needs someone to share it with."

Realizing he'd walked into a minefield, Eddie quickly backed out of talk of Josie's house.

"I had a call this morning and must return to Oyster Island," he said. "I'll be back in a day or so."

"We got you covered," I said. "Josie and I are visiting an artist in the Quarter later today who may have information on Lucien D'Arcy."

"Be careful," Eddie said. "I wasn't kidding last night about how dangerous I consider the man."

"Don't go yet," Josie said. "I'm not much of a cook, but I called in an order from Brennan's. They should be here soon."

When the delivery person arrived, Josie, Eddie, and I feasted on eggs Benedict from Brennan's Restaurant in the Quarter.

"Must be nice," Eddie said.

"What?" Josie said.

"Being able to call in for delivery a world-class meal and not have to worry about the price," he said.

"Give it up, and just enjoy," Josie said.

After breakfast, Josie opened the garage door, and we watched Eddie drive away to Oyster Island. When he was gone, and the garage door had closed, Josie glanced at the kitchen.

"I need to tidy up a bit," she said. "Meet me on the upper deck in about twenty minutes?"

"You got it," I said.

The breakfast had made me sleepy, though I couldn't close my eyes when I sat in a lounge chair on the roof. The view from Josie's observation deck stretched out in a dazzling panorama. The glittering expanse of Lake Pontchartrain rippled beneath the brilliant Louisiana sun, where sleek boats cut white trails through the deep blue water, their sails billowing in the gentle breeze.

From this perch, I could see the yacht basin, a gleaming cluster of polished hulls and fluttering flags. Seagulls circled lazily overhead; their sharp cries carried on the wind as they swooped and soared in graceful arcs, occasionally diving toward the shimmering surface for a quick meal.

Behind the gulls, a lush green landscape blended with the vibrant hues of the lake while the distant skyline of New Orleans shimmered on the horizon, a faint reminder of the world beyond this tranquil sanctuary.

The air smelled of salt, mingling with the faint scent of magnolias and the faint tang of marshland. I leaned on the railing, watching the light dance on the water, harmonizing with the gentle lapping of the waves below.

It was a perfect day—serene and unhurried, with nature's splendor on full display and the kind of beauty that could steal the breath from your lungs. When Josie joined me on the roof, her old robe was gone, replaced by a sheer nightgown that did little to hide her athletic body.

"I like to sunbathe in the nude."

She smiled when I said, "Hey, don't let me stop you."

Josie laughed. "Why were you so interested in that man last night?" she asked.

She nodded when I said, "You mean Steve?"

"He was sort of 'out there,' if you know what I mean," she said.

"He caught my attention," I said.

"How so?"

"Brain transferal," I said.

"That's purely science fiction," Josie said.

"It may have something to do with Eliza's disappearance," I said.

Josie rolled her pretty eyes. "You amaze me sometimes," she said.

"How so?"

"Steve seemed like a total loser to me," she said.

"Sometimes losers play the most important roles," I said.

A breeze was blowing in from Lake Pontchartrain. Josie's nightgown rippled in the breeze as she stood beside me against the railing. In addition to being Frankie Castellano's only child, Josie was wealthy in her own right. A successful real estate agent, she was a member of the million-dollar club.

"Whatever," she said. "I have a showing in Metairie and can't go with you to visit the art studio."

"No problem," I said.

"I'll drop you off before my showing and pick you up at Bertram's when I finish."

"All of our investigation will occur in the Quarter," I said. "It's probably best if I stay at my own apartment."

Josie's smile disappeared. "Please don't go. This monstrosity of a house gets lonely when there's no one here but me."

I enjoyed Josie's company, though I didn't see the logic in staying so far away from the French Quarter.

"Well..."

"Please?" Josie said.

Her smile returned when I said, "Why not? It isn't that far from here to the Quarter."

The longer we remained on the observation deck, the more I doubted my decision. Josie parading around nearly naked didn't help, and I found myself having to concentrate on our conversation. Josie acted as if everything was normal, and I did my best not to stare. She finally took pity on me.

"I'm going to dress for my appointment. Meet me on the first floor in thirty minutes, and I'll drop you on Dumaine."

When Josie came out of her bedroom, she was dressed as a successful real estate agent in an expensive business outfit with all the correct accessories. On the way to Dumaine, she caught me staring.

"What?" she said.

"Did anyone ever tell you how gorgeous you are?"

"Where did that come from?" she asked.

"Sorry," I said. "Guess it was a sexist thing to say."

"The client I'm showing the property to is a true sexist. I was half naked in front of you all morning, and you were a complete gentleman."

"Sounds as if I should accompany you," I said.

"I can take care of myself, Wyatt Thomas."

I grinned and said, "Of that, Josie Castellano, I have no doubt."

When Josie stopped to let me off, she unexpectedly leaned over the console and kissed me.

"It's you who needs to be careful. See you at Bertram's in a few hours."

I watched the big vehicle disappear around the corner before turning to see where Josie had dropped me. Midnight Impressions was a loft-style studio tucked behind an ornate wrought iron gate in a narrow alley just off Dumaine Street.

The building was old, with ivy creeping up the brick façade and floor-length curtains veiling its tall windows. Inside, the space was dim, with light filtering in from angled skylights, giving the place an ethereal atmosphere.

Many canvases of various sizes lined the walls, some leaning haphazardly against weathered bookshelves. A collection of sculpting tools, brushes, and paint jars sat across an old wooden workbench. The faint smell of turpentine and aged wood lingered in the air. A woman stepped from the shadows.

"May I help you?" she asked.

"I'm Wyatt Thomas. I'm looking for Giselle."

"May I ask for what reason?"

"I'm interested in her paintings," I said.

"I'm Sabine Moreau. Giselle isn't here right now. May I show you some of her work?"

Sabine was a slight woman in her late thirties, with delicate features contrasting her jet-black hair cut sharply above her shoulders. She wore an oversized linen shirt splattered with paint and a pair of olive-green pants. Her eyes were an intense gray, and there was an air of mystery. She moved with a quiet grace, her voice low and almost whispery, as if accustomed to keeping secrets.

"Please do," I said.

"I'm Giselle's assistant, handling the studio's daily affairs and dealing with visitors."

"When does Giselle do her painting?"

"She only works in the wee hours after midnight. I never disturb her when she's creating."

Sabine smiled when I said, "Is she a vampire?"

"That's a question you'll have to ask her. Follow me. I'll show you some of her paintings."

Sabine led me into the studio's gallery area, her footsteps barely audible on the wooden floor.

"These paintings are all examples of Giselle's unique style," she said with a gesture.

The paintings were dark and unsettling, with eerie themes. One depicted a barren landscape where the moon cast a greenish glow. In the center of this world stood a single person—a girl with flowing red hair, her pale skin almost translucent, dressed in a tattered white gown.

The young woman's expression was sad, her eyes vivid and wild, as though she was both lost and searching. The girl bore an uncanny resemblance to Eliza. Around her, shadows danced like living creatures, elongated and grotesque, while ethereal flowers bloomed at her feet, their petals curling inward like claws.

Another painting revealed a distorted carnival scene with grotesque clowns and a carousel spinning in a nightmarish fashion. The same red-haired girl stood apart from the chaos, her eyes glowing with a supernatural intensity.

"These are Giselle's latest paintings," Sabine said.

"The model is stunning and seems so real," I said.

Sabine chuckled and said, "Giselle has an eye for pretty girls."

She shook her head when I said, "Is the woman a professional model?"

"Giselle doesn't 'see' people the way we do. She... dreams them, or they come to her in fragments, like whispers from somewhere else. She says nothing of where they come from. Only that they must be painted."

Sabine grinned when I said, "Give me a break! My guess is she's a street waif, maybe even underage."

"Possible," Sabine said.

"Don't bullshit me."

"You could be right," she said. "The girl's probably a runaway Giselle picked up off the street. Giselle is tight with her money, and my guess is that she bought the girl's dinner in exchange for her doing the modeling gig."

She nodded when I said, "Cheapskate, huh?"

"I'm Giselle's most valuable asset," Sabine said. "You'd be surprised how little she pays me."

"Maybe we can change that. You don't know this model?" I asked.

"Giselle only works at night. The young woman was long gone before I got to work. Why are you so interested in her?"

"I buy and sell art, and I'm not a collector," I said. "The more background information I can supply my clients, the more they pay for the paintings."

"Uh-huh!" she said.

Sabine's expression told me she wasn't buying my story, though she was buying my act as a sleazy art dealer, and I decided to play up the sleaze by handing her a crisp hundred-dollar bill.

"In my business, I need all the help I can get, if you know what I mean."

Sabine nodded and stuffed the bill into a pocket in her green pants.

"The girl in the painting is beautiful in a kinky way," she said. "I can understand why someone might desire her."

"We're on the same wavelength," I said. "I'll make it worthwhile if you tell me where to find her."

I'll ask some of my contacts," she said.

Sabine thought I wanted to connect with Eliza for carnal purposes, and I didn't disavow her opinion of me. After giving her my best, sleazy grin, I gave her another hundred.

"There's more where that came from if you can hook me up with the girl."

Sabine nodded and said, "I'll see what I can do."

"I'm also interested in the two paintings with the red-haired chick. How much is Giselle asking for the two of them?"

"Five thousand dollars each," she said.

"I don't have lots of money, but my clients do. I'd rather see the money go into your pockets than your cheapskate boss's."

"Then give me a thousand, and I'll sell the two paintings for three thousand."

I had to dig deep to come up with Sabine's thousand dollars.

"Perfect," I said. "Here's your commission. What time do you leave?"

"Five," she said.

"I'll be back before then to pick them up and with the rest of the money."

"How do you know you can trust me?" Sabine asked.

She grinned and nodded when I said, "Because we understand each other. We're partners now, and there'll be another five hundred bucks in it for you when I return."

"I love partnerships," she said. "Let's drink to it."

Sabine produced a bottle of Crown Royal and poured us a glass.

"Cheers," she said with a smile.

I chugged the Crown Royal, kissed her on the mouth, and said, "Here's hoping that in the future, we can share more than ill-gotten gains."

Chapter 7

I left Midnight Impressions feeling dirty and more than a little drunk, the walk to Bertram's on Chartres doing little to alleviate the feeling. I sat at Bertram's bar, hoping he didn't realize it.

"You off the wagon again?" he asked.

"I had a little nip in the line of work," I said.

"I can smell your breath from here. Where you been?"

"I'm good," I said. "I'll be lots better when you give me a glass of lemonade."

"Uh-huh!" he said.

Bertram pushed the glass of lemonade across the counter, his stoic expression reminding me of my nanny's comment when she learned I'd stolen a dollar from my mother's purse.

"Thieves go to hell," she'd said.

My cell phone rang, erasing the thought from my head. It was Josie.

"I sold the property. I'll be at Bertram's in five minutes to celebrate," she said.

I had enough money in Bertram's safe to pay for the two paintings. It didn't matter because he was across the bar waiting on customers.

"Pull up front," I said. "I bought something that will interest you. We need to pick up my purchase."

I had barely reached the sidewalk when I saw the Range Rover drive around the corner. Josie smiled and waved after pulling to the curb.

"Where to?" she said when I climbed into the passenger seat.

"Midnight Impressions," I said. "I bought two paintings and have to pick them up. And Josie, I need to borrow twenty-five hundred bucks."

Josie didn't ask questions but wasn't smiling as she counted the money on the Range Rover's posh leather console. Sabine, waiting with the two paintings, smiled when I gave her the money.

"Here's hoping this is the first transaction in a long and prosperous relationship."

Sabine smiled as she wrapped her arms around my waist and pulled me toward her.

"One request," she said. "Let me share the girl with you when we find her."

She laughed out loud when I said, "You got it, sweet britches, but you may have to take sloppy seconds."

I could smell the whiskey on her breath when she kissed me. I felt even dirtier when I left Midnight Impressions with the two paintings and put them into the backseat of Josie's vehicle.

"Please explain," she said.

"You'll understand when you see the paintings," I said.

"I thought you were a teetotaler," she said. "Have you been drinking?"

"Is it that apparent?" I asked.

"You're slurring your words and have lipstick on your collar. You know the money doesn't mean much to me. I hope you aren't taking advantage."

"I have money in Bertram's safe," I said. "I'll pay you back when we get to the bar."

Josie's frown seemed painted on her pretty face, and she didn't turn down my offer to repay her. She let me off at the curb.

"I'll park the Rover and join you. I think you have some explaining to do."

Bertram's frown hadn't disappeared when I propped the two paintings against the bar, and I remembered why I had gone on the wagon.

"Another lemonade, or would you rather have a shot of Blackjack?"

The glass of whiskey had gone straight to my head, and it was apparent everyone could tell. I didn't try to explain. Josie, her arms clasped tightly against her chest, was still angry when she joined me at the bar.

"Now," she said. "Let's hear your explanation."

"First," I said. "Look at the two paintings."

Her angry expression mellowed, and she said, "Is that Eliza?"

"It's her," I said. "Eliza recently modeled for Giselle."

"What does it mean?" she asked.

"That we're on the right track."

Bertram ducked under the bar for a look. "Has Eddie seen these?"

"Not yet. He had to return to Oyster Island, and I haven't called to tell him," I said.

"You purchased the two paintings from Giselle?" Josie said.

"Giselle's a night person and never paints until after midnight. Her assistant, Sabine Moreau, showed me these two paintings and told me they were Giselle's latest creations," I said.

"The young woman in the picture is Eddie's niece," Josie said. "How did Eliza end up in Giselle's studio?"

"My question exactly," I said. "Sabine told me Giselle's subjects aren't real and appear to her in dreams."

"Bullshit!" Bertram said.

"That was my reaction," I said. "I played the part of a shady art dealer and offered Sabine a bribe. She fell for it and told me the woman in the painting was likely a runaway Giselle had picked up off the street. She wanted five grand each for the two paintings but took less when I gave her a kickback."

"Why did you do that?" Josie asked.

"She thought I wanted to have sex with the street waif and offered to find her for me if..."

"If what?" Josie said.

"If I gave her more money under the table and let her participate when I had sex with the girl. She wanted to seal the deal with a toast. I reluctantly complied."

"Uh-huh!" Bertram said.

"Get me twenty-five hundred dollars from your safe," I said. "I need to repay Josie."

"No way," Josie said. "These paintings are easily worth five thousand dollars each. I paid for them. They're mine."

"You think this Sabine woman will tell you where Eliza is?" Bertram asked.

"I don't trust her any farther than I could pick her up and throw her," I said. "Still, we can't take the chance that she won't."

When Bertram left the bar to deliver a pitcher of beer to some customers, Josie gave me a look.

"Maybe you were right about staying here at Bertram's," she said. "I'm taking the paintings to the lake house. Can you bring them to the sidewalk when I pull up outside?"

"Of course," I said.

When Bertram returned, he said, "Where's Josie?"

"She left. I'm taking the paintings to her when she pulls up outside and honks."

"She didn't seem too happy with you," he said.

"That, I can't help. I was only playing a part," I said.

"Sounds like a part you enjoyed playing," Bertram said.

"What was I supposed to do? I'm a private dick and not a knight in shining armor."

Bertram could hear the anguish in my voice, and his demeanor changed.

"She'll come back around. What now?"

"I'm revisiting La Porte Mystique," I said. "I don't believe Madam Elzora told us everything she knows."

Josie's horn honking outside on the street interrupted our conversation. After waving goodbye to Bertram, I loaded the two paintings into the back of the Range Rover. She didn't bother speaking or giving me a wave before driving away.

I realized why I was a bachelor as I headed toward St. Louis and La Porte Mystique. I was halfway there when my cell phone rang. It was Eddie.

"What the hell did you do to piss off Josie so badly?" he asked.

"Long story," I said. "Bottom line is she kicked me out of her lake house, and it looks like I'm on my own with the investigation."

"Bummer!" he said. "She told me you found proof that Eliza is in the French Quarter."

"She's here," I said.

I hesitated before speaking when he asked, "Is she in danger?"

"It's possible she's living on the street. You know what that means. Want me to call the police?"

"Don't do it," he said. "If Lucien D'Arcy is involved, and I think he is, it would only put her in more danger. I'll be back in New Orleans tomorrow, and together, we'll think of something."

"I'm on it."

"I know you are," he said. "Do what you can, buddy. I'll be there tomorrow."

I had much to think about as I walked the rest of the way to La Porte Mystique. As I approached the botanica, the air turned still, charged with an energy that felt as tangible as the old wrought-iron gate barring the entrance. Perched on the gate's twisted black metal was Calypso, Madam Elzora's raven, its glossy feathers catching glimmers of sunlight that seemed to darken rather than illuminate.

Its head cocked to one side, and the bird fixed its dark eyes on me, a gaze that felt ancient, knowing. Its beak opened, and in a voice rough as gravel yet unnervingly clear.

"The moon's shadow still lingers. Cross the gate, and she'll see you through."

The raven fluffed its feathers, giving a final low squawk that seemed to echo within the walls of the mystic shop.

I wondered what the raven was doing outside the little shop as I entered through the old wooden door, causing the brass bell to jingle. As before, the air inside was thick with the scent of incense, herbs, and the metallic tang of ritual. The shop was dim, with only flickering candlelight casting dancing shadows on the walls. Madam Elzora smiled when she appeared from behind the black curtain.

"You have returned. Did you find the young woman you sought?"

"Not yet." Her smile grew broader when I said, "Only more questions than answers."

"Isn't that the way it always is?"

"Your raven is outside. You aren't afraid she'll fly away?"

"The French Quarter is Calypso's home. She comes and goes as she pleases," Madam Elzora said.

"She spoke to us when we left the previous time I visited and again a moment ago."

"Calypso is sentient; you should heed what she tells you."

"What exactly did she tell me?" I asked.

"Sometimes, there's more than one answer," she said. "Now, why have you returned to my little shop?"

"The crystal skull. It's very valuable. Why did you trade it to us?"

Madam Elzora laughed. "The skull always returns to its rightful owner. You are simply borrowing it. Now, tell me why you are here."

"Josie and I visited After Midnight. The bartender told me of an artist named Giselle. I visited her studio earlier today and purchased two paintings that portrayed a young woman. Giselle's assistant informed me the model was likely a street waif."

"In the French Quarter, many young people live on the street. Some don't survive."

"Is Eliza alive?" I asked.

"I can help, though I want something in trade," Madam Elzora said.

"What?

"Your mother's ring," she said.

Madam Elzora's words were like a punch in the face. My parents were never affectionate. Neither my father nor mother ever told me they loved me. The closest thing to it was when my mother was on her deathbed. She pulled her wedding ring off of her finger and handed it to me.

"Keep this ring forever," she had said. "As long as you have it, we'll have a bond."

The ring was in my pocket, the gold worn thin by years of wear. I pulled the only thing of real value my mother had ever given me from my pocket and handed it to Madam Elzora.

The old voodoo woman smiled and said, "Now, I will give you something in return. Before I do, you must submit."

"To what?" I asked.

"An ear piercing," she said.

She nodded when I said, "You want to pierce my ear?"

"Yes," she said.

"But why?" I asked

"From which to hang an obsidian charm—a crescent-shaped stone known as the Moon's Eye."

"Why should I let you?" I asked.

"To enhance your ability to see beyond the veil of the living," she said.

"How will your stone help me do this?" I asked.

"The Moon's Eye grants those who wear it fleeting glimpses of spirits, unfinished business, and secrets bound to the city's past."

Madam Elzora had a silver lancing device in her hand when I said, "I don't know."

The old mambo rubbed numbing salve on my earlobe and then used the device to pierce my ear. She showed me the Moon's Eye and looped it through my ear. I immediately began to feel something.

"You will experience visions, fleeting but potent," she said.

"Visions of what?" I asked.

"Long-buried secrets and shadows of those who met tragic ends. Each time you use the amulet, it drains energy from your soul."

"How will it manifest itself?" I asked.

"You'll know, but beware," she said. "The charm's power is both a blessing and a curse."

I wondered what I had gotten myself into and said, "What if it becomes too much?"

"Then you must return to La Porte Mystique. I put it on you, and only I can remove it."

Chapter 8

J osie had mixed feelings when she returned alone to her house on Lake Pontchartrain. After Eddie had jilted her, leaving her alone at the altar, she had yet to fully recover emotionally. She'd thought she could trust Wyatt, though his actions when securing the two paintings seemed to suggest otherwise. Still, she disliked staying alone in the large lake house. To make matters worse, the stormy weather of the previous night had returned.

It was still early, lightning flashing over the lake and rain pounding the floor-to-ceiling windows as she closed the door to her bedroom and opened a bottle of vodka. She filled a tumbler with ice and poured straight vodka over it. The crystal skull pulsated a gentle blue as she sat on the edge of the bed, the alcohol warming her as she sipped from the chilled glass.

Josie liked to sleep in the buff and was thankful there were no window peepers on the narrow strip of land abutting Lake Pontchartrain. It mattered because there were no curtains on the windows. She liked it that way, lying in bed and watching the fireworks over the lake and the city's distant lights.

The weather was warm. When Josie finished her vodka, she didn't bother pulling the sheet over her. She lay in the room's darkness, lit only by lightning out over the lake, the rumble of intermittent thunder and pulsing of the crystal skull the only sounds. She soon fell deeply asleep, the vodka and crystal skull propelling her into a vivid dream.

The crystal skull on Josie's bedside table caught the moonlight, casting an eerie glow around the room. She was suddenly outside her house, rain falling on her bare shoulders as she wandered through a misty New Orleans alleyway. Flickering like restless spirits, gas lamps illuminated her path.

She floated down a French Quarter street surrounded by tourists moving slowly through darkness and thick ground fog. Even when they brushed against her, no one seemed to notice or care that she was naked. She wafted over the cobblestone pathway, soon finding herself in a dark studio lighted only by the flickering flames of red candles dripping blood instead of wax.

In the dim light of the studio, she found herself drawn to the figure of Giselle, naked as she was, her skin splattered with globs of bright paint as she stood in front of a massive canvas, utterly absorbed in her work.

Giselle's back was turned, but there was an almost otherworldly stillness as she stroked the brush over the canvas with an unsettling grace. Dark hair draped her shoulders like a shadow, silky yet wild, framing her pale figure. The faint scent of old paint and something metallic, thick and heavy, hung in the air.

As Josie took a cautious step closer, Giselle whipped around with unnatural speed, her eyes flashing a piercing shade of amber that glowed in the low light. Her face, beautiful but gaunt, carried a seductive and terrifying hunger. High cheekbones cast eerie shadows, giving her an almost skeletal appearance. When her lips curled into a smirk, Josie caught sight of two elongated fangs, sharp as needles and gleaming against her bloodless lips.

Giselle tilted her head, studying Josie with an intensity that felt like she could pierce through her soul.

"What do you think of my work?"

Giselle's voice dripped mockingly as she gestured to the canvas, where Eliza's full-length portrait loomed in grotesque detail. Eliza's body was twisted and contorted in an almost serpentine pose, her arms elongated in unnatural ways.

Crimson hair flowed like blood over Eliza's bare shoulders, and her eyes stared vacantly into the dark as if pleading for release. Josie felt her skin prickle as she realized that Eliza's painted eyes, filled with a terror that felt disturbingly real, almost seemed to follow her.

Giselle's hand caressed the portrait as she chuckled, revealing her fangs fully. She whispered, her voice chilling and reverberating around the room.

"Beauty demands sacrifice, don't you think?"

Josie stumbled back, her pulse racing as Giselle's amber eyes narrowed, glittering with both menace and amusement. She followed Giselle into the shadows in time to see her sink her fangs into the pale skin of Eliza's neck. As blood dripped from the puncture wounds, Josie extended her hand, trying to speak. The words refused to issue from her mouth.

Behind them, an ominous figure appeared: a tall man with dark hair slicked back from his forehead. His skin was deathly white, his eyes glinting red, and drops of blood dripping from his fangs.

"You have something of mine," the grotesque vampire creature said.

"Who are you?" she asked.

"I'm Lucien, though I think you already knew that," he said.

"What do you want from me?" she asked.

Giselle and Eliza laughed as Lucien floated through the mist toward her. The creature's gnarly nails scratched her neck when his long fingers, cold as a dead man's, wrapped around her throat.

"You know what I want," he said.

Josie awoke with a start, not bothering to dress as she sprang from the bed. She took a moment to glance at the crystal skull on the nightstand. It seemed almost alive and was pulsating crimson red.

She rushed into the living area and turned on the lights, unmindful that she was perhaps putting on a strip show for voyeurs aboard the sailboats moored in the yacht basin.

She'd brought the two paintings into the room and had propped them against the couch. At least, she thought she had. They were gone. Rushing to the garage, she checked inside the Range Rover in case her memory was faulty. It wasn't.

Realizing someone had entered her house and taken the paintings, she immediately checked all the doors to see if they were locked. Then it hit her. Whoever had taken the paintings might still be in the house. Returning to her bedroom, she checked the closet and bath before locking the door. Her hand shook as she dialed the number on her cell phone.

"Wyatt, it's Josie. Can you catch a cab and come to my house?"

Josie's voice was in a state of panic when I answered the phone.

"I'll get there as quickly as possible," I said.

"Please hurry," she said.

"If you're in danger, call 9-1-1."

"I'll wait for you," she said.

I sensed the dangling Moon's Eye as I got dressed. I knew Josie was frightened because I could see her in my mind's eye, holding a butcher knife as she stood naked at the door of her bedroom. I could even see the lightning flashing through her window.

I caught a cab on the sidewalk and was soon banging on Josie's front door. She flung it open, throwing her arms around me.

"Oh, Wyatt, thank you for coming," she said.

Josie shivered uncontrollably as she pulled me into the house and slammed the door behind us. I led her into the bathroom, found a robe, and covered her with it.

"You're shivering," I said. "Sit on the couch. I'll get you something to drink, and you can tell me what happened."

I soon had a pot of coffee brewing. Josie huddled close to me when I brought her a cup and joined her on the couch. She smiled for the first time and warmed her hands on the steaming cup. It was then she noticed the dangling earring.

"What's that?" she asked.

"An earring," I said.

She stared at the dark half-moon and said, "I never knew your ear was pierced."

"It wasn't until a few hours ago," I said.

"What possessed you to have your ear pierced?" she asked.

"I returned earlier to speak with Madam Elzora. She called the black stone the Moon's Eye and told me never to remove it."

"For what reason?" she asked.

"It's magic," I said. "I can see glimpses of the past, present, and future."

"You don't believe that, do you?"

"When you called, I saw you."

"You mean you formed a mental picture of me as we spoke?"

"No," I said. "I saw you just as you were and sensed immediately you were in danger. Tell me what happened."

"I fell asleep with the Crystal Skull on the nightstand beside the bed. It was flashing a gentle blue. I fell into a dream. It was so vivid, it felt real."

"Tell me," I said.

"I was floating through the French Quarter though there were no lights. The people on the street moved slowly, not noticing I was naked. I entered Giselle's studio and saw her painting in the darkness."

When Josie shivered, I said, "Are you okay?"

"I have a bottle of vodka on the nightstand beside my bed. Will you get it for me?"

She smiled and nodded when I said, "I'll also bring the coffee pot. I need another cup even if you don't."

When I returned from Josie's bedroom with the vodka, she laced her coffee, tasting it before she continued.

"Thank you," she said.

"No problem. Please continue your story."

"Giselle was painting and didn't hear me enter her studio. Something metallic, thick, and heavy hung in the air. It took me a moment to realize what it was," she said.

"What?" I asked.

73

After sipping the vodka-laced coffee, she said, "Blood."

"How do you know what blood smells like?" I asked.

"In my dream, I did," she said. "Giselle was gaunt and pale and was painting in the nude. She wheeled around when she sensed I was behind her. Wyatt, she had fangs."

"It was just a dream," I said. "You said so yourself."

"Her eyes were the color of amber and glinted in the light of the candles set around the easel. I thought she was going to attack me. Instead, she disappeared into the darkness beyond the canvas she was painting. I shadowed her."

She nodded when I said, "Someone you recognized?"

"It was Eliza, her arms and legs twisted grotesquely. Giselle and Eliza embraced. It was then that he appeared."

"Who appeared?" I asked.

"Lucien D'Arcy. He was a vampire; his skin was pale white, and his face looked like a grotesque mask. He also had fangs."

She nodded when I said, "He spoke to you?"

"He said I had something of his. He approached me, his dark fingernails scratching me when he put his hand on my neck." Josie touched her neck and said, "his hand was ice cold. When he opened his mouth, I awoke."

"It's okay," I said, pouring her more coffee and lacing it with a liberal shot of vodka.

"I flipped on the lights and ran into the living room. The paintings of Eliza are gone, though all the doors were locked."

Josie was shivering again when she sat her coffee on the table and put her arms around me.

"There must be an explanation," I said.

74

"There isn't," she said. "What'll we do now?"

"Get dressed," I said. "We're going to Giselle's studio."

"It's after midnight," she said.

Quoting Calypso the raven, I said, "'Beware the clock that strikes too late... what you find, you cannot unmake.'"

"Then what the hell are we about to find?" Josie asked.

"Something we can't unmake," I said with a smile.

Josie dressed, and we soon headed toward the French Quarter in her Range Rover. It was late, so we found a place to park near Giselle's studio. We found the front door open and wafting in a midnight breeze when we got there on foot.

"It's dark," she said. "We can't just go in there."

"I have a flashlight," I said.

Josie clutched me so tightly that I could hardly walk as we entered the dark studio. The flashlight cut through the darkness, and the place looked nothing like I remembered after visiting earlier in the light of day.

"That's Giselle's easel," she said.

My voice echoed when I called, "Giselle, are you here?"

No one responded.

"See what's on the other side of the easel," Josie said.

She remained latched to my arm as I pointed the flashlight into the darkness and walked beyond the easel. Josie screamed, seeing something on the floor before I did.

"Oh, my God, Wyatt. It's a body."

A woman's naked body lay on the floor in front of us. I crouched beside it, grabbed a shoulder, and turned her over. After seeing the woman's face, Josie screamed again.

The woman's dead eyes glinted in the light of my flashlight. Her skin was pale and bloodless, her mouth agape in a silent scream.

"She's dead," I said.

"Is it Eliza?" Josie asked.

"Sabine Moreau," I said. "The woman who sold me the paintings of Eliza."

"What'll we do?" she asked.

I didn't answer because I was already dialing 9-1-1 on my cell phone.

Chapter 9

Sometime later, the street was filled with cop cars flashing blue lights and crime tape cordoning off Giselle's studio. Two N.O.P.D. homicide detectives stood over the body while forensic techs were busy collecting evidence. I knew the detectives because Tony Nicosia, my sometimes business partner, had trained them both.

Tommy O'Rear was a rawboned cop with unruly red hair and the shoulders of a football linebacker. Like Tony, he'd grown up in the Irish Channel district of New Orleans.

"What the hell are you doing here, Cowboy," he asked.

"Ongoing investigation," I said.

"At two in the morning?"

"I'm like you and Marlon, Tommy. I don't work regular hours."

"You wearing an earring now?" Tommy asked.

"Long story," I said.

Tommy let the matter drop. His partner, Marlon Bando, was as tall as Tommy, though less athletic and more soft-spoken.

"Who are you, ma'am?" he asked.

Marlon's eyes widened when she said, "Josie Castellano."

She nodded when Tommy said, "Frankie Castellano's daughter?"

"Yes," she said.

"Frankie Castellano isn't involved," I said.

Tommy looked at Josie and said, "Then why are you here?"

"Eddie Toledo's niece has gone missing in the French Quarter," I said. "Josie is Eddie's and my friend. She's helping with the investigation."

"Has Eddie reported his niece's disappearance to the police?" Marlon asked.

"He didn't want to involve the police," I said.

"Why is that?" Tommy asked.

"Eddie had a conflict of interest from his time as Assistant Federal D.A.," I said.

"Uh-huh!" Tommy said. "Do you know the victim?"

"Her name is Sabine Moreau. I met her earlier today," I said. "She was the assistant of Giselle, the artist who owns this studio."

"What's Giselle's last name?" Marlon asked.

"Don't know," I said. "Giselle only paints late at night. Josie and I were here to interview her."

"What did Giselle have to do with your runaway?" Marlon asked.

"Eliza, Eddie's niece, was the subject of two of Giselle's recent paintings. She possibly knows where to find her."

"The victim is drained of blood; the only marks of violence are the fang marks on her neck. Is there any reason I shouldn't suspect you and Ms. Castellano of the murder?"

Tommy smiled and shook his head when I said, "Josie and I aren't vampires."

Tommy glanced at the ceiling and said, "Only in the Big Easy. Lord, help us!"

"I don't envy you and Marlon," I said. "Are we free to go?"

"Marlon and I may have more questions. You going to be at Bertram's later?"

He smiled when I said, "I'll be there and buying."

I clutched Josie's elbow when Tommy waved and nudged her toward the door.

"I don't believe in vampires," Josie said as she started the Range Rover.

"How else are you going to explain a victim drained of blood and not a single drop on the floor?"

"What now?" Josie asked.

"Drop me off at Bertram's," I said.

"You kidding? I'm not dropping you off anyplace that I'm not going."

"Bertram's isn't open."

"After a theft, a murder, and the worst nightmare I've ever experienced, I'm going no place alone," she said.

Josie wasn't lying and clutched my arm up the stairs to my apartment.

"You hungry?" I asked.

"Not really," she said. "I could use a shot of vodka."

"We can sneak downstairs and liberate a bottle from Bertram," I said.

"I have money and don't mind paying," she said. "Here's a hundred. Is that enough?"

"Keep your money," I said. "You can pay Bertram tomorrow."

While I was downstairs, Josie found one of my tee shirts, stripped off her clothes, and lay under my covers. I'd brought a tumbler from Bertram's and poured her a vodka. I stripped down to my boxers and undershirt, found a blanket, and sat in my old recliner.

"You don't have to sleep in the recliner," she said. "The bed's big enough for both of us, and I trust you."

"I don't trust myself," I said. "You know I've always had a crush on you."

"You never told me that," she said.

"Because it's not something you go around broadcasting."

"Do you want me to apologize to you?" she asked.

"You owe me no apology," I said. "I don't expect one."

"You've been a close friend for many years. I shouldn't have mistrusted you," Josie said.

"I'm not a perfect person. I make mistakes all the time," I said.

She patted the mattress and said, "Come lie on the bed with me. I won't bite you."

She laughed when I said, "Maybe I want you to."

I lay beside her on the bed, trying to keep my distance. When my cat Kisses bounded on top of us, we both laughed.

"The vodka has hit me," she said. "I don't think I can keep my eyes open."

Josie's measured breathing informed me she had fallen fast asleep, her arms draped across my chest and her head on my shoulder. We were both exhausted, and it wasn't long before I joined her. Someone pounding on my door some hours later awoke us. It was Bertram.

"Wyatt, you in there?"

"I'm here," I said.

"Eddie's downstairs and wants to talk to you," he said.

"Put a scotch on my tab and tell him I'll be down as soon as I dress," I said.

"I'll tell him," Bertram said as he walked away.

"Oh, shit!" Josie said. "What are we going to do now?"

"Fess up and tell him we spent the night together," I said.

Josie jumped out of bed, whipped off my tee shirt, and began searching for her clothes.

"That won't work. Think of something else," she said.

"I'll lower you to the ground from my balcony, and you can take your car back home."

"No way. I'm not going there alone."

"Then wait outside for fifteen minutes and join us at the bar as if you just arrived from Lake Pontchartrain."

"Eddie won't fall for it," Josie said.

"I don't know what to tell you," I said.

A few tourists gave us the evil eye as I stretched over the balcony to deposit Josie on the sidewalk.

They grinned when Josie said, "Jealous wife."

I dressed and headed downstairs to meet Eddie. He was waiting at the bar, a glass of scotch in his hand.

Eddie looked up from his drink and said, "What the hell, bro! You got your ear pierced?"

Bertram was shaking his head. "You get tattoos with that earring?" he asked.

"Madam Elzora had important information about Eliza and wouldn't give it to me until I consented to wear this magic charm."

"What important information?" Eddie said.

Josie entered the bar before I could answer Eddie's question.

"Look what Cowboy did to his ear," Bertram said.

"I think it's sexy," Josie said. "You and Eddie should both get one."

"I don't think so," Bertram said. "You drinking, or is it too early?"

"I've been dying for one of your martinis," she said.

"At least someone's still sane around here," Bertram said.

When we were all seated at the bar, Eddie said, "I'd like to see the paintings of Eliza."

"A little problem," Josie said.

"What problem?" Eddie asked.

"They were stolen."

Looking shocked, Eddie said, "Who even knew you had them?"

"Lucien D'Arcy, apparently," she said. "He appeared to me in a dream and told me I possessed something of his, and he wanted it back. When I awoke, the paintings were gone."

"Someone broke into your house?" Eddie asked.

Josie shook her head. "There were no open windows or doors. It was as if a ghost took the paintings."

"Josie's right," I said. "She called me. When I arrived, I checked all the doors and windows. Nothing was amiss."

"Part of my dream involved the artist Giselle and Eliza. Wyatt and I went to her studio and discovered a dead body."

Eddie sat up straight on the stool. "Not Eliza, was it?"

"A woman named Sabine Moreau, Giselle's assistant," I said. "We called the police. Tommy O'Rear and Marlon Bando arrived to investigate."

"What was the cause of death?" Eddie asked.

"Loss of blood," I said.

"Punctured artery?"

"There was no blood on the floor. The body was drained of blood, two fang marks on her neck the only visible signs of trauma."

"Crazy," Eddie said. "What now?"

"There's a place in the Quarter called the Eden Club, where 'working vampires' congregate."

"What are 'working vampires?'" Josie asked.

"Like-minded people who have no fangs but share blood using ceremonial razors. They aren't afraid of the light of day, and most have regular jobs," I said. "It's owned by a young woman I know named Hope."

"Hope, huh? You never told me about her."

When Josie gave me a dirty look, I said, "I've never told you about any woman I know."

Eddie grinned and said, "Maybe you should loosen up a bit."

"I don't think so," I said.

"I'm game," Josie said. "When are we going?"

"They're open for tourists and such, though Hope and the regulars don't arrive until after dark," I said.

"Then let's go to my lake house," Josie said. "We can grab some lunch and discuss what we know until it's time to visit the Eden Club."

Before we'd finished our drinks, Tommy O'Rear and Marlon Bando entered the bar. Eddie got off his stool to greet them.

"Tommy, Marlon, long time no see," he said as he shook their hands.

"Good to see you, Eddie. How's life on Oyster Island?" Tommy asked.

"Couldn't be better. You boys need to come down one weekend. Room, booze, and meals are on me," Eddie said.

"You mean it?" Tommy said.

"Wouldn't have said it if I didn't," Eddie said. "Bertram, drinks are on me."

Bertram had already poured an Abita, a shot of Blackjack for Tommy, and a glass of lemonade for Marlon. Tommy killed the shot and chased it with cold Abita before joining us at the bar.

"I needed that," he said. "Marlon and I've been up all night."

"Wyatt told us about the murder," Eddie said. "You know Josie?"

"Met last night," Tommy said. "Now, I see the connection."

"Josie and I are still good friends," Eddie said. "What did your forensic people find?"

"Absolutely nothing," Tommy said. "Might as well have been a ghost who committed the murder."

"Or a vampire," I said.

"Something drained every drop of the victim's blood," Tommy said. "Whatever or whoever killed her didn't spill a drop on the floor."

Marlon remained quiet as he sipped his lemonade.

"What about you, Marlon?" I asked. "What do you think happened?"

"I grew up in Monroe. Far as I know, there are no vampires in Monroe. Don't know about the Big Easy. Things that are common here you never see anywhere else."

"That's a fact," Eddie said.

"Why didn't you report your missing niece to the police?" Tommy asked.

"I was working on a case before leaving the DOJ," Eddie said. "It involved a powerful individual guilty in my eyes of many things. Problem is we could never make any of our charges stick."

Eddie nodded when Tommy said, "And you think this person is somehow connected to your niece's disappearance?"

"I've never seen the man, not even a picture. Lawyers showed up in his place every time we subpoenaed him," Eddie said.

"How did he get away with that?" Marlon asked.

"The man is connected," Eddie said. "Someone, an important judge or a powerful individual we couldn't refute, always provided an excuse for him."

"I understand why you were reluctant to report your missing niece. I probably would have done the same," Tommy said. "It's different now, and we need his name."

Tommy flinched when Eddie said, "Lucian D'Arcy. You know him?"

"I've heard the name," Tommy said.

"And?" Eddie prompted.

"If he's the murderer, we're never going to make the charges stick," Tommy said.

"Because?" I asked.

"Because D'Arcy knows people, and this is the Big Easy, Cowboy. Nobody knows that any better than you."

Chapter 10

E ven though we assured her we would be behind her in his Miata, Josie was reluctant to go home alone. Eddie, an experienced prosecutor, was determined to know everything I knew before reaching Josie's house.

Once in the Miata alone, he said, "Now, explain to me what Madam Elzora told you so important that you let her pierce your ear."

"Madam Elzora has a raven that spoke to me when I visited La Porte Mystique. She advised me to heed what the raven said."

Eddie laughed and said, "You didn't just fall off the wagon, buddy; you jumped off headfirst."

"Funny," I said.

"You need to listen to yourself," he said. "You sound crazy."

"We're not dealing with normality," I said. "Everything I've seen so far suggests something else entirely. If we're going to find Eliza and rescue her, we need to go with the flow."

Eddie was laughing, though I could tell he was serious. "Okay, I'm hip. What did the raven say?"

"She spoke to Josie and me once and only to me twice," I said.

"Tell me," Eddie said.

"When Josie and I were leaving La Porte Mystique, the raven said, 'Beware the clock that strikes too late... what you find, you cannot unmake.'"

"Catchy," Eddie said.

"I don't know. What it said next was even more cryptic. She said, 'The moon's shadow still lingers. Cross the gate, and she'll see you through.'"

"What the hell is that supposed to mean?" Eddie asked.

"Maybe the only way we're going to find Eliza is to visit a place neither of us is familiar with."

Eddie grinned. "I think that weird-looking earring is affecting your brain," he said.

We found the garage door to Josie's lake house open. Eddie drove inside and parked. Josie was in the living room, her expression dumbfounded. The two paintings of Eliza were leaning against the couch.

"What?" I asked.

"The paintings are back," she said. "Exactly where I left them."

Eddie stared at the paintings and said, "Eliza, what have you gotten yourself into?"

"Both of you are staying here tonight," she said. "I'm not remaining in this house alone."

"I'm here for you," Eddie said.

Josie looked at me, smiling when I said, "So am I."

Last night's rain had passed, though stormy weather was never far from New Orleans during springtime.

"I see a bit of sun peeking through the clouds," Josie said. "Let's go to Joe's and have lunch on the sundeck. We can walk from here."

Joe's was a giant wooden building on stilts jutting out over Lake Pontchartrain. It had a marvelous outdoor upper deck with a sweeping view in all directions. We sat on the upper deck, eating raw oysters and bowls of gumbo.

"What's the deal on this vampire club you want us to visit?" Eddie asked.

"Kind of a strange place," I said.

"Tell us about it," Eddie said.

"A friendly young woman named Hope owns the club," I said.

"What does she look like?" Eddie asked.

"Long blond hair, blue eyes, big tits, and killer legs," I said.

"If you boys must talk about women like pieces of meat, I'm returning to the lake house," Josie said.

"Sorry," Eddie said. "At least we're treating you like one of the boys."

"I'm not one of the boys, so stop it," Josie said. "Wyatt, go on with your description."

"The place is called the Eden Club, and there is loud synthesizer music on the first floor, usually occupied by tourists. The second floor is where the bar's regular patrons congregate.

"The vampires?" Josie said.

"They aren't 'true' vampires but 'working vampires' with nine-to-five jobs. At night, they exchange blood with like-minded people using ceremonial razors."

"You have to be kidding," Josie said.

"Not kidding," I said. "Maybe Hope can tell us how to find a real vampire club."

After a lazy lunch, we returned to the lake house.

"Now, all we have to do is wait until dark," Eddie said.

"No way," Josie said. "We can't go to a French Quarter vampire club looking like tourists."

"What difference does it make?" Eddie asked.

Josie shook her head and said, "All the difference in the world. We're not going like this, and when I went to the ladies' room, I called someone to transform us."

"Who?"

"Lazarus Delacroix," Josie said.

"Who is that?" Eddie asked.

"Everyone in the New Orleans theatre scene knows Laz. He has a flair for the dramatic and a deep understanding of the city's subcultures."

"Is he coming here?" Eddie asked.

Someone knocked on the front door, and Josie said, "That's probably him now."

Josie opened the door and welcomed the man with hugs and kisses.

"Wyatt and Eddie, this is Laz Delacroix, quite possibly the industry's greatest wardrobe and makeup guru."

Laz had jet-black hair styled with a dramatic wave. A touch of powder enhanced his already pale complexion, and his dark eyeshadow gave him a smoky gaze that felt piercing. His wardrobe was eclectic—black silk scarves, lace gloves, vintage rings on every finger, and a floor-length Victorian-style coat with intricately embroidered cuffs.

"Josie, you are too kind," he said.

"Laz is known for his Gothic-meets-haute-couture aesthetic," Josie said. "He specializes in creating looks that speak to each person's darker alter ego."

Laz smiled and rubbed his hands as he looked at Eddie and me.

"You didn't tell me I would be working with such gorgeous men," he said.

Josie laughed. "Laz has a background in theater costume design and makeup artistry and has worked with everyone from avant-garde fashion houses to local drag queens and alternative musicians."

"You aren't going to make us look like drag queens, are you?" Eddie asked.

"You have a problem with drag queens?" Laz asked.

"No," Eddie said.

Josie smiled again and said, "Laz is known for his incredible transformations but also for his somewhat supernatural aura; locals joke that he must have some vampire blood in his veins."

Laz patted his vintage leather makeup and styling kit and said, "Don't know about that, but I go nowhere without the rare pigments, powders, and accessories I've gathered from all over the world."

"I need a scotch," Eddie said. "Can I get you something to drink, Laz?"

"I'll wait until Romy and Silas arrive," Laz said. "Besides being my wardrobe and makeup assistant, Romy is an excellent bartender. We never work anywhere without our wet bar."

"Love it," Eddie said.

"I left the garage door open," Josie said.

"Perfect," Laz said. "Romy and Silas were right behind me and got snarled in traffic."

As dusk settled over the lake house, a matte-black van with custom Gothic script spelling out 'Delacroix & Co. Wardrobe and Makeup' pulled into the driveway, its headlights cutting through the growing darkness. Josie motioned them into the garage and then shut the door.

With a soft hiss of the brakes, the van parked, and Laz's two assistants emerged.

"Romy and Silas, this beautiful woman is Josie, and these handsome men are Eddie and Wyatt," Laz said.

Romy and Silas were every bit as eclectic as Laz. Romy, a petite woman with lavender-dyed hair cut into a blunt bob, wore an oversized black sweater adorned with silver chains and a pair of vintage Doc Martens. Bracelets and charms that jingled softly as she moved stacked her arms.

Silas, tall and lanky with silver piercings along his brow and nose, was dressed in a tailored black vest and trousers. His nails were painted metallic silver to match his accessories.

Romy pulled a portable wet bar from the van, and Silas began rolling out clothes racks. Josie led them to the living room. After folding out various shelves and sorting bottles of alcohol, Romy smiled.

"The bar is open," she said.

"Do you always do your work with a traveling bar?" Eddie asked.

"Wardrobe and makeup are works of art and require not just copious amounts of alcohol for all, but specific cocktails conducive to the process," Laz said.

Romy began mixing a complex cocktail. When it was ready, she handed it to Laz, who sipped it.

Josie took a sip and said, "It's beautiful. What is it?

"A Negroni Sbagliato," he said. "It's a twist on the classic Negroni but made with sparkling prosecco instead of gin. Would you like to taste it?"

"Wonderful," she said.

"Romy, make Josie a Negroni Sbagliato," Laz said.

Romy made another and handed the concoction to Josie. The drink was striking in its presentation—dark amber with an orange slice garnish.

"Just the right balance of bitter, sweet, and bubbly," Josie said.

Romy began distributing cocktails with names like Corpse Reviver No. 2 and black Manhattan. Laz wasn't happy that I was drinking straight orange juice. The group was soon on their way to contented alcoholic highs. Probably a good thing as Laz began issuing orders.

"Now," he said. "Everyone strip."

"Right here?" Josie said.

"Yes," Laz said.

"Down to our underwear?" Eddie asked.

"All the way," Laz said. "When I dress someone, they are perfect, including their underwear."

Romy's specialty drinks had worked magic, and Eddie and Josie happily complied with Laz's orders. I wasn't so lucky, feeling everyone's eyes were on me as I stripped off my clothes.

Josie had a silly grin on her pretty face as Laz assessed her naked body. He was soon rummaging through boxes, looking for the perfect undergarments for her. He chose a matching lingerie set for her that blended sensuality with a dark aesthetic.

A black lace balconette bra with intricate detailing and a high-waisted lace thong suited her look perfectly, allowing for the right mix of allure and sophistication. She was hot, and I could hardly take my eyes off her.

Laz turned his attention to Eddie, patting his cheek. "Did anyone ever tell you you look like a young Marlon Brando?"

"No," Eddie said.

"You could play the part of Terry Malloy in our fall production of *On the Waterfront*."

"I can't act," he said.

"Nonsense," I said. "You're an ex-prosecutor. You'd be perfect."

"At least I wasn't a bleeding-heart defense attorney," Eddie said.

"Boys, boys!" Josie said. "Go outside if you're going to fight."

Laz studied Eddie's body and said, "For you, I'm going with low-rise briefs in a comfortable fabric with subtle but edgy detailing, like a skull or snake motif subtly embroidered near the waistband. Put these on."

Eddie pulled on the briefs and said, "Kind of snug.

"Snug and fitted," Laz said. "Just the thing to complement your rebellious look."

"They're cute," Josie said.

She smiled when he said, "Not the reaction a man wants when someone is staring at their private parts."

Laz ignored them, turned his attention to me, and said, "You're too good-looking, and I adore your earring."

"You're making me blush," I said in my best sarcastic voice.

"For you, I have the perfect undergarment," he said.

"Let me guess," I said. "Red bikini briefs."

"Hardly," he said. "Black boxer shorts with subtle luxurious detailing, like a hint of lace trim or a satin waistband."

"Not bad," I said when I tried them on.

"The classic style adds a touch of elegance that will help you embody your mysterious night persona."

Josie, Romy, and Silas applauded. "Bravo, Laz. You've done it again," Romy said.

Romy began dispensing more drinks as Laz stared at Josie, his chin in hand.

"You don't need the bra," he said, removing it and tossing it on the couch.

He, Romy, and Silas soon had her dressed in a black lace bodysuit, high-waisted leather pants, and a velvet jacket. Her makeup was bold, with dark eyeliner and deep red lipstick. Her choker channeled a Victorian-meets-modern vampire look. He topped things off with high heels and slicked-back hair.

With help from Romy and Silas, Laz dressed Eddie in a sleeveless leather vest with silver accents to play up the vampiric edge. He added fingerless gloves and chunky silver rings with skulls and snakes, amplifying his grunge vibe. He added dark eyeliner and contouring for makeup, giving him a chiseled look, and styled his hair into textured spikes.

He held a mirror up for Eddie and said, "What do you think?"

"My mom wouldn't recognize me," he said.

Laz turned to me and said, "Last but certainly not least."

He and his assistants got to work. Before dressing me, they added smoky eye makeup and a touch of concealer to make me look mysterious enough to pass as a club regular.

"Josie says you're a detective. Sexy," Laz said. "I want to keep the detective vibe but have you embrace a Gothic twist."

Laz and his assistants soon had me dressed in a tailored black blazer, jeans, and a deep maroon shirt with a faint sheen for a darkly dapper touch. He added a vintage silver ring and a dark onyx necklace. A pair of classic leather boots and tousled hair completed my look.

After celebrating with more of Romy's cocktails, Josie said, "Laz, you're a genius. Our outfits are perfect."

"Glad to help," he said. "You need to convince Eddie to audition for the lead in some of our upcoming productions." Before leaving, he said, "Wyatt, I love your earring."

When Laz and his assistants were gone, Josie said. "We're definitely locked and loaded. Ready to pull the trigger?"

Chapter 11

Darkness fell over Lake Pontchartrain as we backed out of the garage and headed toward the lights of New Orleans. The Eden Club lay buried in the heart of the French Quarter, practically humming under the pale streetlight that spilled onto the door from the narrow alley outside. Crimson lighting pulsed through its grimy windows like blood flowing through veins, luring tourists and curious locals alike.

Inside, loud synthesizer music throbbed across the black-and-red walls, and clusters of people—some draped in black lace and leather, others wearing oversized goth crosses or plastic fangs—flocked around the bar, snapping selfies and knocking back blood-red cocktails. I knew better than to mistake these visitors for the club's regulars; the real Eden started on the second floor.

I led Josie and Eddie up the narrow staircase, past posters of classic vampire movies framed against the faded walls. We entered a darker lounge where the vibe felt less like Halloween and more like a hushed ritual.

Soft laughter and the murmur of quiet conversations floated over the room as small groups leaned close, whispering conspiratorially in candlelit corners. Patrons here were different: a peculiar crowd in odd attire, black the predominant color. Everyone's eyes seemed predatory. The way they held themselves was a blend of strangeness and danger. Quiet exchanges of blood pricks and ceremonial whispers practiced primarily for show but occasionally in eerie seriousness interrupted their conversations.

Hope, the club's owner, and primary bartender, stood behind the bar, watching us with a bemused smirk. Her braided blond hair spilled over her shoulders, framing her striking blue eyes and that dangerous smile I remembered. Dressed in a sleek black dress that hugged her figure, she looked like the vampire queen she embodied for her patrons.

"Wyatt Thomas," she said, her voice lilting as she leaned forward. "Love your earring. Thought I'd have to send out a search party. And here you are, bringing friends."

She glanced at Josie and Eddie, her gaze sizing them up as if she were measuring them for dark secrets.

I smiled. "Can't keep away from the nightlife, Hope. You know that." I motioned toward Josie and Eddie. "This is Josie and Eddie. Figured I'd show them around, see if the old place still had its charm."

Hope raised a brow and gave Eddie a wry smile. "Charm, huh? This place has all the charm of a mortician's waiting room."

"Nonsense," Eddie said. "I already love the place."

"How about something to drink, handsome?" she said.

Eddie smiled and said, "Thought you'd never ask. I'll have a scotch, neat."

Hope grinned and said, "You can't visit a vampire bar without trying our club special."

"Why not," Eddie said.

Hope poured three glasses of a dark red cocktail that might have been wine—then again, with her, it was always best not to ask.

Evocative music lilted through the dimly lit club. "Love the music," Josie said. "Don't believe I've ever heard the song, but it's so catchy and..."

"Haunting?" Hope said.

Josie nodded and said, "Yes."

"The song is *Paper Trails* by Darkside. Don't you love it?"

The song faded away, replaced by another. Josie glanced at Hope and said, "Who?"

Hope smiled and said, "*Bela Lugosi's Dead*. Sung by Bauhaus."

"Perfect," Josie said.

Hope nodded. "I'm guessing you didn't just stop by for the ambiance. What's the latest in the world of gumshoes and gangsters, Wyatt?"

I lifted my glass, giving her a measured look. "This looks wonderful, but I'm an alcoholic. Got any iced tea?"

"Seems I remember you drinking a club special or two," she said.

I smiled and said, "Another time and place."

"The night's young," she said. Hope glanced at Josie and said, "Lady, you are drop-dead gorgeous. Is that what it takes to hook up with the two most handsome men in New Orleans?"

"We're only friends," Josie said. "Eddie's niece has gone missing in the French Quarter. Wyatt and I are trying to help him find her."

"New Orleans is dangerous after dark," Hope said.

I smiled and said, "You don't have to wait until after dark. New Orleans is always dangerous."

"That's a fact," Hope said.

"Heard a rumor there's a new club around here, somewhere more underground than Eden. A 'real' vampire club."

Hope let out a low laugh. "You think I'd allow competition? If there's a 'real' vampire club, it's either a figment of some drunken goth's imagination or one of my little birds got restless." She leaned forward, her voice dropping to a murmur. "But I might have heard of a few new 'underground' places. You sure you want to know?"

Eddie, intrigued, piped up. "So, this isn't just for the costumes and razors, huh?"

Hope smirked, giving him a once-over. "Some of us like to dress up, and some like a little bite."

"What do you like?" Eddie asked.

Hope tapped her lips. "I'm here for the fun, but a few folks take it seriously. You might say they believe in...higher stakes. What's your niece's name?"

"Eliza Castellano," Eddie said.

"Have a picture of her?"

Eddie removed Eliza's photo from his wallet and handed it to her. She took the photo and studied it. Josie had taken pictures of Giselle's painting featuring Eliza.

"Giselle's paintings," Hope said.

"You know Giselle?" I asked.

"She drops by occasionally," Hope said.

"What can you tell us about her?" I asked.

"Some people in the Quarter are best to steer clear of," Hope said. "We call them 'night people.'"

"Night People? Why do you call them that?" Eddie asked.

"Because you never see them in the cold light of day," she said.

"Are you suggesting they're real vampires?" I asked.

"I'm not suggesting anything," Hope said.

"Giselle appeared to me in a dream," Josie said. "She had fangs like a vampire."

Josie nodded when Hope said, "Real fangs?"

"There was also a man, and I use that term loosely, who said his name was Lucien D'Arcy. You know him?"

Hope nodded. "The Prince of Darkness. I've never seen him nor anyone I know that has, if that tells you something."

The song ended, and another began. Josie looked at her and asked, "Who?"

"*Angel* by Massive Attack," Hope said.

"Why haven't I heard any of these songs?" Josie asked.

Hope smiled, reached across the counter, and caressed Josie's hand.

"You aren't listening to the right channels. What you need is a bit of indoctrination."

"Sounds dangerous," Josie said.

"Life is dangerous. Want to taste it?"

Josie didn't answer, allowing Hope to pull her under the counter. She didn't move when Hope kissed her and then yanked the top of her lace bodysuit down to her waist. From a pocket in her dress, Hope produced a tiny ceremonial razor.

Eddie's eyes grew large. He looked at me and said, "What's happening?"

"They're about to exchange blood," I said.

Hope lowered the top of her dress, revealing her large breasts.

"Do you trust me?" she asked.

Josie didn't move. "Yes, though I don't know why."

"I'm going to make a tiny cut above your heart. I promise it won't hurt or leave a permanent mark." Josie nodded when she said, "Ready?"

Josie closed her eyes as Hope squeezed the cut until a single drop of blood appeared. Then, smiling, she showed Josie her tongue before licking away the drop of blood. Josie's eyes rolled back in her head, and for a moment, I thought she'd swooned. She hadn't and was smiling when she opened them.

Josie's eyes were dewy, her grin silly when she glanced at Eddie and me to see if we were looking. Eddie's mouth was open, his eyes unbelieving when she winked at us.

"How was it?" Hope asked.

"It took my breath away," Josie said.

Hope handed the ceremonial razor to Josie and said, "My turn."

Josie made the tiny cut just above Hope's heart, squeezing it until a single blood drop appeared. The two women touched tongues, and then Josie licked away the drop of blood. Hope's eyes closed as she tilted her head toward the ceiling.

"Exquisite." Hope glanced at Eddie and said, "You're next, pretty boy, though I'm in sensory overload right now."

"Whoa!" Eddie said.

Hope pulled up Josie's bodysuit and said, "Girl, you're giving me ideas."

Josie's mad grin didn't disappear as she ducked under the bar and rejoined Eddie and me. Hope regained her composure and poured us another drink. Engrossed in the performance, we didn't notice the appearance of a person joining us at the bar. Eddie jumped when he saw the man. I knew who he was and smiled.

"Malik," I said. "It has been a while."

Malik, the man beside Eddie, had long hair and stood at least seven feet tall. His leather overcoat, from a different era, almost covered his heavy boots.

"Wyatt," he said. "Good to see you."

"This is Eddie and Josie. Josie just performed the blood exchange ceremony with Hope," I said.

"I've seen Hope perform it dozens of times, though it never grows old," Malik said. "What brings you here?"

"Two things," I said. "Eddie's niece is missing, and there was a murder in the Quarter last night at Giselle's studio," I said.

"Not guilty," Malik said. Who was murdered?"

"Giselle's assistant, Sabine Moreau. She died from loss of blood."

"It wasn't me. I only suck the blood of homeless people."

Hope brought Malik a mixed drink and gave me a sideways glance as he paid for it with the small change he fished from his pocket.

"What are you drinking?" Eddie asked.

"A grim reaper," Malik said. "Kahlua, 151 proof rum, grenadine and ice. No real blood, but I love them."

"Are you a real vampire?" Eddie asked, wincing when Malik showed him his fangs.

"I arrived here in New Orleans almost three hundred years ago," he said.

"Get out of here!" Eddie said.

Malik laughed. "I know. I have a New Orleans accent. After three hundred years, what do you expect?"

"There's no black or white when it comes to the French Quarter," Eddie said.

"When it comes to colors, black and white are rare," Malik said. "They only exist in unfiltered sunlight or the depths of a black hole. Who are you looking for?"

102

Eddie showed Malik the picture of Eliza. "My niece. Have you seen her?"

Malik shook his head. "There's a disappearing house on the end of Bourbon Street. Runaways often find their way there."

"A disappearing house?" Eddie said. "What's that supposed to mean?"

Malik shook his head. "You can't explain the supernatural. I should know. Sometimes the house is there; most of the time it's not."

"Have you ever visited?" Eddie asked.

"Lots of times," Malik said.

"Can you take us there?" Eddie asked.

"Maybe some other time, perhaps. I have business tonight, and the hour is late."

Malik laughed when Eddie said, "Please tell me more."

"Like I said, not tonight. I'm hungry and have to go," Malik said. "I enjoyed meeting you."

When the giant of a man was gone, Josie said, "Where is he going?"

"Hunting," I said. "For human blood."

I nodded when Eddie said, "Is he a real vampire?"

"As real as they get," I said.

Hope had finally regained her composure and said, "Forget Malik. You three are hot. Want to party with me?"

"What do you have in mind?" I asked.

"There's a music venue called Musik Azul not far from here. A singer named Rene is performing. He's one of the Nocturnes."

"What's that?" I asked.

"It's what the Night People call themselves. Want to meet him?"

"Sure," Eddie said.

Josie flashed Hope a smile and said, "I'm game."

"Me too," I said. "Can you just leave the Eden Club unattended?"

"No way, silly boy," she said. "My backup bartender is on her way. I'm high as a kite and feeling no pain. When she gets here, I'm ready to blow the place."

Chapter 12

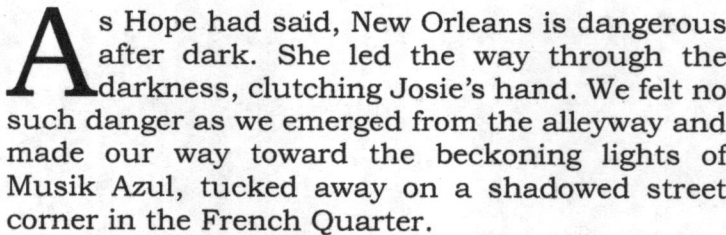

As Hope had said, New Orleans is dangerous after dark. She led the way through the darkness, clutching Josie's hand. We felt no such danger as we emerged from the alleyway and made our way toward the beckoning lights of Musik Azul, tucked away on a shadowed street corner in the French Quarter.

The silence of the Quarter was broken when we entered Musik Azul's almost hidden door. Music flooded over us, the venue feeling like a secret whispered among those who knew its rhythms. Inside, the walls were painted in moody blues and rich purples, chipped and faded in places, lending the place a gritty charm.

Candle-lit tables were scattered across a floor that creaked with history, and the scent of spiced rum, leather, and a hint of old wood lingered in the air. Small chandeliers cast a dim glow over patrons seeking refuge from the Quarter's more commercial establishments.

"The clientele was an eclectic mix of artists, musicians, and curious souls," Hope said. "Some are Night People—those who linger at the edges of society, with pale skin and an almost ethereal presence."

"What brings them here?" Eddie asked.

105

"They're drawn to Musik Azul for its haunting atmosphere," Hope said. "Some are locals who've been coming here for years, older musicians with stories etched in their lined faces, and younger drifters who crave the edge the place offers."

"And tourists?" I asked.

Hope grew introspective. "Tourists rarely stumble into Musik Azul. Those who do are immediately captivated by its raw authenticity. They usually stay long enough to feel they've glimpsed something hidden."

"Like what?" Josie asked.

"A piece of the Quarter's soul that doesn't make it into the guidebooks," Hope said.

"Is that Rene on stage?" I asked.

Hope nodded. The venue pulsed with blue light, casting shadows that stretched and swayed along the walls. A smoky haze mingling with the scent of incense and whiskey hung in the air, curling around dimly lit chandeliers. The stage was modest but commanded attention.

Behind the grand piano sat Rene, a man with sharp features and a compelling and unnerving aura. Dark curls fell over his eyes as his fingers drifted effortlessly across the keys, every movement slow and deliberate as if he felt the music in his bones.

When we grabbed a table near the piano, Rene spotted Hope across the dimly lit bar, nodded, and smiled. He was singing something darkly soulful—a song that felt like it was reaching into the shadows.

Josie and Hope were still holding hands, and Josie asked, "What's the name of the song?"

"*Strange Weather.*"

The song's haunting melody and lyrics about love and loss perfectly captured the mysterious vibe of the club and the Night People gathered there. Rene's raspy voice turned the lyrics into something deeply personal, almost confessional, with a rawness that tugged at everyone's attention. His voice was like gravel smoothed over by whiskey and regret, each word hanging heavy in the air.

"Will you take me across the channel?" he sang. *"London Bridge is falling down... Strange weather, I'm having strange weather..."*

The song echoed through the room, each note resonating like a secret exposed, thick and somber, instilling the sense that everyone was drawn to his voice and held by the spell he cast.

Rene's voice was a gravelly murmur that smoothed out into an unexpected sweetness when he hit the higher notes. As he sang the blues-infused ballad, I imagined the Night People in the room, with their pale skin and piercing gazes, watching him perform with something akin to reverence.

Hope saw something in my eyes and said, "His voice unlocks a part of them, some echo of an old longing usually buried under layers of careful detachment."

Eddie leaned close and said, "Didn't expect this place to feel so... heavy."

I nodded and said, "Like everyone's carrying a secret they'll take to the grave."

"I love it," Josie said.

"It's the kind of place where the past hangs in the air, like perfume that won't fade," Hope said.

Josie, swaying slightly to the music, grinned and said, "Hope knows how to pick a scene, doesn't she?"

"Got that right," Eddie said. "Rene's voice could haunt the dead. Almost does, by the look of the crowd."

Hope nudged Eddie. "Shh, no more talking. Let Rene do his thing."

Hope leaned back in the chair, her gaze fixed on the stage as if caught in a trance as the song finished on a drawn-out note. Rene's hands rested on the keys for a beat longer than necessary before lifting his head and locking eyes with me.

My earring was suddenly going crazy, flashing visions through my brain as Rene continued staring at me. The place had exploded with applause and noisy approval. Rene smiled, his gaze intense, like he'd seen something in me that no one else could. He raised his whiskey glass with a knowing smile and spoke directly to me. Though I couldn't hear him, I read his lips.

"Here's to the night," he said.

Hope raised a brow, her fingers tapping to the faint jazz that had resumed in the background as Rene weaved through the crowd toward our table.

"He's coming over," she said. "Get your questions ready."

Rene's presence was magnetic and eerie, like a gust blowing from another world. He greeted us with a conspiratorial nod and an unsettling smile before sitting beside Hope. His gaze focused on Josie, and he didn't seem to notice Eddie or me.

"Who's your gorgeous friend?" he asked.

"Josie. We exchanged blood earlier, and now I'm in love with her," Hope said.

"I see why," Rene said, glancing at Eddie and me for the first time. "Introduce me to your other friends."

"Rene, this is Eddie and Wyatt. We're looking for someone. I thought you might be able to help."

"Who are you looking for?" he asked.

"Eddie's niece, Eliza. She's gone missing in the Quarter," Hope said.

"Why would you think I might know where she is?" Rene asked.

"She modeled for Giselle. Josie has pictures on her phone."

Hope released Josie's hand so she could access the photos on her phone. Rene leaned close when she used her fingers to enlarge them.

"I may have seen her," he said.

"Was she okay?" Eddie asked.

"The young woman I recall seeing was in no distress. Perhaps she wants to be here," Rene said.

"Her mother is worried," Eddie said. "I'd like to talk to her. Do you know where she might be?"

"There are many doors, though only a few have keys," Rene said.

"What's that supposed to mean?" Eddie asked.

"The Quarter functions as two parallel worlds—one that tourists see during the day, full of musicians, colorful balconies, and lively street performers, and another at night, where the true 'Night People' emerge," Rene said. "Isn't that what Madam Elzora told you?"

Eddie's blank stare was unnerving. "Okay," he said.

"Eliza may have crossed the boundary between these worlds, becoming entangled in a dangerous game she didn't understand," Rene said.

"You're talking gibberish," Eddie said.

Rene stood and said, "You can't appreciate a symphony if your brain is limited to a three-chord progression."

"Wait," I said. "Madam Elzora's raven told me something. Perhaps you can help me understand what she meant."

Rene smiled and said, "What did Calypso tell you?"

"She said, 'The moon's shadow still lingers. Cross the gate, and she'll see you through.' Who'll see me through?"

"The keeper of the gate," Rene said.

"Madam Elzora?"

"Who else would it be?" he asked.

"Then why didn't she tell me that in the first place?" I asked.

"She told you Eliza was seeking the darkness. She showed you the door and sent you in search of the key to unlock it."

Rene's frown returned when Eddie said, "Enough with the bullshit! If you know where Eliza is, tell us."

I felt the Moon's Eye earring buzz against my neck, like an old friend urging me to pay attention.

"Some things aren't made to be neat and only make sense on the edge."

Rene's words left me feeling strangely exposed, and I asked, "Is that where we are?"

Ignoring Eddie, Rene leaned forward, his fingers tapping lightly on the table.

"It's where the best mysteries lie. Where you find things that can't be taught." His gaze lingered on me. "But you know all about mysteries, don't you, Wyatt?"

I felt a strange pull, like the ground had tilted under my chair.

"What are you getting at?" I asked.

"You're not just looking for a girl, my friend. You're searching for something deeper. Aren't you?"

A chill rippled through me as the Moon's Eye began to burn hot against my skin, its pulse quickening like a drumbeat, louder and louder until it seemed to echo through my very bones. Josie noticed my unease.

"You all right, Wyatt?" she asked.

I rubbed my neck, though the sensation didn't subside. "Just... the earring."

Rene watched me, a knowing glint in his eyes, and leaned in close.

"Sometimes, when you walk the path you're meant to walk, things you thought were dead begin to stir. And places you thought didn't exist show themselves on the other side of a veil."

"What the hell are you talking about?" Eddie asked.

"Let him finish," Hope said, her expression intent.

Rene shifted his gaze back to me. "I can show you a place, Wyatt—where all the questions you carry with you will finally be answered. But you'll need to come alone."

As I listened to Rene's words, the earring burned even hotter, a sensation like an insistent warning. I clenched my jaw against the pressure building in my head.

"And where exactly is this... place?"

Rene smiled, unfazed by the tension simmering around us.

"You'll know it when you're there, but it must be on a night like this. A night when the world isn't quite awake, and the shadows are thick enough to drown in."

The bar suddenly grew colder, and the dim light cast jagged shadows across Rene's face. My earring practically screamed a pulsing alarm that rattled in my ears like a warning bell. I met Rene's gaze, unsure if I felt fear or curiosity. I already knew I'd be going, no matter the risk.

"I'm ready anytime," I said. "What about now?"

"This isn't the door, though I've given you the key, and I have another set to perform," he said.

"Now what?" Eddie asked.

Hope blew Rene a kiss as he launched into a piano intro to another haunting song.

"Clear our tab and get the hell out of here," she said. "Rene told us what we came here to ask him."

"You have to be kidding me," Eddie said. "We still have no idea where Eliza is."

Hope glanced at me and said, "Wyatt does."

Even though it was very late when we left Musik Azul, sounds of music, laughter, and crowd noise echoed from the direction of Bourbon Street. Josie didn't ask if Hope was coming with us to the lake house. It was understood. When the garage door shut behind us, Josie led Hope into her bedroom and closed the door.

"Want to tell me what you learned back there?" Eddie asked.

"I don't have an answer for you because I don't know myself," I said.

"Then what did Hope mean?"

"Don't know," I said. "Maybe I'll have a chance to ask her in the morning."

"Hell, bro," Eddie said. "It is the morning."

"Then get some sleep. I'm returning to La Porte Mystique tomorrow and talking to Madam Elzora again."

The little bedroom on the third floor was cozy, the covers warm. Lightning flashing across the window awoke me sometime before daylight, replacing the darkness. When I opened my eyes, I saw Hope standing naked beside the bed. She smiled as she slipped under the covers and embraced me, her soft body warming me from the chill of the morning.

"There's something I haven't told you," she said.

"Like what?"

"Certain people in the Quarter may be supernatural. They are called Nocturnes."

"Is Rene a Nocturne?" I asked.

"Yes," she said. "And so is Giselle. Her life is in danger if Eddie's niece is involved with the

Nocturnes. Rene indicated as much when he said she was looking for the darkness."

"And that's why we need to find her," I said.

"It may already be too late."

"You think she's dead?" I asked.

"Or undead," she said.

"Then why did Rene offer to help us?"

"He recognized something in you and wants to possess your soul."

Chapter 13

Hope wasn't beside me in bed when I awoke to bright sunlight shining through the windows. As I descended to the first floor, laughter pealed from downstairs. Hope, Eddie, and Josie were dressed and waiting for me.

"We thought you were going to sleep until noon," Eddie said.

"It's only eight, and we didn't get much sleep last night," I said.

"Some of us didn't get any," Hope said with a smile. "I'm starved and couldn't find a damn thing in the kitchen to cook."

"I usually just call out," Josie said.

"This is the Big Easy," I said. "We can get a world-class breakfast on almost any street corner."

"We've already voted," Hope said. "I haven't seen Bertram in a while and he makes the best breakfast in the French Quarter."

"That's a fact," Eddie said.

"I'm in," I said.

Josie opened the door to the spacious garage and said, "I'm hungry, too. Let's hurry."

As Josie's sleek Range Rover rolled away from the lake house, the gentle morning light danced across Lake Pontchartrain, casting silvery reflections that sparkled like jewels. The fresh

114

spring air, fragrant with hints of jasmine and cypress, drifted through the open windows, carrying the earthy scent of the lake and the whisper of a distant breeze.

Eddie and I were in the backseat, and I admired the view as Josie navigated the big SUV along the winding shoreline. The towering oaks draped with Spanish moss created an enchanting canopy overhead. The sky was a cloudless blue—a painter's dream—unfolding like a vast canvas above us.

Hope sighed with contentment, taking in the sights of wild azaleas blooming alongside the road, their fiery colors strikingly contrasting with the lush greenery. The countryside was alive with spring's vibrance, the air filled with birdsong and the rustling of reeds swaying in rhythm with the gentle gusts.

As we crossed the city, the sights grew denser and livelier. The Range Rover glided smoothly onto the highway, the lake slowly receding behind us, giving way to the iconic skyline of New Orleans.

The unmistakable sounds of the Crescent City started to seep in—honking horns, the low rumble of streetcars, and, faintly, the distant strains of jazz that seemed to float up from the pavement. As we entered the French Quarter, I glanced out the window, catching glimpses of wrought-iron balconies draped with lush ferns and flags fluttering in the soft spring breeze.

Bertram's awaited us on Chartres Street, nestled among the pastel-painted buildings and hidden courtyards. Josie found a parking spot not far from the bar.

With a touch of Louisiana warmth, she opened the door onto the cobblestone street and said, "We're here, y'all."

As always, I felt the magic of the French Quarter settle over me—a world apart, vibrant, and alive, as if the very stones beneath our feet had a thousand tales to tell. Despite the early hour, Bertram's was doing a brisk business. It didn't stop him from smiling and rubbing his big hands together when we entered from the sidewalk.

"Well, lookie here!" he said. "If it ain't three of my favorite customers and pretty Miss Hope. How you doing, baby?"

"Like a pig in fresh slop," she said, grinning.

Bertram was already mixing drinks, stopping when Hope leaned over the zinc countertop to hug him.

"I hear that," he said. "Want one of your vampire drinks?"

"I'm off work," she said. "A martini is what I need."

The savory aroma of a Cajun breakfast feast filled the kitchen in the back of Bertram's bar. He had everything going—cast-iron skillets sizzling with andouille sausage and shrimp, thick slices of French bread browning in butter, and a pot of cheesy grits bubbling away on the stove. Over it all, the unmistakable fragrance of dark roast coffee, mingled with the heady scent of rosemary, thyme, and garlic, filled the bar with a warmth that felt like home.

We sat at the bar, sipping our drinks as Bertram brought out steaming plates piled with shrimp and grits, topped with poached eggs and garnished with chopped green onions. Alongside were buttery biscuits, freshly baked and still warm, waiting to be slathered with homemade cane syrup.

I leaned back, letting out a low whistle. "Bertram, you might've outdone yourself this time."

Hope reached for a biscuit, breaking it open with a satisfying tear. "You're spoiling us, Bertram. I could get used to this."

"Careful," Bertram chuckled, handing over a plate to Eddie. "Get used to it, and you'll be here every morning, eating me out of house and home."

Eddie grinned as he forked a generous bite of shrimp and grits.

"Bertram, if you served this every morning, I'd put up a cot in the back and never leave."

Josie laughed, stirring sugar into her coffee, and said, "That's the danger with good cooking around here. Folks start showing up; before you know it, they're family."

Hope nodded, savoring a forkful of grits. "Well, that's not such a bad thing in my book. After all, family is the people with who you share meals."

I gave Bertram a nod. "Or who shares your meals. Guess we're all part of the Picou family now."

Bertram grinned, wiping his hands on his apron. "Long as y'all clean up after yourselves, you're welcome anytime." He winked, grabbing his coffee cup and settling in behind the bar. "But don't even think about asking me to make beignets. That's where I draw the line."

Laughter filled the bar, and for a moment, everything felt easy and right—a group of friends, a great breakfast, and nothing on our minds but the warmth of good company and the taste of Bertram's fine Cajun cooking. Things changed when N.O.P.D. homicide detectives Tommy O'Rear and Marlon Bando joined us.

Bertram poured Tommy a cold Abita, which he had on tap, along with a shot of blackjack. Like me, Marlon was a teetotaler, and he smiled when Bertram sat a glass of chilled pineapple juice on the bar before him.

"My two favorite homicide detectives," Bertram said. "Want some breakfast?"

"Thought you'd never ask," Tommy said.

Tommy and Marlon tore into Bertram's breakfast as if they hadn't eaten in a while. Their clothes looked lived in. I noticed, and so did Bertram.

"Long night?" he asked. "You two look as if you didn't get much sleep."

"Because we didn't get any," Tommy said.

"What's the problem?" Bertram asked.

"That's why we're here. The body of our murder victim disappeared from the morgue." Tommy looked at me and said, "Know anything about it?"

"Why ask me?" I only met the woman once."

"Because we have no other place to go; no clues, no body, no nothing," Tommy said.

"Bodies don't just disappear," Eddie said.

"This one did," Marlon said.

"Someone must have taken it," Eddie said.

"No way," Tommy said. "The morgue is secure. No one goes in or out without someone knowing it."

"It's as if the body vanished into thin air," Marlon said.

"Was there an autopsy performed?" I asked.

"Scheduled but never completed. The only info we have on the body was from our initial examination," Tommy said.

"Are we talking about the woman you and Josie discovered?" Hope asked.

I nodded. "Josie and I found the body of Sabine Moreau drained of blood."

"The victim of a vampire," Hope said.

Tommy and Marlon quickly focused on Hope and her comment about vampires.

"Who are you, ma'am," Tommy asked. "And what do you know about vampires?"

"I'm Hope, the owner of the Eden Club, the Quarter's only vampire bar."

"Your customers are vampires?" Marlon asked.

"Working vampires," Hope said. "People who have an interest in the vampire lifestyle, though, hold down day jobs and don't have fangs."

"Do you suspect any of these working vampires of murder?" Tommy asked.

"No way," Hope said. "It's more of a cultural thing."

Eddie turned his attention to me and said, "Tell me again how you and Josie happened to find the body of the deceased."

I smiled and said, "Ever the prosecutor. I visited the studio of reclusive artist Giselle earlier in the day and spoke with Sabine Moreau, Giselle's assistant. She informed me Giselle only works late at night."

"Why did Josie go with you?" Eddie asked.

"The Crystal Skull caused me to have a disturbing dream," she said.

"Crystal Skull?" Tommy said.

"An ancient artifact Josie traded for when we visited Madam Elzora," I said.

"Who is Madam Elzora?" Tommy asked.

"A voodoo mambo who owns La Porte Mystique, a botanica not far from St. Louis Cemetery No. 1," I said.

"How is Madam Elzora involved in this case?" Tommy asked.

"The name of her shop was written on an AMTRAK schedule," I said. "We're looking for Eddie's niece, Eliza. The note was in Eliza's handwriting and was our only clue."

"Where is this Crystal Skull?" Tommy asked.

When Josie flashed me an apprehensive glance, I remembered she'd left the Crystal Skull in my room upstairs. She hadn't taken it when I lowered her to the street below my balcony.

"It's in my room," I said.

"Can you get it?" Tommy asked.

My cat Kisses purred and rubbed against my leg when I entered the door to my apartment. I gave her fresh water and food before looking for the Crystal Skull. I clearly remembered seeing it last on the nightstand.

The Crystal Skull was gone and my Moon's Eye earring sending distressing signals to my suddenly overloaded brain.

"Where is it?" Eddie asked when I rejoined everyone at the bar.

"Vanished," I said.

Bertram, Josie, and Eddie exchanged glances.

"Impossible," Bertram said. "Ain't nobody been up those stairs except me since you last left."

"Do you remember seeing the skull when you fed Kisses?" I asked.

Bertram nodded. "It was on the nightstand beside your bed."

Marlon smiled wryly when he said, "Maybe the same person who took the victim's body stole your Crystal Skull. What's the address of this voodoo botanica?"

I wrote the address of La Porte Mystique on a bar napkin and handed it to Tommy. Having finished their breakfasts and drinks, he and Marlon looked considerably better than when they'd entered the bar.

"It's starting to sound like our murder and your missing person investigation are linked," Tommy said. "If you learn anything interesting, keep us informed."

"Will do, Lieutenant," I said.

Bertram began clearing the bar of plates and utensils as Tommy and Marlon exited the bar.

"What now?" Eddie asked.

"Madam Elzora informed me that she's the true owner of the Crystal Skull and that it will ultimately be returned to her."

"Maybe she took it," Eddie said.

"I done told you," Bertram said. "No one except me has been in Wyatt's room since he was last there."

"Sounds as if we need to revisit La Porte Mystique," Josie said.

"Let's wait awhile," I said. "At least until Tommy and Marlon are gone."

"How in hell did a body disappear from the morgue?" Eddie asked.

"If she was drained of blood, maybe she's the victim of a vampire," Hope said.

"There are no real vampires," Eddie said.

"Malik is," Hope said.

"Then maybe he killed Sabine Moreau," Eddie said.

I shook my head. "Malik's victims are street people who no one ever reports as missing. It's what has kept him under the radar for so long. He wouldn't have killed someone who would involve the police," I said.

"Maybe we should ask him," Eddie said. "He hinted about the disappearing house on Bourbon Street where other vampires congregate. If he wasn't just pulling our legs, maybe he'd take us there."

"It'll have to wait until Rene shows me the mysterious place where all my questions will be answered."

"No need to wait," Eddie said. "You check out Rene, and I'll check out Malik."

"Not without me, you're not," Josie said. "I'm coming with you."

"Me too," Hope said. "If there's another vampire club in the Quarter, I want to visit it."

"Sounds like a plan," I said. "Right now, it's a long time until it's dark, and I didn't get much sleep last night. I'm going upstairs and remedy the situation."

Chapter 14

After Wyatt had gone upstairs, Eddie, Hope, and Josie continued drinking. The day was sunny, and regulars and tourists were starting to fill the bar.

"Another drink?" Bertram asked when their glasses neared empty.

Eddie handed him a credit card and said, "Clear our tab. It's about time we visited Madam Elzora's."

"Good," Bertram said. "I got other customers to attend to." He looked at Hope and said, "Baby, don't make yourself so scarce next time. I love that pretty face of yours."

Hope leaned over the bar and hugged him. "And I love yours," she said.

Hope stopped when they reached the front door. "I need sleep, and I'm not going with you to La Porte Mystique."

Josie kissed her and said, "Then we'll see you later tonight."

Hope grinned. "Neither of you got any more sleep than I did, and there'll be lots of time after you visit the botanica before I open the Eden Club."

"What are you suggesting?" Josie asked.

Hope handed her a business card with directions scribbled on the back.

"This is my address," she said. 'When you're finished at La Porte Mystique, join me. I'll leave the door open."

Hope held Josie's hand a moment too long before turning and walking away.

"You two have a thing going?" Eddie asked.

Josie grinned and said, "You jealous?"

"Just asking," Eddie said.

"A girl crush," Josie said. "Nothing serious."

"Uh huh," Eddie said, deciding not to press the subject.

It was a glorious day in the French Quarter as they set out on foot to La Porte Mystique, birds chirping in the trees.

"This is the first time, you know?" Eddie said.

"For what?" Josie asked.

"Since I left you..."

"Waiting at the altar?" Josie said, finishing his sentence.

"I've apologized more than once. Let me do it again," he said.

"No need," Josie said, looking away. "I'm over it."

Eddie grabbed her shoulder. "I'm not. I need to explain. I wasn't ready. It wasn't right for me and wouldn't have been good for either of us."

"I've come to grips with it," she said. "Now that I have, I'm glad it happened like it did. I wanted a father for Jojo so badly that I let it impair my good judgment."

"I tried my best," Eddie said. "When the time came, I couldn't go through with it."

"Like I said, it's okay. Since Jojo's real father came forward and accepted him as his son, Jojo's been on cloud nine. He's in Florida now, spending time with his father, his new stepmother, and his half-siblings. He won't return to New Orleans until school starts in the fall."

"And you're okay with it?"

Josie smiled. "Having the time of my life. Children are a heavy responsibility."

"I imagine," Eddie said. "Maybe you and I can get back together in the meantime."

"Don't press your luck, Eddie Toledo. That's never going to happen. You're still an asshole, and lucky I didn't kick you in the nuts."

Eddie smiled, extended his hand, and said, "Friends?"

Josie nodded, shook his hand, and said, "Yes, and that's all we'll ever be. Meantime, I'm here to help you find Eliza."

The brass bell on the door tinkled as Josie and Eddie entered La Porte Mystique. As before, the air was thick with incense and dried herbs. Eddie glanced in awe at the potions and remedies lining the shelves on the walls.

"What's that smell?" he asked.

"Sage," Josie said. "Someone's burning it to rid the botanica of evil spirits."

"I hate it," Eddie said. "It might just get rid of me."

"You'll survive," Josie said. "Do you see what I see?"

On a cabinet sat the Crystal Skull, glowing azure blue.

Someone behind them said, "The magical skull returned to its rightful owner."

It was Madam Elzora.

The old woman's face told the stories of many lifetimes. Deeply wrinkled and tanned to a shade that resembled well-worn leather, her skin had a textured look, weathered by age and the Louisiana sun, giving her an almost mystical appearance.

Her eyes were sharp and penetrating, glinting with wisdom and secrets as if she'd seen both the past and the future. Crow's feet fanned out around them, but her gaze was lively and astute. She wore a vibrant indigo turban, its fabric intricately knotted and adorned with hand-sewn charms and feathers. A few locks of gray hair escaped from beneath, adding to her untamed look.

Her clothing was rich with the symbols of her craft: layers of earthy-colored robes draped with strings of beads in shades of red, black, and white, each amulet telling its own tale. Small charms dangled from her neck—crosses, tiny animal bones, and moon-shaped trinkets softly clinking as she moved.

Her hands, twisted with arthritis and covered in intricate henna patterns, were wrapped in rings bearing stones of obsidian and blood-red garnet, adding to her commanding presence. Bracelets woven with leather and copper, some bearing engraved veves, adorned her wrists and marked her as an experienced practitioner of the craft of voodoo.

"You traded it to me," Josie said. "Why did you take it back?"

"I took nothing," the old woman said. "The Crystal Skull was here when I awoke. Whatever service you required was performed. Now, it has returned to me. Who is this person with you?"

"Eddie Toledo. Eliza's uncle," he said.

A smile crept over the old woman's face, and she said, "Ah, yes."

"You know something?" Eddie asked.

Madam Elzora's voice changed when she spoke, her New Orleans accent replaced by the sing-song patois of an antebellum field worker. She leaned in close, the rattling of her amulets the only sound in the dimly lit room. Her gaze settled first on Eddie, then drifted to Josie with a knowing heaviness.

"You two... I seen your faces before, many times, many places. In dreams, shadows, lifetimes that ain't this one."

Eddie exchanged a glance with Josie, raising an eyebrow.

"You're saying Josie and I have met before?"

Madam Elzora chuckled, like dry leaves rustling, and held his gaze.

"Oh, you ain't just met, child. You were born into the same family, a brother and sister once. Bound by blood, but torn by fate."

Josie shifted in her seat, a chill creeping up her spine.

"A brother and sister? But... We're—"

"Soulmates, I know. This lifetime, you're something different. The spirit's a funny thing. It don't care what this world says is right. You and him, you were bound from the start. Different lives, different forms... but the same souls."

Eddie's expression turned serious, the words settling heavily on him.

"And... that's why we feel this way? Why we're... locked together?"

Madam Elzora nodded, her eyes glinting with something neither Josie nor Eddie could name.

"Locked, yes. The love between you... it can't be broken, even if it ain't meant to be. This world got its rules, just like the last. You two were never to be, not in that life nor this one. But that don't stop what the soul knows. You're bound together... for better or worse until your time here is done."

Josie felt a tightness in her chest, a mix of relief and sorrow that she couldn't explain.

"So, this is... this feeling... it's not just in my head?" Josie said.

Madam Elzora smiled, her wrinkled hand reaching to rest on Josie's.

"Child, it's in your spirit. You carry each other in there. Ain't no breaking that bond. Just learn to live with it, same as you done before."

Madam Elzora's words hung between them, and for a moment, neither Eddie nor Josie spoke. The room felt thick with memories they couldn't name but could almost feel lingering in the air between them like a secret melody.

"If what you say is true, then I want more than ever to help Eddie find his niece," Josie said.

Eddie's Rolex was his prize possession, given to him after a decade of service with the Department of Justice. Madam Elzora glanced at it. The old voodoo mambo rested her hand on the watch.

"Beautiful timepiece," she said.

"You know something about Eliza?"

"Maybe," Madam Elzora said.

Eddie removed the watch from his wrist and handed it to her.

"From me to you," he said.

Madam Elzora's New Orleans patois had returned when she said, "The old vampire gave you a clue."

"The disappearing house on Bourbon?" Eddie said.

"A dangerous and fascinating place. You mustn't go there alone. Take the old vampire with you. He will keep you safe. I must go now."

"Wait," Eddie said. "Is the disappearing house where we'll find my niece?"

"I don't open doors; I only disperse keys," the old woman said. "What you find when you open the door is up to you."

"How is it up to me?" Eddie asked.

Madam Elzora grinned and said, "Maybe Calypso will tell you."

The ancient voodoo mambo disappeared behind the black curtain as Eddie and Josie locked eyes.

"What now?" she said.

"See what the bird tells us, and then get the hell out of here," Eddie said.

Josie nodded toward the large black bird and said, "Good, because she's waiting for us."

Calypso sat perched on a shelf near the front door. She cocked her head, her sharp black eyes glinting in the dim light. After ruffling her feathers, she spoke in a deep voice.

"By unseen will, it came and went,
Its fleeting presence a tale well-spent.
But skies grew dark, and fate took hold,
A spell was cast, both fierce and bold."

Eddie shook his head and said, "I don't understand. Are you talking about the disappearing house?"

Calypso watched them closely, testing their resolve. Then added, softer, "In that house, truth wears many faces. Look for the child—but know she may not be the only one waiting."

The brass bell on the door to La Porte Mystique tinkled as they exited Madam Elzora's botanica.

"Strange," Josie said.

"Everything about that place is strange," Eddie said.

"There was no one there but us," Josie said. "Same as last time when Wyatt and I visited."

"So?" Eddie said.

"How does she stay in business without any customers?"

Eddie rubbed the wrist once occupied by his Rolex.

"Tell that to our watches. The old woman's making out like a bandit," he said. "What now?"

"Like Hope said, it's a long time until midnight. Her house isn't far from here, and if we'll be up all night again, we need some sleep."

Hope's house was nearby. Eddie's jaw dropped when the gorgeous woman opened the door naked and with a yawn. Josie glanced at Eddie's perplexed expression, shook her head, and grinned.

Hope grabbed Josie's wrist, pulled her through the door, and said, "Come in this house."

Eddie glanced around the apartment when he unlocked his gaze from Hope's lush body.

"Cozy," he said.

"I love it," Josie said.

Hope's French Quarter apartment had a vintage charm that reflected her practical lifestyle and love for the area's character. Situated in a Creole-style building, it had tall windows framed by sheer curtains that let in the soft glow of the streetlights below at night.

The worn but polished hardwood floors creaked slightly with every step. An assortment of antique rugs lent warmth to the space. Hope's furniture was an eclectic mix: a velvet armchair by the window, a small but sturdy couch in muted tones, and a low coffee table with chipped edges.

A secondhand turntable sat in one corner, and a few framed photographs and local art pieces adorned the exposed brick walls. In the modest kitchenette, open shelving held mismatched ceramic plates, coffee mugs, and a small stash of spices and spirits.

A single ceiling fan slowly spun overhead, adding to the relaxed ambiance. The place had an understated elegance, with a few personal touches—a guitar leaning against the wall, a vintage floor lamp beside the armchair, and a shelf lined with well-loved books.

Despite its simplicity, Hope's apartment felt comfortable and lived-in, a quiet retreat from her life at the bustling Eden Club.

"I love your place," Josie said.

Hope yawned again. "Wait till you see my bedroom. My four-poster isn't gigantic, though plenty large for all of us."

Hope grinned when Eddie said, "I think I need a drink."

Hope pointed to the liquor bottles on a cabinet in the kitchenette.

"This ain't the Eden Club, so pour your own." Grabbing Josie's hand, she pulled her toward her bedroom. "And Eddie, when you've had your drink, doff your clothes and join us."

Chapter 15

Flickering neon filtered through my open balcony door when I awoke, a slight breeze wafting the curtain. It was late, nearly midnight. My kitty Kisses was nowhere around, probably tomcatting in her favorite French Quarter alleyway. I smiled, realizing she and I weren't that different.

The night was chilly as I followed the darkened sidewalk toward Musik Azul, and I was glad I'd thought to wear a warm scarf and sports coat. The people on the sidewalks thinned as I neared the music venue where Rene would be playing.

Musik Azul was as I remembered it, and hearing Rene's voice filling the room was almost like stepping into a hidden part of New Orleans that most tourists only dream of. There was something about that kind of music, in a place as dark and timeless as Musik Azul, that felt like magic, pulling everyone into a shared moment. If only Josie could be here with me, tucked into a candlelit corner, letting that song wash over us!

Rene was finishing a set, his gravelly voice haunting as he told a story with his song. When he spotted me, he completed the song and nodded to a door in the back. As I joined him, a chill wind blew down the dark alleyway behind the bar.

"Where are we going?" I asked as we left the noise of the bar.

"A place in the Quarter tourists never visit," he said.

"There aren't many places in the Quarter I haven't visited," I said.

"Where I'm taking you is a hidden place known only to those attuned to the city's supernatural undercurrents, a city unlike any that you know, and a secret shrine called La Grotte de la Vérité."

"The Grotto of Truth," I said. "Is that what I'm going to find?"

"Like beauty, truth is in the eyes of the beholder, and almost everyone sees it differently. I'm curious to learn how you see it."

"Can't wait," I said.

Rene led me through the winding alleys of the French Quarter to an old iron door hidden in plain sight between two crumbling brick buildings. When he said an incantation and pushed open the door, we stepped into a place that felt familiar and otherworldly—a shadowy reflection of New Orleans, where time and reality blurred.

It was New Orleans, only different, dark, and diffused in color.

"This is unreal," I said.

"An alternate plane of reality holding remnants of what the city might have been in forgotten eras, and here, anything is possible."

We stepped onto cobbled streets under a sky that seemed trapped in twilight. Maybe I was dreaming, but we were in an uncanny version of the Quarter that pulsed with an eerie energy.

The journey into the parallel universe began subtly as a dream one barely notices has shifted. As we stepped out of the dimly lit alleyway, the familiar scents of the French Quarter—jasmine, fried beignets, and aged bourbon—warped into a faint metallic tang. The Quarter was still there, though not quite. Gas lamps cast an unnatural glow, their flickering flames refracted in hues of green and blue, making the cobblestone streets ripple like water. Though the light sources were unclear, shadows danced on the buildings like the moon hung in fractured pieces across the sky.

The wrought-iron balconies sagged under the weight of impossible flora. Vines of ghostly white wisteria coiled around railings and spilled downward, their blossoms shimmering with an eerie bioluminescence. In place of Mardi Gras beads, the branches held strings of what appeared to be glowing orbs, pulsing faintly like beating hearts. The air buzzed with a low-frequency, unsettling, and rhythmic hum, as though the city was alive and breathing.

Distorted people, almost too tall, limbs too long, and faces veiled by a shimmering haze, moved through the mist-laden streets. Some nodded as we passed, their eyes flickering like oil lamps, while others seemed to vanish the moment they turned their heads.

The shops bore uncanny facades: the once-colorful doorframes were now etched with spiraling runes that glowed faintly. A bookstore called *Pages of Yesterday* displayed books in its window, but the titles shifted constantly, the words dancing into illegible shapes before settling briefly into familiar scripts.

Even the soundscape had changed. The soulful jazz drifting from unseen brass bands felt warped, slowed down, and layered with an unidentifiable wail, like a distant cry submerged underwater. Though their tones clanged hollow, the cathedral's bells rang, each chime sending subtle tremors through the ground beneath our feet.

"Is it always like this?" I asked.

Rene, unfazed, adjusted his hat and smiled. "Always and never. The Vérité bleeding through— the Quarter's reflection, stripped of its disguises. Stay close. The truth is not always kind to strangers."

As we continued, the air grew colder, and the streets narrowed, guiding us like veins to the heart of this spectral mirror of the French Quarter. Ahead loomed an arched doorway embedded into the earth itself, its stone surface slick with moisture and marked by a sigil that glowed faintly red.

La Grotte de la Vérité waited beyond, though I couldn't shake the feeling that we were already inside something much older—and much hungrier—than the city we'd left behind. A staircase beneath the old stone slab led down to the damp air of the cavernous depths.

"The catacombs," he said.

"Impossible," I said. "New Orleans is below sea level."

Rene only laughed. "You will see," he said.

We descended silently, Rene carrying a small lantern he'd produced from some unknown place. I felt the walls pressing in, the age and weight of the city surrounding me. The passages twisted and turned, leading ever deeper until a faint hum filled the air, like whispered secrets from the past.

The grotto was an underground chamber lined with crumbling stone archways and carved symbols that glowed faintly in the dark. At its center was a still pool of water, reflecting our images with an unsettling clarity.

"Approach the pool," Rene said.

As I peered into the still water, visions began to unfold as if time had melted away, revealing his world's hidden motives, spectral presences, and unresolved mysteries.

"This is crazy," I said. "It must be a dream because this place can't exist."

"A parallel universe, if you will. Only the invited ever experience it."

"Why me?" I asked.

"You have questions, and the grotto reveals answers only to those willing to confront the most complex truths."

"What truths?"

"Questions that have haunted you your whole life," he said.

"I'm fine with my past," I said. "I thought you were helping me find Eliza."

"You're a Traveler and have experienced many pasts," Rene said. "Before becoming one of us, you must accept your fate."

"What the hell are you talking about?" I asked. "I'm not here for myself," I said.

"You are rudderless. If you have no destination, no map will guide you there," he said.

"I have a destination. I know what I'm looking for."

Rene shook his head and said, "Do you? This space straddles the boundary between worlds and reveals truths beyond ordinary perception."

"What exactly do you want me to become," I asked.

"A Nocturne," he said. "You've been chosen."

"This place confuses me," I said.

"Clarity will soon replace your confusion. Sit by the pool and stare into the water. You must do this alone."

Rene's lantern cast flickering shadows that danced like spirits on the cavern walls. The Grotto of Truth wasn't what I expected—no statues, no altars, just a still pool of water, dark as ink and rimmed with jagged stones. The air hung heavy with the scent of damp earth and something faintly metallic.

"What must I do alone?" I asked.

"Stare into the water," Rene said, his voice reverent, almost fearful. "You'll see what you need to see."

I crouched at the edge, reluctant but unable to refuse. The water was unnaturally still, its surface reflecting my face with unnerving clarity. At first, there was nothing but my reflection, distorted by the dim light. Then, ripples began to form, concentric circles spreading outward from some unseen source.

The first face appeared. My mother. Her features were soft, her eyes brimming with sorrow I didn't understand. She didn't speak, only mouthed words I couldn't hear before fading.

Then, my father. He looked younger than I remembered, a wide-brimmed hat shadowing his piercing eyes. "Keep looking, son," he said, his voice echoing in my mind rather than my ears. "You've only scratched the surface."

And then he—my grandfather, Governor Charles Wyatt Thomas, a titan of Louisiana politics in his time. His face emerged sharp and clear, his gaze piercing the veil between worlds. His death had been a mystery—an assassin's bullet ended his reign abruptly, leaving a legacy tangled in shadows and whispers of conspiracy.

"Grandpa," I muttered, my throat dry. "How is this possible?"

"Possible is a matter of perspective," he said, his voice low and commanding. "You've seen too much of this world to doubt that now."

"Why are you here?"

"To tell you what must be done," he said, his expression hardening. "Join the Nocturnes, Wyatt."

I frowned. "Grandpa, I don't even know what a Nocturne is."

"Power," he said, the word heavy with promise and threat. "Only a few control the universe. Most are controlled and too stupid to know it. The Nocturnes stand at the pinnacle. Join us. I need your youth."

I staggered back, shaking my head. "You're dead, Grandpa."

"Maybe not," he said, a ghost of a smile playing on his lips. "Life and death are smaller things than you realize." His image shimmered, breaking apart like a reflection in disturbed water. "Think about it. You can be more than you ever dreamed—or continue being less than nothing."

The pool stilled. The cavern fell silent.

I turned to Rene; his expression was unreadable. "What the hell is a Nocturne?"

"You'll find out," Rene said. "When you're ready."

The lantern light seemed dimmer now, the shadows deeper. I shivered, though the air was warm. Something had shifted, and I couldn't shake the feeling that my grandfather wasn't entirely gone—or altogether wrong.

Another image appeared, confounding me. It was Desire, the only woman I'd ever truly loved. Her image rippled in ever-increasing circles. Her hand was outstretched as if attempting to take my hand and pull me into the pool with her or perhaps have me save her from the cold depths of death. I heard Rene moving behind me and turned to look. No one was there, and Desire's image was gone when I gazed again into the pool's stillness.

Desire's image was gone, though it had appeared, chilling my soul. The image of Josie, Hope, and Eddie appeared. They were in a grand hall amid dozens of opulently dressed revelers. I sensed something was dreadfully wrong.

I staggered to my feet, my heart pounding as the visions dissolved. I sensed a shift in the air, a warning deep in my bones.

"Rene," I said, "I must return to the Quarter."

"Go?" Rene's brow furrowed. "You've only just begun to see—"

"No time. They're in danger. Eddie, Josie, and Hope. I feel it."

Before Rene could protest, I bolted from the grotto, my mind racing as I navigated the labyrinthine corridors back to the surface. When I burst into the French Quarter, the familiar chaos of the streets disoriented me for a moment before I regained my focus. There was only one person who could help now.

Chapter 16

Eddie awoke in an old four-poster bed he didn't immediately recognize. It took him a moment to realize that he was alone. Getting out of bed, he searched the dark room until he found his clothes.

The ethereal memory of lying between Hope and Josie's warm bodies still caused his skin to tingle. When he exited the bedroom, he found them grinning as they held hands on Hope's overstuffed couch.

"You aren't waiting on me, are you?" he asked.

"If we were, we'd be backing up," Hope said.

"Funny," Eddie said.

"We're not laughing at you," Hope said. "You are quite the man."

"As I remember, I was doing more watching than participating," he said.

"Oh, you participated," Hope said. "To that, I can attest. If we're going to a party, we must dress more suitably."

"We only have the clothes we arrived in," Josie said.

Hope nodded and said, "No problem. As owner of the Eden Club, I've collected an eclectic wardrobe for both sexes. Let's go look."

140

Hope had a unique rack of clothes in her extra bedroom. She, Josie, and Eddie were soon sorting through them, each finding something catching their fantasy.

When they were dressed, Hope said, "You ready to hit the Eden Club?"

"I'd rather revisit your bedroom," he said.

"There's time for that after we visit the disappearing house," Hope said.

"How can you be so sure there is such a place?" he asked.

"If Malik said there is, then I believe him," she said. "I called my sister, Nyx. She replaced me as bartender last night and will do it again tonight. I'll sacrifice the tips, though I won't miss the excitement of accompanying the two of you to Malik's disappearing house."

Hope, Josie, and Eddie's attire reflected their anticipation for the strange and mysterious evening ahead. A plunging neckline highlighted Hope's floor-length black dress. A choker adorned with an iridescent opal caught flashes of green and purple as she moved.

Josie's black leather pants clung to her body like a glove. A white lace blouse, mimicking Hope's plunging neckline, completed her look. She layered the outfit with a cropped leather jacket and stiletto heels.

Eddie had a little gangster in him, so he chose a charcoal-gray blazer over a black button-up shirt. His dark jeans were cuffed at the ankle, revealing polished black boots.

Lightning lit the sky as they entered the almost hidden doorway to the Eden Club. Their carefully chosen outfits drew glances and whispered admiration, setting the tone for what promised to be a night steeped in the strange and extraordinary. Hope's replacement bartender was waiting for them at the bar.

"I'm Nyx," she said. "Hope's sister."

"Little sister," Hope said. "Growing up, she was an insufferable brat."

Nyx's ash-blonde hair was tied in a ponytail. A classic beauty, she needed no makeup.

"I see the resemblance. I'm Eddie, and this is Josie."

Nyx smiled and said, "Now I see why Hope wants the night off."

Hope's little sister wore white shorts and an Eden Club T-shirt. She was a slenderer version of Hope, and like her sister, her legs were world-class. Eddie couldn't stop staring, and both Hope and Josie noticed.

When he sensed them glaring at him, he said, "I can't get over your baby sister's piercing blue eyes."

Nyx grinned when Hope said, "You weren't looking at her eyes."

Nyx said, "Cocktails?"

"Martinis for me and Josie. Scotch for Eddie," Hope said.

"Any particular brand?" Nyx asked.

"Monkey Shoulder if you have it," Eddie said.

"We have everything," Nyx said.

Haunting music poured from hidden speakers, adding to the vibe of the dimly lit vampire club. Hope, Josie, and Eddie sat at the bar. To the annoyance of Hope and Josie, Eddie and Nyx continued to flirt.

"Has Malik been in yet?" Hope asked.

"No," Nyx said. "You know I can't stand that creepy man."

"He's not exactly warm and cuddly," Hope said.

"Unless you like reptiles," Nyx said.

Hope smiled and turned around when a deep bass voice said, "Are you talking about me?"

"Mr. Malik," Hope said. "My sis is tending bar tonight."

"Oh?" the large man said. "Other plans?"

"We were hoping you'd take us to the disappearing house," Hope said.

"Don't know about that," Malik said. "I have my own agenda for later tonight."

Hope clutched his hand and said, "I can make it worth your while."

Malik's eyes widened, and he said, "Really?"

Nyx interrupted their conversation when she handed Malik a drink and said, "Here's your grim reaper, Mr. Malik."

Nyx made a face when Malik said, "Is your little sister included in the bargain?"

"Just me," Hope said.

Malik chugged the grim reaper and tossed four quarters on the bar. "Fine," he said. "I'll take care of my business now and return in a few hours."

When he'd exited the bar, Josie said, "You won't go through with your promise, will you?"

"I'll wiggle out of it somehow," Hope said.

"Sounds like you just wiggled into it," Eddie said.

Nyx grinned and said, "Don't expect me to bail you out."

"I'll get us into the disappearing house. I'm counting on the rest of you to help me get out of my promise to Malik," Hope said.

The trio was well-lubricated when Malik returned. After drinking another grim reaper, he said, "Are we ready?"

"Let's do it," Eddie said.

The quartet emerged from the Eden Club and stepped onto Bourbon Street, alive with its usual mix of neon lights, raucous laughter, and jazz pouring from open doorways—the scent of spilled beer mingling with the faint sweetness of pralines from a nearby shop. Bourbon Street's chaos seemed almost comforting as Malik led the group southward, navigating the shifting tapestry of tourists and street performers.

The further they walked, the livelier the noise seemed—until, strangely, it didn't. Somewhere past St. Ann Street, the lights grew dimmer, the crowd's buzz muted. It was like an invisible curtain had dropped, leaving them in a shadowed corridor where time and sound felt distorted.

The group turned onto an unassuming side street where gaslights flickered unnaturally, casting elongated shadows that danced like spectral fingers. In the darkness of the non-commercial end of Bourbon Street, Malik raised a hand to halt them. There it was, a vacant lot between houses.

"This can't be right," Eddie said. "There are no vacant lots in the French Quarter."

"Watch and learn," Malik said, his voice lower, almost reverent.

And then it appeared—a flickering vision, barely solid, of a Creole townhouse. Its shutters were askew, its wrought iron balcony draped with cobwebs, yet it seemed alive, pulsing faintly with light that shimmered between the physical and ethereal. The house looked like it had been plucked from another era and stitched imperfectly into the present.

Malik knocked on the peeling door with a rehearsed rhythm. It swung open, revealing a dimly lit foyer that smelled faintly of jasmine and decay. Inside, everything seemed slightly off-kilter—doors too tall, chandeliers swaying as if caught in an unseen breeze.

The ballroom was like stepping into the abyss—dark, decadent, and otherworldly. The air was thick with the scent of aged wine and spiced incense, mingling with an underlying tang of blood that prickled the senses. Crystal chandeliers draped from the vaulted ceiling, their light refracted by clusters of black diamonds, casting fractured shadows that danced ominously across the marble floor. The crowd of vampires gathered beneath them was a tableau of ageless beauty and sinister intent, their eyes gleaming with predatory hunger.

Malik hesitated at the threshold, his normally imperious demeanor faltering. "I'm not exactly welcome here," he said, his gaze sweeping over the throng.

"Why not?" Eddie asked, his voice barely audible over the eerie strains of a violin being played somewhere unseen.

Malik's lips curled into a sardonic smile. "I came here from France over three centuries ago. These New World vampires don't trust outsiders— especially one as old as me. To them, I'm an interloper, a relic of a bygone age."

Hope glanced at him sharply, her curiosity piqued but tempered by unease. "Then why are we here?"

"You'll see," Malik said, his tone cloaked in a peculiar mix of reverence and disdain.

The trio followed him through the milling crowd. As they passed, all eyes seemed to turn toward them, some curious, others openly hostile. Malik pressed forward, his head held high despite the whispered curses and sneers trailing after him.

At one end of the room was a magnificent dais, an opulent stage raised above the crowd like a dark sun around which the gathering revolved. The throne atop it was a work of grotesque beauty—

crafted from blackened gold and encrusted with blood-red rubies, it seemed almost alive, pulsating faintly as though imbued with a heartbeat. On the throne sat a towering figure, his presence as commanding as the throne itself.

"That's Lucien D'Arcy," Malik said, his voice low and tinged with something close to fear. "The Prince of Darkness."

Lucien was a mountain of a man, his skin like polished alabaster, his eyes a blazing inferno of amber. His power radiated from him like a storm, coiling in the air and brushing against the room's edges. Around him, his favored minions flitted like shadows, each a masterpiece of seduction and menace.

"Sabine Moreau," Josie said, her gaze locking onto a pale figure. "She's alive."

Malik smirked and said, "Not quite."

Sabine glided across the dais like a phantom, her ice-white gown trailing behind her like smoke. She settled beneath D'Arcy's throne.

Next to Sabine stood Marceline, a statuesque figure with a crown of raven hair and a gaze that pierced through the dimness. Giselle, a gorgeous red-haired woman with dark eyes that seemed to drink in the light, moved with a predatory grace.

But it was the figure seated beside Lucien who commanded the most attention. Draped in layers of black veils, the figure exuded a chilling authority. The veils obscured all but the faintest outline of a face—pale, delicate, and inhumanly still. Whispers rippled through the crowd, too low for human ears to decipher, but Malik's expression hardened as he stared at her.

"Who is she?" Josie dared to ask, her voice barely a whisper.

Malik's answer came after a long pause, his voice tight. "The Widow of Midnight, the Shadow

Queen. She was human once. She's older than me. But one thing is certain—she's more dangerous than anyone else in this room."

As they watched, Lucien rose from his throne, his imposing figure casting a shadow that seemed to stretch impossibly far. He surveyed the room with a lazy arrogance, his gaze lingering on Malik and his companions for a fraction too long. A thin smile curled his lips, and with a flick of his hand, the crowd parted to make way for him.

"Malik," Lucien said, his voice deep and resonant, like the tolling of a cathedral bell. "It's been far too long. Tell me, what brings you to my domain... and with such interesting company?"

Malik bowed slightly but did not kneel, a defiance that made the air tense.

"A matter of mutual interest, Your Highness," he said carefully.

Lucien's smile widened, revealing teeth that gleamed like polished ivory. "Then, by all means, speak. But tread carefully—my patience for old ghosts grows thin."

The veiled figure beside him shifted slightly, her unseen gaze landing on Malik. Though her features were hidden, the weight of her attention was suffocating, a reminder that no one was truly safe in this den of darkness. Malik stepped forward, his voice low and deliberate, as if the words carried the weight of centuries.

"Old ghosts, Lucien? Is that what you think this is? Fragments of the past lingering to haunt your evenings? No, this is something far older... something far worse. You thought you could bury it, didn't you? But the truth has claws, and it's digging its way out—starting with the pact you broke and the blood you owe."

Malik paused, letting the silence stretch, his dark eyes unblinking as they bore into Lucien.

"You tax my patience, old vampire. I've spared you because of sentiments beginning to fade," Lucien said. "I'd advise you not to continue pressing your luck."

"The debt remains. And it's not just your soul they're after, Lucien. It's everyone you've ever touched. Shall I continue? Or is your patience for the truth even thinner than for ghosts?"

"Guards," Lucien's commanding voice said.

Anticipation rippled through the crowded room as Lucien's minions appeared from the darkness.

"The master has summoned his soldiers," someone said.

Lucien's soldiers, the Obsidian Vanguard, stood in eerie stillness behind their master, their dark armor catching the flickering light. Even Malik, confident and sharp-tongued, felt the weight of their gaze—or perhaps the unnatural void where their eyes should be.

"I get your gist, Lucien, and I shall go now." Malik avoided the confused looks of Hope, Josie, and Eddie and said, "I've kept my side of the bargain. Come with me or resign yourselves to your fate."

"You can't leave us here alone," Hope said.

"I can, and will," he said.

Without waiting for a reply, Malik walked to the door and disappeared into the night.

Chapter 17

Josie, Eddie, and Hope froze in place as Malik disappeared out the door and into the night. The crowd around them also paused, waiting for Lucien to speak. When he did, his deep voice echoed through the ballroom.

"Malik, the vampire, isn't welcome here," he said. "The three of you can stay and enjoy the festivities."

Once Lucien was back on his throne, a murmur arose from the ballroom, ending in applause and noisy accolades. Orchestra music began again, and the revelers started dancing.

"What now?" Josie asked.

"Join the party or run for the door," Eddie said.

"Lucien said we are welcome here," Hope said. "Let's stay."

An empty table on the edge of the ballroom beckoned, and the trio waded into the throng of dancers, intent on securing it. The laughter was a low hum. Some revelers were clad in elaborate masks, their faces completely obscured. The air was thick with the smell of absinthe. The orchestra suddenly quieted, replaced by the faint notes of a haunting piano melody threading through the room like smoke.

Eddie, Hope, and Josie made it to the table ahead of another group of partygoers. The table was in a dark corner of the ballroom, providing them with a great vantage point to view the action, yet dark enough to keep them out of view. A waiter brought them champagne.

"I'd rather have a scotch," Eddie said.

"There's plenty of scotch at the Eden Club if we make it out of here alive," Hope said.

Hope's words frightened Josie. "Wish you hadn't said that," she said.

The guests' movements were fluid yet disjointed, as though they were half a beat behind the room's rhythm—waiters glided through the crowd, offering glasses of a bubbling liquid that seemed to glow faintly. The guests sipped with exaggerated pleasure, their smiles stretching too wide.

Josie whispered to Eddie. "Do you feel it? It's like... they're watching us, even when they're not looking."

"I feel it," he said.

"Check out the art on the walls," Josie said.

The macabre paintings seemed to change— scenes of serene bayous shifting to storm-lashed waters, then surreal depictions of creatures with too many eyes and mouths. A grand staircase wound upward into shadows, its steps lined with a crimson carpet resembling spilled wine or blood. A man approached them, his face hidden beneath a silver mask adorned with intricate swirls.

"Welcome," he said. "You've arrived at the perfect time."

"What time is that?" Eddie asked.

The man smiled when he removed his mask, revealing his real fangs.

"Any time after midnight is special here," he said.

Eddie looked at Hope and Josie, unease etching his face. "I have a distinct vibe. Maybe we should call it a night and get the hell out of here."

Overhearing Eddie's comment, the man in the mask tilted his head and said, "You're exactly where you're meant to be."

"I don't know," Eddie said.

Josie clutched Hope's hand. "Eddie's right. Let's go."

"It's okay," Hope said. "You wanted to see a real vampire club, and this is it."

"It's not okay," Eddie said. "Let's head for the door."

The air in the old house seemed alive, charged with an unnatural electricity. The dim lighting flickered as Hope, Josie, and Eddie left the table and waded onto the dance floor. The haunting strains of a forgotten waltz played softly in the background, though everyone had stopped dancing. Eddie nodded his head toward someone across the crowded ballroom.

"Wait," he said. "Something's about to happen."

"What?" Josie asked.

Eddie shook his head. "Don't know," he said. "Brace yourself."

The pulsating rhythm of the music reverberated through the cavernous room, the flickering lights casting the dancing guests into a whirl of masked faces and glittering costumes. Hope, Josie, and Eddie stood near the crowd's edge, their unease growing. Then, without warning, the music stopped, its jazzy notes cut off as though strangled. The silence that followed was almost deafening.

An insistent beat of voodoo drums replaced the lively music, the primal sound filling the room and rattling through the darkness. The dim lighting grew darker, shadows stretching and deepening as though the house was alive, feeding on their fear. A figure emerged from the clinging darkness, moving with an almost inhuman grace.

"It's Marceline," Eddie said, his voice barely audible above the relentless drumming.

The beautiful bartender from After Midnight danced into view, completely naked, save for an array of long gold and silver necklaces that swayed and clinked with her every movement. Her lithe form glistened with sweat, the droplets catching what little light remained, making her appear otherworldly, like some pagan goddess summoned from the depths of the bayou.

As the crowd surged forward, encircling her, Marceline's movements grew more frantic, her bare feet pounding the floor in time with the drums. Her head was thrown back as long hair whipped around in wild arcs. Each twist and turn of her body seemed to pull the watchers deeper under her spell.

Josie clutched Hope's arm, her nails digging in. "What is this?" she said.

"Voodoo," Hope said.

The drumming reached a fevered crescendo, a bone-rattling roar that seemed to come from everywhere. Marceline's body contorted in a final violent spin before she froze in place, her arms raised. The drums stopped abruptly, leaving a heavy silence that felt like a shroud.

From the shadows, two figures emerged, clad in ceremonial garb adorned with feathers and bones. Between them, they escorted a cloaked figure draped in black, the fabric swallowing all light. Marceline's serviteurs brought the shrouded figure to the center of the room, the tension palpable as the crowd parted, creating a perfect circle. The attendants tugged the black cloak free, and a collective gasp rippled through the room.

"It's Nicolette," Josie said.

"Who is she?" Hope said.

"The replacement bartender at After Midnight when Eddie left with Marceline," Josie said. "Wyatt and I spoke with her."

"She's scared to death," Hope said.

"For good reason," Josie said. "So am I."

"From the looks of things, she's about to be a victim," Eddie said.

"Do something," Josie said.

Hope clutched Josie's hand, preventing her from interrupting the drama in the giant ballroom.

"There's nothing we can do," she said.

Nicolette trembled, her terrified eyes darting around the room, seeking escape but finding none. Dressed eerily like Marceline—her skin bare save for the glittering chains of jewelry that adorned her trembling frame, she looked fragile and vulnerable.

Josie inhaled sharply. "No," she said. "This can't be happening."

Nicolette tried to speak, her lips moving, though no sound came out. The crowd's gaze turned to Marceline, her eyes glowing red. She approached Nicolette like a predator stalking its prey. Josie suddenly cried out, her voice shattering the oppressive silence.

"Somebody, do something!"

The room seemed to react to Josie's scream, the walls closing in, the shadows growing darker. Marceline ignored her. Stepping closer to Nicolette, she reached out, her fingers brushing against the younger woman's cheek in a mockery of tenderness.

Nicolette's breath came in shallow gasps as Marceline drew her into an embrace, her lips close to Nicolette's ear, whispering something no one else could hear. Then, without warning, Marceline's head snapped to the side, her mouth opening wide to reveal glistening fangs. Nicolette's scream was cut short as Marceline sank sharp fangs into her neck.

The room erupted into chaos. Guests cheered and clapped, their masks hiding their twisted glee. Josie shrieked, clutching Hope, her face pale as death.

Nicolette's body went limp, her hands falling to her sides as Marceline drank deeply, the blood running in rivulets down Nicolette's collarbone. When Marceline finally released her, Nicolette's lifeless form crumpled to the floor. Marceline turned to face the room, her mouth and chin smeared with blood, her eyes glowing bright red.

"You're next," she said softly, her voice carrying a promise of doom as her gaze locked onto Eddie, Hope, and Josie.

Marceline leaned forward, her crimson lips curving into a predatory smile. Nicolette, her once-vivacious replacement, now looked pale and hollow-eyed, her gaze fixed hungrily on Eddie. Someone left the dais and walked through the dancers to face Hope, Josie, and Eddie.

She smiled when Josie said, "You're Sabine Moreau, the dead woman in Giselle's studio."

Sabine's dark eyes glittered with amusement. "Not dead, undead," she said.

Giselle, the red-haired beauty whose mysterious canvases had likely lured so many into the house's grasp, joined Sabine. Her laughter was soft but unnervingly sweet, chilling Josie.

"This house has secrets," Sabine said. "You'll soon be sharing them."

Hope tightened her grip on Josie's hand, her heart pounding. The room fell silent as someone appeared at the top of the winding staircase. It was Eliza, her pale figure draped in a flowing gown of deep emerald, her red hair gleaming, her expression one of serene detachment. She glanced down at the room, her gaze lingering briefly on Hope, Josie, and Eddie before turning and disappearing into the shadows.

"Was that Eliza?" Josie asked.

Eddie nodded, his voice echoing through the ballroom when he shouted Eliza's name.

"Eliza, it's Eddie. I've come for you."

"She's alive," Hope said.

"Maybe not in the way you think," Marceline said. "Eliza belongs to this house now, just as you soon will."

The flickering light of ornate candelabras danced along the cracked walls of the disappearing house—shadows twisted in eerie shapes cast by the cloaked figures that filled the room below. The air was heavy with the scent of blood, wine, and decayed roses, and the distant murmur of sinister laughter echoed like an undercurrent of menace.

Hope gripped Josie's arm, Eddie's gaze fixed upward. Breaking from the shadows, he bolted up the stairs, his boots thudding against the iron steps. The room stilled as several cloaked revelers turned to watch him ascend. A few smirked knowingly, though most simply returned to their macabre festivities.

"Let him go," Marceline said. "He'll be back."

At the landing, Eddie reached Eliza. Up close, the sight of her broke him. Once neatly braided, her hair hung loose and tangled around her shoulders. The delicate silk of her dress was torn, the hem brushing the floor. Her vacant stare terrified him.

"Eliza," he said again, softer this time, taking her by the shoulders.

She flinched at his touch, blinking slowly as if trying to recognize him.

"Eddie," she said, her voice thin and dreamlike. "You shouldn't be here."

"And you should?" His voice cracked. "Look at you! You're not yourself. Come on, we're leaving—now."

Her lips parted, and for a fleeting moment, he thought she might agree. But then, she pulled back, her movements sluggish though deliberate.

"I can't," she said.

"What do you mean you can't?" Eddie's grip on her hand tightened. "You don't belong here, Eliza. These... these people—this place—it's not you."

She smiled faintly, but it was an empty thing. "You don't understand, Eddie. I'm... part of this now."

"Like hell you are." His jaw clenched as he glanced at the crowd below, their eyes glinting like predators in the dark. "They've done something to you. Drugged you, brainwashed you—I don't know. But this isn't you. Please, Eliza." His voice softened, turning to a plea. "Come back with me. We'll fix this together."

Her expression wavered for a moment, and her glassy eyes brimmed with tears that didn't fall. She cupped his face, her touch cold as marble.

"You can't save me, Eddie," she said. "I've already chosen."

"No." He shook his head vehemently. "You don't mean that. You don't know what you're saying."

A sharp laugh echoed from below, and Eddie saw a pale man with a wolfish grin watching them.

"Oh, but she does," he said, raising a blood-red goblet in mock salute.

Eddie's eyes darted back to Eliza, his panic rising. "Listen to me. Your mother and I love you. I'm not leaving without you."

Eliza's hand fell from his face, and she stepped back toward the stairwell leading further into the shadows.

"Goodbye, Eddie," she said softly, her voice breaking on the final word.

"No!"

He lunged for her. She had already slipped away, her pale figure swallowed by the darkness.

"Eddie!" Hope's voice jolted him from his shock, and he looked down to see her and Josie waving frantically. The cloaked figures closed in, their fangs gleaming in the dim light.

Eddie couldn't move, his legs feeling rooted to the ground, his soul tethered to where Eliza had stood.

"Eddie, now!" Josie's urgent shout finally snapped him back to reality.

After a last glance into the shadows, he fled down the stairs, his chest heaving with suppressed anguish. He reached Josie and Hope as the vampires closed in, their movements deliberate, like a pack of wolves encircling their prey.

"You'll see, it's not so bad," Giselle said, her voice light, almost comforting. "The house always chooses the worthy."

"Worthy of what?" Eddie said.

Lucien's deep baritone voice issued from everywhere and nowhere. "Of eternity."

The vampires stopped, fangs flashing as their lips peeled back in unison. Eddie, Hope, and Josie were pressed back-to-back, the air around them crackling with growing menace.

Marceline leaned in close to Eddie, her breath cool against his neck. "Soon, you'll understand," she said.

Hope clenched her fists, her breath coming in sharp gasps. "We're not joining you," she said.

Sabine tilted her head, her dark hair falling like a curtain over one shoulder.

"Toss your ceremonial razor, sweet cakes. You're about to become a real vampire."

Chapter 18

Malik's lair was precisely as I remembered—
a decayed opulence that masked its true
menace. I banged on the heavy door until
it creaked open, revealing the old vampire lounging
in a high-backed chair, a glass of crimson liquid in
his hand.

"You're persistent," he said, raising an
eyebrow. "I like that. But shouldn't you be
elsewhere? Perhaps staring into your precious
truths?"

I stepped inside, my urgency dispelling any
thought of pleasantries. "Help me," I said.

"Or what?" he asked.

"Or Hope, Josie, and Eddie will die."

Malik tilted his head, studying me with
amusement. "And why should their lives concern
me?"

"Because they went to the disappearing
house," I said. "You took them there, and now
they're trapped."

"How do you know?" he asked.

"I saw what was unfolding as I stared into La
Grotte de la Vérité," I said.

"Perhaps you should refrain from self-
discovery."

"You're probably right about that," I said. "Now, I'm more worried about my friends."

Malik's smirk faded, replaced by something darker. "Foolish children," he said. Setting his glass aside, he rose, his movements fluid and predatory. "Very well, Wyatt. But know this—once we enter that house, no one, not even I, can guarantee our safe return."

I met Malik's gaze and said, "Then let's not waste time."

"One thing before we go," he said.

The hulking man opened a wooden chest in the corner of his room and rummaged through it until he found a beautiful ceremonial sword.

"Excalibur," he said. "The magical and mystical sword."

My stare was incredulous when I said, "Get out of here! King Arthur's actual sword?"

"Louis XIV collected antiquities, and he bestowed Excalibur to me," Malik said. "It's genuine and possibly the only weapon powerful enough to repel Lucien's Obsidian Vanguard."

"Who are they?" I asked.

"A troop of supernatural soldiers with unnatural strength. They only respond to Lucien's commands. The sword is our lone advantage."

Malik nodded when I said, "You have a plan?"

"One that may work or else result in the death of all of us," he said.

"Then let's hurry," I said. "We might already be too late."

Malik's boots echoed against the damp cobblestones of Bourbon Street as we sprinted through the darkness. The gas lanterns overhead flickered dimly, their light barely piercing the night. Malik carried the sword with a grim determination, its ancient blade gleaming faintly as if aware of its destiny.

"Tell me again, Malik," I said, struggling to keep pace. "This house—it's alive?"

"A living entity," Malik said, his deep voice cutting through the silence. "Its heart is Lucien, the Prince of Darkness. The house obeys his will, drawing in victims and trapping them in its labyrinth."

"And the vampires?"

"Minions. Servants to Lucien's hunger. And then there's the Obsidian Vanguard." Malik glanced at me, his dark eyes serious. "Lucien's elite guards forged in shadow. Almost invincible."

My pulse quickened. "Almost?"

"Excalibur," Malik said, gripping the hilt of the impressive sword. "It is the only weapon that can hold them off long enough for us to save your friends."

We hurried to the darkened end of Bourbon Street, and there it was—a sagging mansion that seemed to flicker between existence and nothingness. An otherworldly glow seeped through the cracked windows. Malik handed me a lighter.

"What's this for?" I asked.

"There's a curtain in the ballroom behind which no one except Lucien and those close to him has access. Use the lighter to flame the curtain."

"To what purpose?"

"Redemption," he said. "If you do as I say, we'll have a slim chance of survival."

Malik's lips curled into a sardonic smile when I said, "Right behind you, boss."

"The house responds to a special knock," Malik said. He demonstrated by tapping his palm. "You'll do the honors because the house would recognize me and ignore my knock. It'll open the door for you, and I'll wait in the shadows until it does."

When we reached the door, I clutched the lighter, the metal cool against my palm. My Moon's

Eye earring was flashing red. I couldn't see it, though I could feel it.

"Remember the plan," Malik said. "And when we're inside—lead your friends to the curtain and set it ablaze."

I nodded and rapped sharply against the door in the precise sequence Malik had shown me. The heavy portal creaked open, revealing a cavernous room teeming with movement.

Dozens of pale faces turned toward us, their eyes gleaming with hunger. Hope, Eddie, and Josie stood frozen at the center of the chaos, terror etched into their faces. Ready to strike with his magical sword, Malik stepped into the fray with a warrior's poise.

The vampires hesitated, their snarls turning to murmurs as Excalibur began pulsing with a fierce light, casting shadows across the grotesque gathering. Then, with a battle cry, he plunged into the crowd, the sword cleaving through undead flesh and bone.

On the raised dais at the far end of the grand chamber, Lucien stood imperiously, flanked by the veiled queen and a contingent of dignitaries, their faces shadowed and unreadable. Below, a sea of Nocturnes hissed and jeered, their pale faces glimmering like phantoms under the flickering light of the chandeliers. Marceline and Sabine fled from the scene on the ballroom floor, retreating to the dais, where they joined Lucien's ruling contingent.

Malik wasn't done. With a roar that cut through the din, he pushed further into the fray, Excalibur gleaming like a shard of the sun in his hands. The vampires recoiled instinctively from the weapon's light, their shrieks piercing the air as Malik swung the blade with practiced precision.

One by one, they fell, their bodies disintegrating into ash before they hit the floor. On the dais, Lucien's calm façade had fractured. He slammed his fist against the edge of his ornate throne, his voice a vicious snarl.

"Enough! Guards—secure the dignitaries and remove them from this rabble. Now!"

As if conjured by his words, the Obsidian Vanguard appeared, their angular armor glinting menacingly. They moved precisely, forming a protective phalanx around Lucien, the veiled queen, and the other dignitaries. One by one, they began leading them through a door in the back of the dais that led to safety. Malik caught sight of them from the corner of his eye.

"Coward!" he roared, leveling Excalibur at Lucien. "You hide behind your lackeys while your empire crumbles around you!"

Lucien's crimson eyes locked on Malik with a fury that could have scorched the air. Stepping forward, his pale face twisted with rage, his words issuing from his fanged mouth like the crack of a whip.

"You dare challenge me, Malik? Mark my words—you and your little friends will pay dearly for this insolence. I will rain vengeance upon you that will echo through eternity!"

"Don't wait!" Malik said. "Come fight me now unless you're the coward I accuse you of being."

The Obsidian Vanguard ushered Lucien from the dais even as his threats echoed through the chamber, their heavy boots striking the stone floor in unison. The veiled queen paused briefly at the escape door, her head tilting toward Malik as though committing his face to memory.

Malik saw her looking and yelled at her. "That's right, broken down whore! You recognize me, don't you? I made the queen a promise, and I've waited an eternity to fulfill it."

When she replied to Malik's threat, the woman's voice was sharp and cracked with age.

"What do you know about promises? The Sun King loved me and not the dried-up prune he was married to."

"How dare you insult the queen," Malik said. "I promise you will pay."

Lucien's enraged voice echoed off the ballroom walls like a curse. "Run while you can! You cannot escape me!"

I followed Malik into the fray and asked, "Do you know the identity of the veiled woman?"

He didn't answer my question.

By now, the Obsidian Guard had reached us, and Malik had no time to answer my question. When I reached Eddie, Hope, and Josie, I grabbed Josie's hand.

Malik's voice was a command that brooked no argument when he roared, "To the curtain!"

"No time to explain," I said. "Follow me."

The vampires had given way to Malik's attack, replaced by the Obsidian Vanguard. The old vampire was almost surrounded, though holding his own as I focused on the black curtain across the ballroom. Josie, Hope, and Eddie wasted no time following me. We darted through the crowd, dodging snapping jaws and clawing hands. I flicked the lighter when we reached the massive black curtain draped along the far wall.

The tiny flame seemed feeble against the oppressive darkness, though it roared to life when it touched the fabric. Fire raced upward, devouring the curtain in a cascade of heat and light. I glanced toward the ballroom to see Malik sprinting toward us, the Obsidian Vanguard directly behind him. The vampires screeched and recoiled, their retreating forms merging into the smoke and flame.

Malik's voice was urgent when he said, "Hold on to each other. Now!"

The ground trembled ominously, and the chamber walls flickered like mirages. Whatever held this strange house together was weakening. As the Obsidian Vanguard advanced toward us, Malik grabbed my hand and plunged his other into the flames and smoke. As he did, a loud explosion rocked the room.

The walls and floor shuddered, the air thick with the acrid stench of burning fabric. As if by an invisible force, we were yanked backward, and the ballroom dissolved around us in a whirlwind of smoke and ash. When the chaos settled, we found ourselves in a smoldering pile on Bourbon Street, the oppressive silence replaced by the distant hum of nightlife.

Toxic black smoke had filled our lungs, and we were all coughing, our lungs burning. Everyone was present when I counted heads, shaken but alive.

"What happened?" I asked.

"The house expelled us," Malik said, his grip still firm on Excalibur. "It saved us from the Obsidian Vanguard."

"Are you okay?" I asked. "You grabbed the burning curtain with your bare hand."

He smiled and said, "I'll live, or at least remain undead."

I turned toward the lot where the mansion had stood. Only emptiness remained—a vacant lot shrouded in shadows. The house was gone, leaving no trace of its sinister presence except for the smoldering curtains at our feet.

Malik grinned and sheathed the ancient sword. "We'll meet Lucien again," he said. "This was just the beginning. There will be an encore."

"You think Lucien will send the Obsidian Vanguard for us?" I asked.

"Except for the Nocturnes, Lucien's minions, including the Obsidian Vanguard, can only exist in the disappearing house," Malik said. "We aren't done with the Nocturnes."

"What about Eliza?" Eddie asked.

"Give her up," Malik said. "She is doomed."

Eddie turned toward the vacant lot. "I can't do that," he said.

Grabbing Eddie's arm, I wheeled him around.

"The house is gone," I said.

"I have to do something," he said.

"Now that we know where she is, we can work on a plan to get her out," I said.

"She may not live that long," Eddie said.

"Your niece is in no imminent danger," Malik said.

"How can you be so sure?" Eddie asked.

"Lucien has a plan for her," Malik said. "Right now, he doesn't have the means to implement his plan. Eliza is safe until then."

"What plan?" Eddie said.

When Malik didn't answer, I said, "You know the woman behind the black veil, don't you?"

"That is none of your business," Malik said.

I rested my hand on his forearm and said, "I'm on your side. At this point, we're all in this together."

"I need a drink," Hope said. "Malik can explain when we get to the Eden Club."

"No, I can't," he said. "This adventure has left me thirsty for more blood. I must satisfy my hunger before the dawn arrives."

We watched as Malik trod away into the night.

"What was that about?" Josie asked.

"What?"

"Your question to Malik implied you think he knows something about the woman in the black veil."

"I believe he does," I said.

"So what?" Hope asked.

"If he does, it means he knows more about the disappearing house and Lucien D'Arcy than he's letting on," I said. "He may also know why Lucien has latched on to Eliza."

"He made it clear that he's not going to tell you," Josie said.

"There are other ways of convincing him to talk," I said.

When Josie and I stared at Hope, she said, "Forget about it! I have no intention of having sex with that cretin."

Chapter 19

The Eden Club was rocking when we reached it, Nyx serving drinks at a table. Hope couldn't wait. Ducking under the bar, she poured me a lemonade and scotch for Eddie and then began mixing martinis for Josie and her. Nyx grinned when she returned to the bar.

"I didn't expect you back tonight," she said. "Are you taking over?"

"All yours, little sister. I saw you flirting with that cute guy sitting at table two. I needed a drink and didn't think I could wait."

"Thanks," Nyx said. "The tips were just starting to get good."

"If you're making good tips, the bar's doing well. That's all I care about," Hope said.

"Someone was here looking for Josie and Wyatt," Nyx said.

Nyx had my attention. "Who?" I asked.

Hope's pretty sister found a business card on the counter. "Steve Vincenzio," she said.

It took me a moment to remember the strange older man with supernatural tattoos we'd met during our visit to After Midnight.

"Did he say what he wanted?" I asked.

"Just that he needed to talk," Nyx said, handing me the card.

When Eddie reached for the card, I yanked it away. "Wait your turn, big boy," I said.

"Who is Steve Vincenzio?" Eddie asked.

"The night we visited After Midnight," I said. "When you disappeared with Marceline, Josie and I sat with an eccentric older man. He told us that he'd had a similar experience with her."

"I doubt that," Eddie said.

"He had a conservative haircut and wore dress pants and a pinstriped button-down shirt. He didn't seem the type to have his chest tattooed with voodoo veves."

"Where are you going with this?" Eddie asked.

"He told us Marceline targeted him when she learned who he worked for."

"And who is that?" Eddie asked.

I glanced at the business card and said, "NeuroGenesis Systems, a software development company whose tagline is Redefining Identity, Redefining Humanity."

"What the hell is that supposed to mean?" he asked.

I shook my head and said, "No idea."

"Why would Marceline be interested in such a company?" Eddie asked.

"She wasn't," I said. "Her boss, Lucien D'Arcy was."

"Because?" Eddie said.

"I have no idea. Perhaps he was here to tell us," I said.

"I'm still shaking from the attack in the disappearing house," Josie said.

Hope sat her martini on the bar and embraced her. "Oh, my poor darling," she said.

"I'm sorry," Josie said. "I've never been so frightened."

"We're safe now," Hope said. "Josie needs some consoling, and I'm taking her to my apartment."

"Don't worry about Eddie and me," I said. "Nyx will take care of us."

"Count on it," Hope said as she led Josie out the door and down the stairs.

The sun was rising when Nyx tabbed out the bar's last customer and locked the door. She quickly mixed herself a mojito.

"I'm wired," she said. "Wish we could go somewhere to get breakfast and take the edge off."

"Bertram's isn't far from here," Eddie said.

"Bertram's?" Nyx said.

"He mixes a mean mojito and cooks the best Cajun breakfast in the French Quarter."

"Eddie isn't lying," I said.

"It's so early," Nyx said.

"Not too early for Bertram," I said. "He wakes up with the chickens and must have been a rooster in another life."

Bertram handed Nyx a credit card and said, "Ignore my nutty friend and tab us out, pretty baby. I'm too tired to sleep and craving some of Bertram's grits and grillades."

Bertram was alone at the bar when we entered. His Cajun smile ignited when he saw Eddie.

"My favorite customer," he said. "Who's this pretty little girl with you?"

"Nyx," I said. "Hope's little sister."

"Miss Hope never told me she has a little sister," Bertram said.

"You know Hope?" Nyx asked.

"She's a friend of mine," he said.

Bertram's dog, Lady, wandered into the bar. Nyx bounded off her stool and hugged her.

"What a beautiful collie," she said. "What's her name?"

"Lady," Bertram said. "Been with me longer than any of my exes."

As if understanding the Cajun bartender's words, Lady barked.

"She's gorgeous," Nyx said. "I want her."

"Well, that's impossible, pretty lady, but I can fix you a mojito."

Nyx smiled and said, "Guess that will have to do."

Eddie sipped the scotch Bertram had poured him and said, "You cooking breakfast today?"

"Don't I always?" Bertram said.

"I love your grits and grillades," Eddie said. "Can you surprise us with something else?"

"Sure," the Cajun bartender said. "What's up with you three?"

"Problems finding my niece Eliza. A hearty breakfast will help us concentrate on a solution."

"How about a flavorful boudin and eggs breakfast with Cajun-style hash browns and buttery biscuits?" Bertram said.

"Sounds wonderful," Nyx said. "I'm an amateur cook. Can you share the recipe with me?"

"Ain't no recipe, pretty baby," Bertram said. "I cook the boudin until its casing is slightly crispy and the savory rice-and-pork filling bursts with Creole spices. The eggs are scrambled soft with heavy cream and topped with freshly chopped green onions."

"Yum!" Nyx said.

"That ain't all," Bertram said. "The hash browns are made with shredded potatoes, caramelized onions, and bell peppers, seasoned with cayenne and paprika. On the side, a small jar of my pepper jelly glistens on the table, ready to slather onto the flaky biscuits."

"Love it," Nyx said with a smile.

The French Quarter morning seeped through Bertram's bar's cracked shutters, the aroma of spiced sausage and buttery biscuits drawing me,

Nyx, and Eddie like moths to a flame. Humming a low Cajun tune, Bertram set down a platter heaped with steaming boudin and scrambled eggs.

"Eat up," he said with a flourish and a wink. "Ain't nobody can solve mysteries on an empty stomach, especially y'all city folk."

Nyx, barely in her twenties and as striking as her older sister, Hope, but with a naughty edge, dove into her plate with relish.

"Bertram, this is heaven."

Nyx's blond pigtails bounced as she gestured with a biscuit slathered in pepper jelly.

Eddie raised his fork in salute before popping a bite of boudin into his mouth.

"If you keep cooking like this, Bertram, I might move back from Oyster Island."

I chuckled, leaning back in my chair, my plate already half-empty.

"You could make a killing running a breakfast joint in the Quarter," Nyx said. "Tourists would line up around the block."

Bertram snorted, flipping a dishtowel over his shoulder. "Cooking for y'all's reward enough for me. Besides, the tourists don't know about a boudin from a bratwurst. Pass me that coffee pot, will you, Miss Nyx?"

Nyx obliged, handing it over with a grin. She studied me for a moment, her dark eyes dancing with curiosity.

"So, Wyatt, what's next on the agenda? Solving another mystery, or will we just let Bertram fatten us up first?"

I smirked, reaching for another biscuit. "First, we eat. Then we solve. Priorities, Nyx."

As laughter filled the room, Bertram leaned against the counter, arms crossed, soaking in the camaraderie.

"Y'all keep talking. Me? I'm going to enjoy the sight of three of the hungriest folks I've ever seen. Makes my heart glad. That's what it does."

Nyx raised her mojito in a mock toast. "To Bertram, the real hero of the morning."

The toast was met with hearty clinks of coffee mugs, the sound mingling with the bar's warmth, and the unspoken bond of friends—family, in everything but name.

We all turned when someone behind us said, "Something smells good. Any chance there's more where that came from?"

It was Tommy O'Rear and Marlon Bando, looking like they'd been up all night.

"Boys," Bertram said. "There's plenty more. Grab a stool, and I'll get you some plates."

Tommy and Marlon soon enjoyed boudin and scrambled eggs, and Tommy drank Abita with a shot of whiskey and Marlon pineapple juice.

"What are you three doing up so early?" Tommy asked as he chugged his shot of whiskey, following it with a drink of Abita.

"I could ask you the same?" I said.

"Another murder," he said. "Same scenario as before. The man's body was drained of blood; the only mark of violence was the fang marks on his neck."

"You here for breakfast, or are we implicated?" I asked.

I expected him to laugh. Instead, he said, "He had your name scrawled on a slip of paper in his shirt pocket."

"Were you able to ID him?" I asked.

"A man in his sixties named Steve Vincenzio." When Tommy saw the look in my eyes, he asked, "You know him?"

"We met," I said.

"Where at?" he asked.

"He's somehow connected to our search for Eddie's niece. We met in a late-night club called After Midnight. You know about it?"

"Lots of strange people hang out there," he said with a nod.

"That's a fact," I said.

"What else?" he asked.

"Nyx is the bartender at the Eden Club. Vincenzio was there last night asking about me. Said he needed to talk to me."

"About what?" Tommy asked.

"No idea," I said.

I didn't bother telling him I'd seen Sabine Moreau and that she was alive, or at least undead.

"This stiff isn't getting away," he said. "I posted a guard at the morgue's door."

Tommy finished his breakfast and his beer.

"More eggs?" Bertram asked.

"We're good," Tommy said. He glanced at me and said, "If you learn anything that can help us, call me."

"You got it, Lieutenant," I said.

Tommy and Marlon were barely out the door when Eddie's cell phone rang.

"Got to go," he said. "Problems on the island. I'll be back as soon as I can. What's your plan?"

"Find out why Steve Vincenzio wanted to talk to me," I said.

"You think it's important?" he asked.

"He knew something he wanted to share," I said. "It's probably important."

Eddie dapped my closed palm. "I trust you, my friend. Find Eliza for me, and I'll be eternally grateful."

"I'm on it, bro," I said.

Eddie cleared our tab with Bertram before disappearing out the front door.

"Your breakfast was to die for," Nyx said.

"Thank you, baby," Bertram said. Other customers were starting to fill the bar. "Right now, I got business to take care of. Keep your eyes out for Wyatt."

"He's cute," she said. "I think I like him?"

"Can I get you a cab?" I asked when Bertram left the bar.

"I'm staying with Hope, and she's busy," Nyx said. "Can I stay with you?"

"Why not? My apartment is upstairs. You can take the bed, and I'll crash in my recliner."

"You afraid I'll put some moves on you?" she asked.

"You should be afraid of me and not the other way around," I said.

Nyx smiled and said, "You don't scare me." When I opened the door to my apartment, Nyx saw my kitty, Buttercup, lying on the bed.

"Oh, what a beautiful cat," she said.

Buttercup purred when Nyx cradled and stroked her.

"I think you've made a friend," I said.

"I love cats. Hope and I had a cat named Sophie," she said.

"I keep my balcony door open so she can go tomcatting whenever she wants," I said.

As if on cue, Buttercup jumped from her arms and disappeared out the balcony door. Nyx followed her out to the balcony.

"Love the view," she said. "Can I move in with you?"

"The place is a bit small for two people," I said.

"I promise I won't get in the way."

"We hardly know each other," I said. "You're welcome to visit anytime."

Nyx plopped on the bed, plumped a pillow, and closed her eyes.

"I'm usually sound asleep by this time in the morning," she said.

"Knock yourself out," I said. "I'll sleep in the recliner."

She patted the bed beside her and said, "Don't make me feel bad about taking your bed. I'll share."

When I lay beside Nyx, she draped her arms around me, hugging me close. She pulled it out when she felt Steve Vincenzio's business card I had stashed in my shirt pocket.

"What?" I asked.

"I know this company," she said. "I worked as a temp there last summer."

She nodded when I said, "NeuroGenesis Systems?"

"The people who run it are slightly strange," she said.

"How's that?"

"They're trying to develop a way to transfer brains, at least the memories and knowledge stored there," she said.

"You mean from one person to another?" I asked.

"My boss told me they were on the verge of accomplishing the impossible."

"Who was your boss?" I asked.

"His name is Darius Thompson. The company operates out of an old warehouse in the CBD. You can't get in unless you know the code at the front door."

"Do you remember the code?"

"A strange word, though impossible to forget," she said. "Metamorphosis."

Chapter 20

Nyx fell asleep in my arms, her soft breathing the only sound in my little apartment, until the screeching of a cat on the street below awoke me. After carefully unwrapping myself, I went to my balcony overlooking Chartres Street to see if it was Buttercup doing the yowling and if she needed help.

It wasn't Buttercup but a large black stray tomcat that I recognized. I'd named him ABC. Someone had thrown a Lucky Dog into the street, and ABC was squared off with a giant orange tabby, vying for the remains of the wiener and bun. ABC was big, the tabby bigger, and it was apparent who would wind up with the bounty. I was wrong.

When a car backfired down the street, the tabby flinched and turned his head. Long enough for ABC to snatch the prize and race away into the darkness. As if he couldn't care less, the big tabby stretched to his full length and then trotted away to check out Bertram's dumpster in the alley.

Though it was late and I dog-tired, I didn't return to bed. The visions I had seen during my trip to La Grotte de la Vérité had affected me more than I cared to admit. Reclining in my rattan chair, I stared out at distant neon. I fell asleep, awakened when Nyx sat in my lap and hugged me. She was wearing one of my L.S.U. tee shirts and nothing else, her soft body warm against my chest.

"What are you doing out here?" she asked.

"A cat on the street awoke me. I thought it was Buttercup and came out to check," I said.

"Who is ABC?" she asked.

"A stray cat, I recognized."

I grinned when she asked, "Why do you call him ABC?"

"It stands for another black cat," I said.

Nyx smiled and said, "Come back to bed."

"I can't," I said.

Nyx could tell I was troubled and said, "Can I get you something?"

She grinned when I squeezed her and said, "Just you."

"Tell me what's bothering you," she said.

"It's complicated," I said.

"Give me the short version."

It was early morning, an hour or so before dawn. A chill breeze gusting up the street in late April caused Nyx to embrace me tighter.

"Hope took Josie, Eddie, and me to Muzik Azul, an obscure music venue in the Quarter," I said. "A man named Rene was performing."

"I know Rene," she said.

"He said he could tell I was searching for something within myself and offered to show me where I could find answers to my questions. He took me to an alternate French Quarter."

"I have no clue what you're talking about," Nyx said.

"Neither did I. It's like the Quarter, though, part of a parallel universe. I can't begin to tell you how strange it seemed."

"Yes, you can," she said. "Tell me."

I stared at the balcony railing, though I lost my gaze in Chartres Street's dim glow below. The night carried a peculiar stillness, broken only by the faint hum of a distant streetcar.

"I don't know where to begin. It's like trying to describe a dream you're not sure you even had."

"Dreams don't have to have a beginning or end," Nyx said.

"Rene took me to an old iron gate in the Quarter and spoke an incantation. When it swung open, he led me through the gate to another place," I said.

"What other place?" Nyx asked.

"A version of the Quarter, though not this French Quarter. The streets were all there—Bourbon, Royal, Chartres—but they weren't the same. The lamps burned a little too brightly. The shadows stretched a moment too long. The air felt heavier, as if it were thick with memories or ghosts. I don't know. I'd look at a building and swear it wasn't quite solid. They shimmered like so many mirages."

Nyx leaned in slightly, her expression unreadable, and said, "Dreams are different than reality. That's what makes them dreams."

"Rene called it a parallel version of the French Quarter. A place where the past, the present, and the could-have-been all bleed together. He called it the In-Between."

Nyx smiled and said, "Great name for a nightclub."

"I saw faces in the windows—faces I recognized but couldn't place. A woman in 19th-century mourning attire stared at me from a balcony, her veil blowing in a breeze I couldn't feel.

"A jazz band played on a street corner; their notes were muted like they were being played underwater. And the smells—God, Nyx, the smells. One moment, it was beignets and chicory coffee;

the next, it was decay, like old graveyards after a rain."

"Your dream was vivid," Nyx said. "I don't recall ever smelling anything in a dream."

"Neither do I," I said. "What I'm describing wasn't a dream. It's what I experienced when I went with Rene."

Nyx squeezed my hand and said, "I believe you."

"I was in the middle of a dream when the street cats woke me," I said. "It confused me, and I've been thinking about it since I sat here."

"Why the confusion?" Nyx asked.

"Because it seemed as accurate as my trip through the In-Between. It makes me wonder where my dream ended and reality begins."

"I'm listening," Nyx said. "Tell me."

"In my dream, that's really a dream, or at least I think it is; we came to the river, or what I thought was the river. The water was black as ink, and there were no boats, no lights, just this endless expanse of darkness.

"Rene told me we had to cross it. A ferryman was waiting. He wasn't human, Nyx. He was this thing, cloaked and silent, his eyes like burning coals. He didn't ask for money; he just looked at us like he was weighing our souls."

"What you had was a death dream," Nyx said.

"Was I foreseeing my own death?" I asked.

It unnerved me when Nyx didn't answer my question, saying instead, "Sorry I interrupted you. Please continue."

"When we reached the other side, everything changed. The air was colder, the stars brighter, but they weren't the stars I knew. They moved and shifted, almost as if they were alive. The path ahead was narrow, winding through a swamp filled with trees that seemed to breathe. Their roots curled toward us like fingers, and the water...It whispered. Words I couldn't understand, but they crawled under my skin."

Nyx shivered. "Is what you're telling me real or a dream?"

I shook my head. "Don't know. I wonder if the entire thing wasn't a dream that morphed into something else when it cycled through my mind. There's more. You want to hear?"

Nyx kissed me and said, "Continue. I'm going nowhere."

"Things grew crazier when we reached La Grotte de la Vérité, the Grotto of Truth. "It was carved into a rock face that seemed to rise out of nowhere, glowing faintly like it had swallowed the moonlight. Rene commanded me to go in alone. Said the truth is something you have to face by yourself.

"Inside, it was just me and my reflection. Or at least, I thought it was my reflection. But the longer I looked, the more I realized it wasn't me—not entirely. It was who I could have been or maybe who I still could be.

"The lines between us blurred, and for a moment, I felt everything. Every decision I'd ever made, every path I'd ever taken—or not— hit me at once. I saw people I've loved and hurt and faces I'll never know."

When I stopped talking, Nyx said, "I want to hear."

"My face emerged on the water's surface, but as I stared, my features changed—aging, then fading, reappearing with scars I didn't recognize. I was dressed in clothes from another era.

"A flickering candle, burning down to the wick, appeared, perhaps my own—tried to shield me from an unseen wind. The candle's flame sputtered and grew weaker, reminding me of my mortality and the urgency of finding answers before time runs out."

"What else?" Nyx asked.

"A secret doorway leading nowhere," I said. "A shadowy doorway at the edge of the water's surface, a door slightly ajar. I felt an overwhelming urge to open it, sensing that the last truth lies beyond. But as I reached for the handle, the door shifted further away, slipping into darkness as if the grotto warned me that some truths may never be fully known.

"Each vision left me with a sense of unease, as if the grotto was giving me not just answers but hints of the high cost of seeking them. These glimpses of truth haunt me."

"Poor baby," Nyx said, squeezing closer.

"My mom and dad spoke to me, and then my grandfather. All three are dead. My grandfather was once the governor of Louisiana. An assassin's bullet killed him."

"Oh, Wyatt, I'm so sorry," Nyx said, touching my cheek.

"I never knew him. He died before I was born," I said. "What he told me was disturbing."

"What did he tell you?" Nyx asked.

"He wanted me to join the Nocturnes," I said. "I told him I don't even know what a Nocturne is."

"What did he say to that?" Nyx asked.

"He said, 'Only a few control the universe. Most are controlled and too stupid to know it. The Nocturnes stand at the pinnacle. Join us. I need your youth.' You're dead, Grandpa, I said. 'Maybe not,' he said. 'Life and death are smaller things than you realize.'"

When I hesitated, Nyx said, "What else?"

"'Think about it. You can be more than you ever dreamed—or continue being less than nothing.'"

Nyx touched my cheek again. "His words hurt you."

"Deeply," I said.

"Don't let them. Hope told me all the Nocturnes are vampires."

"You think my grandfather is a vampire?" I asked.

"If he were, he'd be alive, or at least undead," Nyx said.

"What a horrible thought," I said.

"I didn't mean to upset you further," Nyx said.

"Not your fault," I said. "My grandfather wasn't even the strangest thing I saw in the pool."

"What was?" Nyx asked.

"A woman named Desire," I said.

I nodded when Nyx said, "Your lover?"

"Someone I thought I loved. Now, I'm not so sure," I said.

"Tell me about her," Nyx said.

"A woman from my past. I haven't seen her in years," I said.

"Tell me," Nyx said.

"Desire was the daughter of a client I met during a case I was working on. She had a twin sister named Dauphine. When Dauphine committed suicide, Desire became a nun. To my knowledge, it's where she still is."

I nodded again when she said, "You loved her?"

"More than I can explain. She bore an amazing resemblance to Josie."

"Josie is a beautiful woman," Nyx said. "Is that why she's your girlfriend?"

"Josie isn't my girlfriend. We're just friends," I said.

"Hope thinks there's more to it than that," Nyx said.

"There's not," I said. "I've purposely avoided anything other than friendship with her. She may look like Desire, but looks aren't who people are."

"Josie is attracted to you."

"Who told you that?" I asked.

"I'm a woman. I know how women think," she said.

Nyx pulled away from me, tears in her eyes when I said, "But you don't know how I think." Seeing her adverse reaction, I clutched her hand. "I'm sorry. I didn't mean what I said in a hurtful way."

Nyx stripped off my tee shirt and threw it at me. She was naked, her body enticingly lithesome backdropped by distant flashing neon.

"You're an asshole, and I'm leaving," she said. "I don't want to hear about your girlfriends."

"Whoa! Girl, you have a body on you. Right now, you're my only girlfriend, and I can tell you that no girlfriend I have ever had holds a candle to you."

Nyx grinned when she said, "You're a fucking liar, Wyatt Thomas."

I grabbed her hand, tugged her toward my apartment, and said, "Please don't go."

Chapter 21

Nyx was asleep on my bed when I left my apartment to visit NeuroGenesis Systems in the Central Business District. The weather was sunny, and the old warehouse on Camp Street wasn't far from Bertram's on Chartres, though tourists rarely visit this seedy area of New Orleans.

The building stood at the center of a busy traffic roundabout for streetcars and automobiles. When I was growing up, the roundabout was named Lee Circle and featured a statue of General Robert E. Lee mounted on his horse, Traveler.

Statues of Confederate generals had become politically incorrect, and the city had replaced Lee's statue with one more presentable. Though they had renamed the roundabout Tivoli Circle, it remained Lee Circle in my mind.

Names had changed, though not the area's seedy and dangerous veneer. The stretch of Camp Street in front of the NeuroGenesis Systems building was a patchwork of cracked sidewalks and faded street signs. A bag lady had staked out her territory along the curb, her shopping cart overflowing with a chaotic mix of blankets, aluminum cans, and weathered plastic bags.

Nearby, a man with a scraggly beard strummed a broken guitar, the dissonant notes blending with the occasional honk of a passing car. The air was thick with the mingled scents of stale beer and urine, and the greasy aroma wafting from a nearby food truck, its peeling paint a testament to better days.

Clusters of street people loitered in the shadows of the surrounding buildings, their conversations a low murmur of slurred words and laughter punctuated by the occasional burst of profanity. The NeuroGenesis building, with its unmarked facade and lack of windows, loomed in stark contrast—a cold monolith amid the chaos.

The windowless warehouse, converted decades ago into an office building, seemed to repel the street life around it, even the most desperate transients keeping their distance as if instinctively wary of the secrets hidden behind its locked doors. The building had been there for as long as I could remember, and I'd often wondered what was inside. I realized I was about to find out as I approached the entrance.

The building's weathered brick facade provided no hint of the potential covert operations inside. I ran my fingers over the small plaque that read NGS, indicating I was in the right place. After punching in the code Metamorphosis, the lock clicked, and the heavy door creaked open.

I stepped into a minimalist reception area lit by dim LEDs. The room was vacant of a live receptionist. Instead, a sleek tablet sat on an empty counter. A subtle mechanical hum vibrated through the walls. Instructions beside the tablet listed options: your name, who you were there to see, and your reason for the visit.

I entered Wyatt Thomas to see Darius Thompson for information concerning an online article I was writing for scuttlebutt.com, a name I concocted. After pressing submit, another screen appeared on the tablet, instructing me to take a seat.

I was the only person in the waiting area, so I sat in one of the three metal and red plastic side chairs. They looked as cheap as if someone had purchased them from a yard sale for ten bucks. There wasn't even linoleum covering the concrete floor. Ten minutes later, the heavy metal door clicked as someone inside unlocked it, and a man appeared.

"Mr. Thomas," he said. "I'm Darius Thompson. You wanted to see me?"

Darius Thompson was forty-something, impeccably dressed, his sharp charcoal suit contrasting against his warm mahogany skin. His eyes were sharp and calculating, and his faint smile felt more like a mask than a greeting.

"I'm a reporter for the Scuttlebutt and have a few questions about an article I'm working on," I said.

"Haven't heard of that one," he said. "Who are you associated with?"

"No one. Scuttlebutt is my creation, and I confess I don't have many website visitors."

Thompson glanced at his Apple watch and said, "I'm swamped today. How did you get my name?

"I have an attractive female friend named Nyx who worked for you a while back. She said you were a wonderful man and wouldn't hesitate to give me an interview."

"Did she now?"

"I promise I won't take more than a few minutes of your time. I only need a few lines to complete my article. I promise it'll not affect you or your company."

Thompson rechecked his watch and said, "Why not? I have a few minutes to kill before lunch."

"Great," I said.

When Thompson punched the keypad beside the heavy metal door, I memorized the code. The narrow halls he led me down were as sterile as the waiting area, recessed LED bulbs casting a dim glow in the sunless building. Only one of the metal doors we passed was marked. A small plaque on the door said, Project Chrysalis-unauthorized entrance forbidden.

Thompson's office was small and at the end of a long hallway. It consisted of a gray metal desk stuffed inside a ten-by-ten cubicle with a single red plastic side chair.

He smiled when I said, "Love the décor."

"Early Goodwill," he said. "NGR doesn't believe in splurging on furniture."

"No problem," I said. "I don't even have an office and publish my blog on the dressing cabinet in my bathroom."

Thompson nodded and rechecked his watch. "I don't have much time. What can I help you with?"

"Of course," I said. "Can you tell me about your job with NGS?"

"I'm the head researcher," he said.

Books on neurology, ethics, and philosophy—heavy on works by Nietzsche and Kafka lined the office shelves. Thompson's desk was topped by only a single inbox except for a few family pictures. What caught my eye was a Manila folder labeled Project Chrysalis resting inside the rectangular box.

"I can see from the books on the shelf behind you," I said. "What specifically are you researching?

"Many things," he said.

"Such as?"

"Things like human potential and new eras of consciousness," he said.

"Can you tell me about Project Chrysalis?"

Thompson stiffened. "How do you know about Project Chrysalis?"

"I saw the plaque on one of the doors," I said. "It said unauthorized entrance prohibited. Sounds as if someone is doing important research behind those doors."

"We have lots of interesting projects, of which Chrysalis is one. I'm afraid that's all I'm authorized to tell you."

"No problem," I said. "I understand. It must feel great to be working on the leading edge of technology."

"I'm lucky to work here," he said. "New job openings are few and far between, and NGS is among the highest paying companies in the industry."

"What else?" I asked. "Anything revolutionary the company is working on?"

"You're persistent, Mr. Thomas," he said with a smile. "Nothing I can comment on that I haven't already told you."

"Can you share anything with me off the record?" I asked.

"The work we do here is highly confidential, and though I can't confirm anything outright, I will tell you that NGS is engaged in revolutionary work that will bridge the gap between life and death."

"Impressive," I said. "Why the secrecy?"

"Powerful benefactors control the destiny of NGS. The research and development we perform are state-of-the-art and cost the company megabucks. The industry would steal our knowledge in a heartbeat if we allowed it to become public."

I tried to adopt a casual posture, hoping my next question wouldn't result in Thompson booting me from his office, and my chair creaked when I leaned back against it.

"You probably heard about Steve Vincenzio. He was looking for me not long before someone drained him dry like a New Orleans hurricane glass. He left your business card. Thought you might be able to tell me why."

My question caught Thompson by surprise. His lips twitched, revealing a flicker of something— discomfort or perhaps amusement.

"Mr. Vincenzio was a valued team member."

"Was?"

"He'd recently resigned for personal reasons. His activities outside work were not my concern. NeuroGenesis Systems operates on the cutting edge of innovation, but I assure you, we have no connection to such grisly events as the deaths of past employees."

"Cutting edge," I said. "Mind giving me the layman's version of what that means? You know, to clear up any confusion."

Thompson's smile reappeared, though it didn't reach his eyes.

"We specialize in cognitive technology— understanding, mapping, and enhancing the human mind. It's no secret. We've published papers on neural interfaces and memory augmentation."

"Sounds like something out of a sci-fi flick. Or a horror show, depending on who's holding the joystick."

Darius chuckled, though there was no humor in it.

"Every revolutionary idea was once misunderstood, Mr. Thomas. But I assure you, our work is strictly within ethical boundaries."

"Like how Vincenzio ended up in the morgue?"

Thompson leaned forward against his desk, his voice dropping an octave.

"You came here for answers, but I think you already have a narrative in mind. I would caution you, Mr. Thomas, against chasing ghosts. NGS is not in the business of entertaining conspiracy theories."

Since Thompson had yet to kick me out of his office, I said, "Let's pretend I'm not a guy who chases ghosts, and I'm just trying to keep his friends from being next on a killer's hit list. You're telling me there's nothing here I should worry about?"

Thompson stared at me for a long moment before answering. "I'm telling you, Mr. Thomas, that you're asking the wrong questions."

"Then what are the right ones?"

Thompson stood and gestured toward the door. "Perhaps you should start with why Steve Vincenzio was looking for you in the first place. Now, if you excuse me, I have work to do."

Thompson ushered me to his door, where an intern and another man were waiting.

"Felix will escort you to the exit," Thompson said.

Felix was young, probably in his twenties. Although he was dressed in faded jeans and a tee shirt, he had a confident appearance. His nametag said his last name was Founteneau.

"You work here full-time, Felix?"

"Graduate student at UNO," he said. "I work here as many hours as I can."

He smiled when I said, "Let me guess: computer science?"

"Good guess," he said.

"Why here?" I asked.

"NGR is on the cutting edge of cognitive extraction and cerebral re-homing," he said.

I grinned and said, "I'll take your word for it. How did you land the job?"

"My thesis adviser recommended me."

"Oh, who is your advisor?" I asked.

"Dr. Ian Lavoie. He used to work here," Felix said.

Felix escorted me and the other man out the door. We stood on the sidewalk as the heavy metal door closed behind us. The man smiled and shook my hand.

"Clint Harrell," he said. "I'm a supplier for NGS."

Harrell's angular features—narrow nose, hollow cheeks, and perpetual five o'clock shadow—made him seem older than his years. His brown eyes darted around, assessing my every move. He was dressed casually in a worn leather jacket, dark jeans, and boots.

The wiry man with the restless energy of someone constantly looking over his shoulder was probably in his late forties. The fact that he was able to breach the front door of NGS suggested he might be someone with insider knowledge.

"Wyatt Thomas," I said. "I was interviewing for a job."

"Good luck on that," he said. "You'll have to go through more background and security checks than the CIA. Still won't matter unless you know someone the higher-ups recognize and trust."

"Like Felix's thesis advisor?" I asked.

Clint nodded and said, "Exactly."

"I got that impression," I said. "Everyone I met is creepy, and I don't want to work in a building with no windows anyway."

"You don't know the half of it," he said.

"Hell, Clint, it's past lunch, and my stomach is growling. There must be a little eatery close by that makes killer oyster po'boys and the like. Join me and give me the straight skinny on NGS."

"I know just the place," Clint said. "I don't have another appointment for two hours, and I could use a beer."

"Have as many as you like," I said. "I'm buying."

Chapter 22

Clint and I navigated the CBD, weaving through the jungle of uneven sidewalks and towering office buildings that cast shadowy fingers over the street. The air was thick with the metallic tang of ozone from recent rain, mingling with the faint aroma of roasted coffee and fried seafood wafting from unseen kitchens.

Traffic groaned and sputtered, punctuated by the sharp whistles of a crossing guard directing a line of oblivious pedestrians. Clint kept up a constant patter, cracking cynical jokes about the corporate suits brushing past us. He gestured vaguely toward a narrow alley as we turned the corner.

"It's just up here. Place ain't much to look at, but it's got the best red beans and rice this side of the Quarter."

The café came into view, a squat brick building crammed between two newer high-rises like a stubborn relic of another era. Its hand-painted sign read *Gertie's Kitchen* in faded green letters, the apostrophe slightly tilted.

The door jingled as I pushed it open and stepped into a space no larger than a shoebox but alive with clinking silverware, the low buzz of conversation, and the unmistakable scent of home-cooked Southern food.

The café was a time capsule, with mismatched chairs and laminate tables adorned with plastic red-and-white checkered tablecloths. The walls were plastered with old concert posters, curling slightly at the edges, and black-and-white photos of jazz legends whose names had faded over time. An extended counter stretched across one wall, lined with chrome stools where regulars sipped coffee from thick ceramic mugs.

The clientele was a mixed bag: construction workers in dusty boots, a couple of office workers hunched over their phones, and a pair of retirees arguing amiably about a past Saints game. Behind the counter, Gertie—a robust woman with a loud laugh and a cloud of gray hair pinned up in a loose bun—was barking orders at her staff.

A harried young waitress named Dee bustled past with a tray of gumbo bowls, her ponytail swinging as she muttered under her breath.

"Table six will riot if I don't get their cornbread out." Catching my eye, she offered an apologetic smile. "The booth near the window is empty," she said.

The booth was perfect. I leaned back and studied Clint as he scanned the menu. He held up a hand when Dee tried to pour him a cup of coffee.

"No coffee, baby. Bring us a cold pitcher of beer and two frosty mugs."

"Make it one mug, Dee," I said. "I have another interview and don't want to be sloshed."

Dee grinned and poured me a cup of coffee.

"You ever been here before?" Clint asked when Dee was gone.

"First time," I said. "I figured a guy like you'd know all the places with character."

Clint chuckled, the sound low and gravelly. "Character, huh? That what you call cheap and greasy? Place like this, you don't just come for the food—you come for the stories. Gertie's seen more deals go down in this room than half the boardrooms in the CBD."

"Bet that's the truth," I said, resting my elbows on the table. "Speaking of deals, Clint, what's NeuroGenesis really cooking up? And don't give me the PR spiel about cutting-edge tech. I've seen enough to know there's more to it."

Dee returned with Clint's pitcher of beer before he could answer. He smiled and nodded when she filled his glass and handed it to him.

"Thanks, baby," he said.

"Oyster po'boys with a side of red beans and rice is our special today," she said.

Clint nodded and showed her a thumbs-up. "That's what I'll have," he said.

"Make it two," I said.

After a long pull of the beer, Clint said, "I don't pry too much, Wyatt. I'm a supplier, not a whistleblower. But I'll tell you this—those folks. They ain't just trying to build better computers. They're messing with people's heads, literally. Neural this, cognitive that. Sounds fancy, but it's got a stink to it, you know?"

I raised a brow. "Stink like what?"

Clint leaned in, lowering his voice. "Like people disappearing, for one. Contractors who don't meet deadlines, interns who ask too many questions. They get reassigned, they say. But I know a dead end when I see one. And whatever they're working on? It's worth more than the rest of us put together. Dangerous kind of money."

As Dee arrived with our po'boys, Clint flashed a grin, his sharp eyes glinting in the light shining through the window.

"What else?" I asked.

"More shit than you can say grace over," Clint said.

"Give me the highlights," I said.

"NGS has a small though secretive client list, including wealthy elites with a penchant for the macabre."

He nodded when I said, "You mean like voodoo?"

"Their employees are a tight-lipped bunch, though more than one has told me about their suspicious night deliveries: Trucks unloading strange equipment late at night."

"What's so suspicious about a night delivery?" I asked. "Trucks don't always arrive on schedule."

"Then why are they delivering crates marked as medical devices to a software development company?"

"Got me there," I said.

"Employees whisper about Project Chrysalis, which supposedly involves mapping the human brain for eternal applications."

"Sounds ominous," I said.

"Not to mention the sudden employee disappearances: Several workers have left abruptly, rumored to have signed lucrative NDAs."

Clint grew silent when our lunch order appeared. He ate with gusto, like a dog, afraid something would snatch it from him before he finished eating. When we'd stuffed the last tasty morsel into our mouths, I offered to buy more beer.

"Can't be too pasted when I reach my next appointment," he said.

I smiled and said, "I've enjoyed our conversation and wouldn't mind hearing more about NGS."

"That's all you're getting out of me for now. But if you're looking to stir up trouble, Wyatt, know you're diving into a deep pool with some nasty sharks swimming around."

I nodded and said, "Wouldn't be the first time, but thanks for the warning."

The day had grown late when I left Gertie's Place, so I hiked the short distance to the nearest bus stop. After hearing the NGS intern Felix speak about Dr. Ian Lavoie, his thesis advisor, I decided to visit the UNO campus and find out what he knew about vampires and computers.

As the city bus rattled to the curb, its brakes hissing like a cornered cat, I climbed aboard, fishing a crumpled bill from my pocket to feed the farebox. The driver, a middle-aged man with salt-and-pepper hair and a face that looked like it had seen every kind of New Orleans character, nodded curtly. I muttered thanks and headed down the narrow aisle, my boots sticking slightly to the scuffed floor.

The bus was a kaleidoscope of humanity, each passenger a story in motion. A wiry young man with earbuds bobbed his head to a beat only he could hear. Across from him, an elderly woman in a wide-brimmed hat clutched a canvas bag filled with fresh okra and sweet potatoes, the scent of earth clinging to the produce. A trio of high school students in uniform chattered animatedly in rapid-fire slang, their laughter cutting through the mechanical hum of the engine.

I slid into an empty seat near the middle of the bus, where the cracked vinyl cushion had long since lost its spring. The air was thick with the mingled aromas of exhaust fumes, fried chicken from someone's Styrofoam box, and the faint tang of sweat—a sensory cocktail uniquely New Orleans.

Out the grimy window, the city unfolded like a patchwork quilt, the bus lumbering past shotgun houses with peeling paint, their porches sagging under the weight of potted ferns and wind chimes—a corner store with a hand-painted sign advertising *Po'boys & Lotto* in chipped letters. At a red light, a brass band blared from a street corner, their syncopated rhythms momentarily drowning out the engine's groan.

I watched as the neighborhoods shifted with each stop. The French Quarter's faded charm gave way to Gentilly's industrial sprawl, where warehouses jostled for space with churches and tire shops. The bus picked up more passengers, each boarding with a glance that sized up the crowd before finding a seat or grabbing a pole to hang onto.

A man in a Saints jersey plopped into the seat beside me, nodding in greeting.

"You headed to Fairground?" he asked.

"No ponies today for me," I said. "I have business at UNO."

The man grunted, his attention quickly diverted to the jingling alert announcing the next stop.

The scene outside softened as the bus neared the sprawling University of New Orleans campus. Live oaks stretched their gnarled branches over the streets like cathedral arches, and their leaves dappled with sunlight. Students with backpacks strolled along the sidewalks, some clutching coffees, others lost in their phones. The bus squealed to a halt, and I smiled at the driver as I exited.

The cool breeze carried the faint briny scent of Lake Pontchartrain, not far from the campus, and I took a moment to survey the sprawling grounds. The journey had been its own small odyssey—a reminder of the city's vibrancy and grit—and now it was time to meet Dr. Ian Lavoie, who might have answers to questions I wasn't even sure I wanted to ask.

The office of Dr. Lavoie felt like a sanctuary for a man who had long traded the thrill of discovery for the caution of regret. I rapped lightly on the half-open door, which creaked as it swung wider.

A hoarse voice tinged with weariness said, "Come in."

Dr. Lavoie sat behind a heavy oak desk, its surface cluttered with books, papers, and a half-drained cup of coffee. The man was in his late sixties, with a wiry frame and sharp eyes that flickered with intelligence and caution. His silver hair caught the fading sunlight streaming through the wide window overlooking Lake Pontchartrain.

"You must be Mr. Thomas," he said, leaning back in his chair with a faint smile. "I was wondering how long it would take for someone to find me."

He nodded when I said, "Felix called you?"

"I think he sensed you would come here," the old man said.

I stepped inside. "You've got a reputation, Doc. Figured you'd have answers to some questions I've been losing sleep over."

The professor gestured to the chair across from him. "That depends on the questions—and how much you're prepared to hear."

I sat, glancing briefly at the bookshelves crammed with titles on neuroscience, artificial intelligence, and human cognition.

"I hear you used to work for NeuroGenesis Systems. Something called Project Chrysalis."

Lavoie's expression tightened, and he emitted a heavy sigh.

"So, they've resurrected that name, have they? I suppose it was inevitable."

"What does it mean?" I asked.

The professor tapped a finger on the desk, choosing his words carefully.

"Chrysalis is about transformation—breaking free from the cocoon of mortality. It started as a thought experiment. A way to untether the mind from the decay of the body. But it became... much more. Too much more."

I leaned forward and said, "Brain transferal?"

Lavoie's lips twitched in a humorless smile. "In a manner of speaking. The idea was to replicate consciousness—extract it, even relocate it. But there were... complications. Ethical ones. Physical ones."

"Complications like Lucien D'Arcy?" I asked.

Lavoie stiffened, his eyes narrowing. "Where did you hear that name?"

"Seems he has skin in the game. I'm wondering why."

Lavoie shook his head slowly. "D'Arcy is more than an investor. He drove the project to places none of us wanted to go. His influence... it was terrifying. If he's still involved, Chrysalis has gone far beyond anything I thought possible."

I pressed. "What exactly did he want?"

The professor hesitated, then leaned forward, lowering his voice. "He wanted what Chrysalis could offer—rebirth. Not metaphorically, but literally. But the process... it wasn't flawless. It required..." He stopped, rubbing his temples. "If he's still pursuing this, there's a room at NeuroGenesis Systems. They called it the Chrysalis room. Everything you'd want to know is there—if you can get to it."

I raised an eyebrow. "Why tell me this?"

Lavoie smiled faintly, his weariness evident. "Because some things shouldn't stay buried. And if he succeeds, the world will never be the same."

I stood. "I appreciate the tip, Doc. You've given me a lot to think about."

Lavoie's gaze followed me to the door. "Be careful, Mr. Thomas. If you go digging where you don't belong, you might not like what you find."

I paused, my hand on the doorknob. "I'm not one for sleeping easy, Doc. Thanks for the warning."

Chapter 23

When I left the UNO campus and returned to the Central Business District, night had fully cloaked the city. The streets were eerily quiet, save for the occasional hum of a passing car or the distant wail of a siren. Camp Street stretched before me like a shadowed gauntlet, its narrow sidewalks flanked by darkened buildings. Even during daylight, the area had a reputation for danger. At night, it exuded menace.

I moved briskly, keeping my senses sharp, and crossed the street. As I neared the NGS building, its exterior seemed unnervingly sterile under the weak glow of streetlights. I hesitated, glancing around to ensure I wasn't being followed, then punched the code into the panel. The door chimed softly and opened. I was soon inside the main building using the code I'd seen Thompson use.

The hallway was dimmer and narrower than I remembered, which caused me to take a wrong turn at one of the intersections. Backtracking, I reached the room marked Project Chrysalis. To my surprise, it was unlocked. I pushed it open, and the sterile chill of the hallway gave way to a disturbing hum and dim blue light emitted by operating machinery.

The room was a macabre tableau. Rows of cylindrical tanks lined the walls, each filled with a viscous liquid. Suspended within were human brains, faintly illuminated from below, their neural networks eerily visible through the fluid. Monitors flickered with jagged lines, the recorded remnants of thoughts and dreams.

I spotted a tablet on the nearest desk. Among the profiles was a name that caused my jaw to drop: Sabine Moreau. Her neural patterns danced across the screen in ghostly oscillations as if the essence of her mind had been trapped in stasis.

"What the hell?" I said, stepping back.

As I scanned the room, my unease deepened. Medical equipment stood in neat rows, some gleaming with unidentifiable fluids. A metallic table bore instruments that looked like they belonged in a torture chamber rather than a lab.

A drawer at a desk near the corner stood out slightly. Tugging it open, I found a jump drive labeled Project Chrysalis. The innocuous object felt heavy in my palm, its implications too dark to ignore.

Plugging the drive into a nearby computer, I watched as a cascade of files opened on the screen. When I skimmed the initial pages, my breath caught. This was what I needed—everything was here. I used the empty jump drive on my keychain and copied the files. A noise outside the room froze me mid-motion. Footsteps, heavy and deliberate, growing louder by the second.

After yanking the drive from the computer, I slipped behind a tall filing cabinet just as the door creaked open. An armed guard entered, scanning the room with a flashlight. The beam danced over the tanks and monitors, illuminating the grotesque contents for a fleeting moment before moving on while I held my breath, pressing my back against the wall.

The guard muttered something unintelligible before flicking off the light and exiting the room. I waited until the echo of footsteps had faded entirely before emerging from my hiding spot, then pocketed my keys and slipped back into the hallway. I could hear the guard's steps as he trod the polished floors, and my heart hammered as I retraced my steps to the exit. When I reached the street, I inhaled deeply, grateful for the humid air despite its oppressive weight. My relief was short-lived.

"Hey, buddy," a voice called from the shadows.

I turned, instinctively tensing. A man stepped into the dim light, a gun glinting in his hand. A hoodie obscured his face, but the threat in his stance was unmistakable.

"Wallet, keys," he demanded. "And whatever else you got."

My pulse was already spiked, and it caused me to hesitate for a fraction of a second as the man waved the gun, his impatience evident.

"Now."

Reluctantly, I handed over my wallet and keys. The thief snatched them, shoved me, and disappeared into the night.

"Dammit!" I said,

By the time I reached Bertram's, the weight of the loss hung heavily on my shoulders. Josie was waiting at the bar, her face lighting up briefly at my arrival before catching sight of my forlorn expression.

"What happened?" she asked, her voice sharp and concerned.

"You wouldn't believe me if I told you," I said.

"Try me," she said.

I glanced at her, then at the bar, where Bertram was wiping down glasses, blissfully unaware of the storm brewing in my mind.

"A long story," I said. "And it's about to get a whole lot more complicated."

Without asking, Bertram placed a lemonade and bowl of gumbo in front of me on the zinc countertop.

"Thank you," I said.

I doused the gumbo with Louisiana hot sauce before taking a bite.

"You look like your mama just took your favorite teddy bear. What's the matter?" Bertram asked.

"I got mugged," I said.

"Where?"

"Over on Camp Street," I said.

"Hell, Cowboy, that area is dangerous even in broad daylight. What were you doing there this time of night?"

Josie's eyes grew larger when I said, "You can't break into a business in broad daylight."

"You broke into a business?" she asked.

"NeuroGenesis Systems," I said.

"What did you expect to find?" she asked.

"NGS is the software development company Steve Vincenzio worked for. I visited their headquarters earlier and discovered they were involved in a secret study called Project Chrysalis."

"How does it relate to Eliza's disappearance?" Josie asked.

"I'm not sure," I said.

"You ain't making no sense, Cowboy," Bertram said. "You been hitting the bottle again?"

"I'm sober," I said.

"What's Project Chrysalis about?" Josie asked.

"Brain transferal," I said.

Josie did a doubletake and said, "Excuse me?"

"The exchange of brains between individuals," I said.

"You serious?" Bertram said.

"I visited a room like a laboratory out of a Frankenstein movie. There were brains in jars attached to computer screens. One of the brains was Sabine Moreau's."

"Impossible," Josie said. "We saw her in the disappearing house."

"Sabine Moreau's body, but was it her brain inside that body?"

"Bah!" Bertram said. "I ain't listening to any more of your horseshit. I got customers to wait on."

"I'm finding this all hard to believe," Josie said.

"Me too," I said. "If I hadn't seen it with my own eyes, I wouldn't believe it either."

Josie squeezed my hand and said, "Oh, Wyatt, I don't mean to be skeptical. I'm not doubting you."

"It's okay," I said. "I'm doubting myself on this one, and I have no idea where it leads us in rescuing Eliza."

"What about your wallet?" she asked.

"This is the Big Easy, and it's not my first mugging, though it's the only time I lost something I can't replace," I said.

"Your wallet?"

"My wallet's probably in the nearest dumpster," I said. "I didn't have much cash, and I don't use credit cards."

"Then what did you lose that's so important?" she asked.

"A jump drive outlining all the secret research surrounding Project Chrysalis," I said. "If I had it, it might tell us where to go. Without it..."

"Let's go get it," she said.

"It's late, and I've already been robbed once tonight."

"Then what do you have to lose?" she asked.

"You stay. I'll go. It's too dangerous for both of us."

"No way you're going without me, Tarzan," she said. "Do you have a flashlight?"

"Just the one on my keychain," I said.

Bertram had returned to the bar. He reached under the counter and produced a large flashlight.

"Take this," he said. "It'll make a good club if someone attacks you."

We were soon out the door, music from Bourbon Street wafting in the air. After we crossed Canal Street, the lights disappeared into shadows. Darkness engulfed us, though the CBD pulsed with the gritty energy of late-night New Orleans.

"Shit, Wyatt! I've never visited this part of the CBD, even in broad daylight," Josie said.

"Still time to turn around," I said.

"You coming with me?"

I shook my head and said, "I'm going dumpster diving. The trash will be hauled off before dawn."

"Then I'm going with you," Josie said.

"Suit yourself," I said.

Streetlights flickered against the shadowy facades of aging buildings, their weak glow barely illuminating the alleyway when Josie and I located the nearest dumpster to where I'd been robbed. The air smelled of stale beer, garbage, and the unmistakable tang of desperation.

I glanced at the dumpster, its rusted edges glinting under the sickly yellow light.

"This has to be the one," I said. "Wait here for me."

Josie used a rubber band to secure her long hair into a ponytail and gave me a wry smile. "I'll do it. Give me the flashlight and leg up."

"No, you don't," I said. "No telling what's in that dumpster."

"Quit whining and give me a lift. You're lucky I'm not charging you overtime."

"I'm not asking you to do this," I said.

"Don't flatter yourself. I volunteered," she said.

"You're going to smell like hell, successful or not," I said.

Josie's laugh echoed softly off the alley walls as she climbed into the dumpster with surprising agility. We cringed as the rank odor hit us in full force. Josie wrinkled her nose.

"If I die here, you better give me a Viking funeral."

"Noted," I said. "Just find the wallet and the jump drive so we can get the hell out of here."

Josie lowered herself into the dumpster with a grunt. Inside, the darkness swallowed her, leaving only the occasional rustle and muffled curse as she sifted through piles of soggy trash.

"Remind me to stop volunteering," she said.

A Camp Street derelict reeking of cheap wine ambled by, his shopping cart rattling over the cracked pavement. He stopped to stare at the scene, eyes darting between me and the dumpster.

"What you looking for?" he said.

I gave him a tight smile and said, "My dignity. Pretty sure it's in there somewhere."

The man barked a laugh. "Good luck with that."

He shuffled away, leaving the alley as Josie's voice cut through the quiet.

"Got something!" she said.

Wallet or jump drive?" I asked.

"Both, I think."

Josie emerged from the dumpster like a triumphant spelunker, holding up the leather wallet and a mud-streaked set of keys, including the jump drive. I lifted her over the edge of the trash receptacle and onto the ground. Her hair and designer dress were a mess. Worse yet, she smelled like she'd just climbed out of the sewer. She glared at me when I took the wallet and jump drive and wrinkled my nose.

"Good work," I said.

"Then why aren't you hugging me?" she asked.

I made a face, held my breath, and wrapped my arms around her.

"Good," she said. "Now, you stink as much as I do."

"Let's get out of here before someone mistakes us for the competition," I said.

"Where to?" she asked.

"Back to Bertram's," I said. "We both need a shower and a change of clothes."

"You think?" she said.

It was late when we reached Bertram's, and most of his customers had gone home. Josie didn't stop at the bar to say hello, heading straight upstairs to my apartment. I held up my wallet and the jump drive so he could see and followed her up the stairs. She was standing naked at the bathroom door, her clothes in a pile at her feet.

"Put these in a trash bag and throw them away," she said. "Then get your clothes off and join me. I don't want to smell you when I leave the shower."

Hot, soapy water was soon pouring over our bodies. It wasn't the first time that I'd seen Josie naked, though it was the first time I'd been naked and so close to her. She was gorgeous and I had difficulty keeping my hands off. With a few words, she changed all of that.

"Don't just stand there like a grade school dork," she said. "Soap me down, and I'll do the same for you."

After drying off, we laughed, winding up on my bed in each other's arms.

"You were awesome back there," I said.

"I'm laughing now, but if you ever tell a soul about me diving in that dumpster, I promise it'll be the last thing you ever tell anyone."

"I hear that," I said.

"What now?" she said.

"Trust me when I tell you that right now, I only have one thing on my mind," I said.

"I can see that," she said. "What then?"

I didn't answer her, and she didn't seem to care.

Chapter 24

Bertram's customers were gone, he and Lady the only two in the bar when Josie and I descended the stairs. I'd changed into a fresh shirt and khakis, Josie in one of my tee shirts, and a pair of jogging shorts that kept attempting to slide off her hips. Bertram handed her a martini and me a glass of lemonade.

"Those are on me if you tell me the story," he said.

"Okay," Josie said. "But I'm swearing you to secrecy."

Bertram passed his finger over his mouth and said, "These lips are sealed."

I shook my head and said, "If you tell the biggest gossip in New Orleans what happened, it's on you if anyone else finds out."

"I went dumpster diving and found Wyatt's wallet and keys."

Bertram chuckled. "I could smell the both of you when you walked in the door. Guess Cowboy didn't have anything more suitable for you to wear."

"No, and I'm going to embarrass us all if these jogging shorts drop to the floor."

She grinned and shook her fist at him when Bertram said, "At least there ain't no poor children in here to be scarred for life in case they do."

"Good one," I said, chalking an imaginary score in the air.

"Follow me, baby," Bertram said. "I got a closet full of clothes. I'll bet we can find something to fit you."

I sipped my lemonade, waiting with Lady until Bertram returned alone.

"That girl's picky," he said. "Might take her a while to find something she likes."

When Josie reappeared, I had to fight back a laugh. Bertram was less charitable and let out a low whistle, his Cajun drawl full of mischief.

"Well, cher, look at you," he said, leaning on the bar with a grin. "Didn't know you was auditioning for the Mardi Gras Edition of Duck Dynasty."

Josie glared at him with arms crossed. She wore a two-size-too-big hunting camo jacket over a neon pink tank top that read *Who Dat Diva*. The bedazzled lime-green leggings she had on did nothing to improve the ensemble. The coup de grâce was the bright yellow Crocs on her feet.

"First of all," she said, tugging the jacket tighter, "this was the best I could do from that treasure trove of horrors you call a closet, Bertram."

Bertram chuckled and slid another martini toward her. I was smirking but trying to keep it together.

"Cher, I been collecting those gems for years. Ain't nobody complained before. Guess you too fancy for the good stuff."

I finally broke, shaking my head, and said, "You look like you just rolled out of a Louisiana thrift shop during a power outage."

"Ha, ha!" Josie said. She plopped onto the stool next to me and shot us the finger. "This is what I think about your attempt at humor."

"Hey," I said, holding up my hands. "Bertram's closet is like the Bermuda Triangle—stuff goes in, but it doesn't come out the same."

That's a fact," Bertram said.

Josie groaned, raising her martini and downing it in one gulp. "Next time I'm dumpster diving, remind me to take extra clothes."

Bertram laughed so hard that Lady barked, her tail wagging. "Don't let her fool you, Wyatt. She looks right at home. If she ain't careful, the locals might make her queen of the crawfish boil."

I leaned over, trying not to grin too widely. "I'm thinking we both better shut up before the pot boils over."

"Good thinking," Josie said.

Before either Bertram or I could reply, Eddie walked in the door.

When he reached the bar and saw Josie, he said, "On your way to a Mardi Gras parade?"

"Unless you want the rest of this martini on your head, don't start in on me," Josie said.

"Yes, ma'am," he said. "You're the most beautiful woman in New Orleans and look great in anything you wear."

Josie's arms unfolded around her chest, and she glared at Bertram and me.

"That's how a gentleman handles a delicate situation," she said.

"Eddie knows what he's talking about," I said. "You look great."

When Bertram grinned and shook his head, Josie glared at him and said, "Don't say it."

"I was just having a little fun, pretty lady. I got another closet full of regular clothes. Let's see if we can't find something more presentable."

"This better be for real," she said.

"I pulled your leg once. This old Cajun knows better than to do it twice in a row."

When Josie reappeared from Bertram's other closet, the transformation was striking. She looked every bit the chic woman she usually presented to the world.

She wore a tailored white blouse tucked into dark high-waisted jeans that hugged her figure perfectly. Over the blouse, she draped a fitted black blazer that added a touch of elegance. She'd swapped the Crocs for stylish ankle boots in soft tan leather, and her hair was pulled back into a sophisticated ponytail.

The outfit was understated but effortlessly classy, with just enough casual flair to suit the bar's vibe. Returning to the room, she struck a mock runway pose and grinned.

"Better?" she asked, twirling once.

Bertram let out a low whistle, this time one of admiration. "Now, that's what I call Cajun couture. You clean up nice, cher."

I leaned back on my stool, pretending to appraise her like a fashion critic.

"Not bad. I'd say an 8 out of 10. But you're missing the Crocs. They pulled the whole look together."

Josie narrowed her eyes, leaning closer to me. "Don't make me go digging through the dumpster again, Wyatt. I'll find something worse than Crocs and make you wear it."

Eddie, who'd been silently watching, finally spoke up. "I don't know, Josie. I liked the first outfit. It had... personality."

Josie grabbed a wadded bar napkin, tossing it in Eddie's direction.

"Personality doesn't mean I have to look like I just escaped a Mardi Gras parade gone wrong."

Bertram chuckled, pouring Eddie a scotch. "Well, I'll show you the good closet next time. Remember, Josie—you survived Bertram's Closet of Chaos and lived to tell the tale. That's something to be proud of."

Josie raised her martini and said, "Here's to surviving—and to never stepping foot in there again."

When everyone's smile had returned, I glanced at Eddie and said, "You weren't gone long."

"Long enough to pay the bills, settle a couple of disputes, and arrange a wedding banquet next weekend. What's happening here?"

"We still don't have Eliza," I said.

"Okay, now that Josie's looking like herself, maybe you can tell me why you went dumpster diving."

"A new wrinkle," I said. "Steve Vincenzio worked for NeuroGenesis Systems. I visited their facilities today in the CBD. I learned some things, though I don't know how they pertain to Eliza. Still, I believe they do. I stole the information on a jump drive while I was there."

"And?" Eddie said.

"I don't know. I was robbed leaving the NGS building, and the robber got away with my wallet and keys," I said.

"Let me guess. That's why you and Josie went dumpster diving."

I nodded. "We were pulling Josie's leg, but I must tell you, she's a wonderful partner. I couldn't have retrieved my wallet and jump drive without her."

"Let's see what you have," Eddie said.

"Good idea," I said. "Let me get my laptop, and we'll watch it together."

When I returned to the bar, Bertram had dimmed the lights, only the golden glow of the antique lamps casting long shadows on the polished counter. I set my laptop on the bar, the faint hum of its boot-up cutting through the soft jazz playing in the background. The jump drive, ominously nondescript, gleamed in my hand before I plugged it into the laptop.

Josie leaned forward on her stool, curiosity bright in her eyes, while Eddie slumped in his seat, arms crossed, skepticism radiating from him. With Lady at his feet, Bertram wiped a glass, his Cajun drawl ready to pounce on anything he deemed too absurd to believe.

The screen flickered, and the presentation began. A sterile corporate logo—Chrysalis Biotechnologies—slid onto the screen, followed by a soothing female voice narrating as diagrams, blueprints, and eerie footage of brains in glass cases filled the screen.

"Project Chrysalis: *The Evolution of the Human Mind.*"

The narrator's voice continued, smooth as silk but clinical:

"Imagine a world where the boundaries of life and death are shattered, where consciousness can transcend the frailties of the human body. Project Chrysalis isn't just a dream—it's a revolution. By wiping a brain clean, like a hard drive, and uploading another consciousness, we offer eternal life to those bold enough to grasp it. Welcome to the future of humanity."

The diagrams grew more detailed, showing neural pathways being 'erased' and overwritten alongside footage of eerily still bodies hooked up to machines. A sterile white room flashed on the screen, and a person lay on a table while technicians in lab coats manipulated glowing holograms.

Bertram broke the silence with a low whistle.

"Well, ain't that a big old pot of gumbo crazy? You telling me these folks think they can play God with a laptop and some jumper cables?"

Shaking his head and rubbing his temples, Eddie said, "This is some sci-fi nonsense. Do you seriously expect me to believe you can delete someone and stick another person in their place? What is this, The Matrix?"

Wide-eyed but skeptical, Josie leaned closer: "But if they've got this far—those diagrams, those labs—it's like... maybe it could be real? I mean, think about it. They already map brains, right? What if they figured out how to rewrite them?"

"It doesn't matter if it's real," I said. "The fact that someone's trying to do it is the problem. What happens to the people they're 'wiping'? What happens if it works and this technology falls into the wrong hands?"

Bertram poured himself a shot and downed it. "It don't take much imagination to see this going sideways."

"Politicians swapping bodies, criminals ditching their faces," Eddie said.

"Hell!" Bertram said. "Your ex-wife could show up in some poor waitress's skin and ruin your life all over again."

"Bertram, you're the only one here with an ex-wife," Eddie said. "I think you've been watching too many sci-fi horror movies."

Josie, standing now, her voice rising, said, "This isn't a joke! If this is real, they're talking about erasing people—erasing their entire existence! And for what? So some billionaire can live forever in someone else's body? It's disgusting!"

I closed the laptop with a heavy thud. "Disgusting, yes. But it's also dangerous. We need to determine what this has to do with Eliza's disappearance."

Eddie, stroking Lady's head as she whined softly, said, "Well, Wyatt, if we're going up against folks who can hit Ctrl+Alt+Delete on a human soul, we better make damn sure we aren't next on their download list."

"That's a fact," I said.

"The question remains: how does this relate to Eliza?" Eddie asked.

"I'm going to find out," I said.

"How?" Josie asked.

"Before Malik and I rescued you from the disappearing house, Rene took me to La Grotte de la Vérité, the Grotto of Truth."

"What kind of malarkey is that?" Bertram asked.

"You stare into the water, ask questions, and it gives you answers," I said.

"Then ask it when you're going to pay me your rent," Bertram said.

I shook my head and said, "Funny, Bertram."

"Just pulling your leg," he said.

"Where is this Grotto of Truth?" Eddie asked.

"In the catacombs beneath a place Rene called the In-Between," I said.

"Yeah, yeah," Bertram said. "Come on, Miss Lady. Let's go get some sleep."

We watched Bertram and Lady disappear into his apartment in the back of the bar.

"When are you going to the Grotto of Truth?" Eddie asked.

"Right now."

"Not without me, you're not," Eddie said.

"Or me," Josie said.

"Then let's go," I said.

Chapter 25

We left Bertram's late, the night warm and humid. Neither Eddie nor Josie spoke as I led them to the rusty iron gate marking the entrance to the In-Between. I said the incantation I'd heard Rene speak and was rewarded when the old gate creaked open.

"How'd you do that?" Eddie asked.

"Magic," I said.

"Yeah, sure," he said.

Beyond the gate, the air thickened with a chill that defied the Louisiana heat, and a silvery mist swirled at our feet. We were soon in a place we recognized as the French Quarter as if seen through the eyes of someone high on hallucinogenics. It wasn't my first time there, though it still overwhelmed my senses.

"What is this place?" Josie asked.

"The French Quarter," I said.

"My ass!" Eddie said.

"An alternate plane of reality. Rene calls it the In-Between. The streets are all here, though they aren't the same."

The scene unfolding before us was a glimmering image like a movie playing at the wrong speed and tinted with erroneous colors. The people on the sidewalks moved in slow motion and didn't seem quite human. Eddie was affected more than Josie and me.

"I haven't experienced anything like this since I dropped acid back in college," he said.

"It gets even weirder," I said.

"Hope not," Eddie said. "I think I'm having a flashback."

"We won't be here for long," I said. "There's a catacomb beneath this French Quarter. That's where the Grotto of Truth is located and where we're heading."

"Impossible," Eddie said. "New Orleans is barely above sea level."

"This isn't New Orleans," I said. "It's the In-Between."

I smiled when he said, "In between what? Heaven and Hell?"

The In-Between shimmered like a mirage; everything about it, the people on the sidewalks, the streetlamps, the balconies draped with glimmering ferns, was an exaggerated version of what Eddie, Josie, and I knew. Josie and Eddie stared wide-eyed, taking it all in.

"Unreal," Josie said.

"Rene called this a place where the past, the present, and the could-have-been all bleed together."

"There's a peculiar under smell," Josie said.

"Something rotten," Eddie said.

"Like old graveyards after a rain," I said.

When Eddie hesitated, grabbing his temples and closing his eyes, Josie clutched his hand.

"What's the matter?" she asked.

Eddie's eyes were closed, his expression pained. "Don't know," he said.

"Hang on," I said. "We aren't far from the entrance to the catacombs. It's different there."

"Keep your eyes closed," Josie said. "I'll lead you."

I could see Eddie was freaking out as the path ahead sloped downward, cobbled with uneven stones that seemed to glisten unnaturally in the dim moonlight. The closer we got to the entrance of the catacombs, the heavier the atmosphere became, as if it bore the weight of dark secrets hidden within.

Josie embraced Eddie when he said, "I think I'm going to scream."

"I'll take you back to the gate," I said.

"No," he said. "I don't think I can make it."

"Then keep your eyes closed," I said. "We're almost there."

Shadowy vines clung to the walls like skeletal fingers, their thorny tendrils reaching out as if to snag unwelcome visitors. And then we were there, the entrance yawning before us—a black maw framed by weathered archways etched with faded symbols.

"Petroglyphs," Josie said. "No modern human put them there. What do they mean?"

I scanned the glyphs, their meanings lost in time, though their intent unmistakable.

"Protection, warning, or maybe something far darker, Eddie said.

Josie and I glanced at each other, wondering how Eddie would know the meaning of the markings on the wall.

As we stepped inside, the temperature dropped sharply, and the scent of damp earth and decay curled in our nostrils. The catacombs stretched ahead, dimly lit by ancient sconces that flickered with an unnatural blue-green glow. Eddie's hysteria disappeared, replaced by an unnerving calmness, though his pained expression disturbed me.

The carved limestone walls bore grooves where centuries of water had etched its mark. We passed alcoves holding crumbling statues, some missing limbs, others frozen in grotesque expressions of agony or despair.

Creatures, some small and some larger, moved beneath our feet. Bats hung overhead, dropping guano as we walked. Josie squealed when she stepped on a rat, scurrying to find its hole.

"Keep moving," I said. "We're almost there."

Further in, the glow intensified, casting distorted shadows that seemed to move independently of their sources. The faint sound of dripping water echoed through the labyrinth, joined by a whisper dancing at the edge of perception. It was the murmurs of the Grotto of Truth. Ahead, a faint light shimmered, its hue shifting from pale white to a pulsing blue. Eddie opened his eyes.

"What is this place?" he asked.

"The Grotto of Truth," I said.

Eddie and Josie exchanged glances, their apprehension momentarily eclipsed by awe as the light grew stronger, illuminating a cavern that seemed alive with its own pulse.

Stalactites hung like jagged teeth from the ceiling, their tips glistening with a phosphorescent sheen. The ground felt warm, almost alive, as though the grotto was breathing, waiting for us to speak or be consumed by silence.

We entered the cavern's heart, where the pulsing light grew almost blinding. The Grotto of Truth's energy was tangible, a swirling force that tugged at our minds and demanded attention. At its center lay a pool of water so clear it appeared to have no bottom. Instead, it seemed to stretch infinitely downward, reflecting not our faces but fragmented images—visions that shimmered and changed before they could be grasped.

"It's beautiful," Josie said. "Almost as if we've reached the center of the universe."

"Or the gates of hell," Eddie said.

My Moon's Eye earring burned against my skin, vibrating with frantic energy, making my jaw tighten. I touched it, feeling the heat pulse in rhythm with the grotto's light. A chaotic thrumming that resonated with the air around us replaced the earring's usual soothing hum.

Josie's voice was barely audible when she said, "Hear that?"

Her eyes were wide, locked on the pool, rippling despite the cavern's stillness. Eddie nodded as if afraid that speaking aloud would shatter whatever fragile connection the grotto was forming.

My heart pounded as I stepped closer to the pool, feeling its awareness pressing against me—not hostile, though certainly not welcoming. Eddie began to shiver as if suffering from an uncontrollable chill, his face growing pale and then gray. Josie cast me a disturbed glance and then embraced him. Pushing her away, he removed his clothes and waded into the water. As we watched, his head sank, leaving only bubbles of air.

Josie jumped into the pool and disappeared into its depths. Moments passed before her head burst to the surface, her arms around Eddie's lifeless body. Grabbing her hand, I pulled them to shore. We laid him on the floor of the grotto, Josie administering mouth-to-mouth. She soon began to cry.

"Oh, my God, Wyatt! He's dead," she said.

I knelt beside them and said, "Let me take over."

Eddie opened his eyes before I could blow my first breath into his lungs.

"Where am I?" he asked.

"Back from the dead," I said. "Josie saved you."

Eddie's expression had changed from fear to calmness. Seeing Josie was drenching wet, he embraced her.

"The pool has answers to our questions," he said.

"How do you know?" Josie asked.

Eddie could only shake his head and show her the palms of his hands. "Ask it," he said.

I gazed into the pool's still water and said, "What does Eliza's disappearance have to do with NeuroGenesis Systems and Project Genesis?"

The grotto's response was silence—heavy, oppressive, and absolute. But then, the water's ripples grew stronger, casting faint images onto the cavern walls. A face emerged from the chaos: Malik. The vampire's pale features twisted into a knowing smirk before fading into shadow. Behind him, a faint outline formed—a woman's silhouette crowned with a glowing veil.

"The Veiled Queen," Josie said as though the name had been plucked from her mind and placed on her tongue.

The Moon's Eye earring burned hotter, a sensation like static electricity coursing through my veins. The grotto wasn't done. The water shifted again, showing a flickering image of an old man standing beneath a crescent moon.

"What the hell?" Eddie said.

"My grandfather," I said.

Grandfather's shadow stretched impossibly long, blending into the darkness until it became something else entirely—something monstrous, with eyes glowing like twin embers. My chest tightened as he mouthed a single word that

resonated in my mind, unbidden yet
unmistakable.

"Nocturne," he said before disappearing.

"What was that all about?" Josie asked.

"My past and future seem to have come full
circle," I said. "That was my grandfather. I'm
unsure what he wants from me."

"Yes, you do," Eddie said.

"What?"

"To join him," he said.

Eddie shook his head when Josie said, "In the
water?"

"He's dead," I said. "How can I join him?"

"That's an answer the pool won't give you,"
Eddie said.

"How do you know?" I asked.

"No clue," he said. "Just watch your ass.
There's danger all around. The grotto is telling us
Malik knows."

"About Eliza?" Josie asked.

Eddie nodded. "About Eliza, the Veiled Queen.
About everything."

I tore my gaze from the pool, my thoughts
racing. The grotto's refusal to answer directly was
a redirection, not a dismissal. As Eddie said, the
answers lay with Malik, though the revelation
about my grandfather burned just as fiercely. If my
family's bloodline was tied to the Nocturnes, it was
a piece of myself I had yet to uncover.

"We need to speak with Malik," I said. "And
soon. But this..." I touched the earring, the weight
of its revelation lingering. "This damn thing is
driving me insane."

"Don't remove it," Eddie said.

"Why not?" I asked.

"Just don't do it," he said.

The grotto's light dimmed as if satisfied that it
had fulfilled its purpose. The cavern felt heavier

now, its energies retreating into the shadows as we returned to the surface. This time, experiencing the In-Between didn't cause Eddie any ill effects. It was dawn when we exited the Enchanted Gate.

"Too late to visit Malik," I said. "He'll be in his coffin. What now?"

"Hope's house isn't far," Josie said.

We were soon standing on Hope's porch, pounding on her door. She was stark naked and yawning as if she didn't care when she opened the door for us.

"Is this how you always greet your guests?" Eddie asked.

"You love it," she said with a smile. She pulled Josie into the house when she saw her drenched hair and dripping clothes. "Baby, what happened to you?"

Hope didn't wait for an answer as she hustled Josie into the bathroom. Eddie and I made ourselves comfortable.

"I'm having a drink," he said. "Want one?"

"Don't you think you'd better ask first?"

"Last time Josie and I were here, Hope told me to help myself," he said.

"When was that?" I asked.

"Before having Malik take us to the disappearing house."

"Guess I was off with Rene," I said.

"Your loss, not mine," Eddie said.

"Anything you want to tell me?" I asked.

Josie and Hope, both wrapped in white bath towels, appeared from the bathroom before Eddie could answer. Hope quickly mixed her and Josie a martini, giving me a glass of water before joining us on the couch.

"Malik won't be up and around for another eighteen hours," Hope said. "I'm going with you, and we need to kill some time until then."

"Good," I said. "I need a few hours of sleep, and my bed calls me."

"Josie and I have a better idea," Hope said. "We're starving. After we dress, you can take us to breakfast."

"I could eat something," Eddie said.

"Me too," I said.

"Afterward, we can come back here and crash until dark," Hope said.

Eddie gave me a wink and said, "Sounds like a plan."

Chapter 26

Eddie's anticipation went unresolved after we returned from breakfast in the Quarter. He slept on Hope's couch and I in her recliner. It was just as well for me as it had been a while since I'd slept more than an hour or two. It was dark outside, Eddie, Hope, and Josie enjoying cocktails when I opened my eyes and joined them.

"Talk about sleeping like a log," Eddie said.

"It's been a while since I had any sleep," I said.

"What the hell have you been doing?" Eddie asked.

Hope grinned and said, "The real question is, who the hell have you been doing?"

Josie and Hope had dressed for the occasion. Changing the subject, I said, "Nice outfits."

Josie and Hope pirouetted for Eddie and me to see. Their black high-neck lace blouses with intricate patterns went well with black leather miniskirts and thigh-high stockings highlighted by blood-red garters adorned with tiny black bows. Their boots made a statement: bold—heeled ankle boots with silver buckles. They'd moussed their hair, and long red fingernails protruded from their open-fingered lace gloves.

"Wow!" Eddie said.

I couldn't have agreed more and said, "Double wow!"

"You lucky boys are going to be the envy of every person in the club," Hope said.

"Got that right," Eddie said. "What now?"

"Malik won't be out of his coffin yet," I said.

"Nyx is bartending at the Eden Club," Hope said. "It's still early, so let's have another cocktail before making our appearance."

"Sounds like a plan," Eddie said.

The Eden Club was rocking when we reached it, Nyx polishing a glass behind the bar. When she saw me, and how Josie and Hope were dressed, she frowned and averted her gaze. Eddie didn't notice, but Hope and Josie did.

"Something you want to tell us?" Hope asked.

"About what?"

"You know what. I haven't seen that look on my little sister's face since her boyfriend in high school blew her off for a pretty cheerleader."

"I haven't blown anyone off," I said.

"Then why did she give Josie a go-to-hell look?" Hope asked.

"Nyx is a stunner, but you two are dressed like celebrity divas," I said. "Maybe she's envious."

"Or maybe you had sex with my little sister," she said. "Don't bother concocting an excuse. I can tell by the look on her face that you did."

When I glanced at Josie, she averted her eyes. Hope didn't miss Josie's reaction.

"Who else did you have sex with?" she asked.

"I haven't done anything wrong here," I said.

Josie turned away when Hope looked at her and released her hand. Seeing a situation brewing, Eddie stepped between me and Hope.

"I don't know what's happening here, but Eliza's life is in danger, and we have important

230

business to attend to," he said. "Stow your attitudes, and let's handle the problem."

"Fine," Hope said, giving me the evil eye. "In the meantime, keep your hands off of my sister."

Hope was correct about one thing: her and Josie's looks were attracting attention throughout the club. Josie wouldn't look me in the eye, Eddie glaring at the both of us. Nyx's smile had returned as she began dispensing drinks.

"You and Josie are gorgeous," she said. "What's the occasion?"

"We're visiting Malik's lair to ask a few questions," Hope said.

"Malik won't be happy when you show up at his house unannounced, even dressed the way you are," Nyx said. "Unless…"

"Unless what?" Hope asked.

"Unless you and Josie intend to offer him your sexual favors."

"Ain't happening, little sis," Hope said.

"You two are gorgeous, though Nyx has a point," Eddie said. "Unless you're willing to have sex with the big guy, it's going to take more than flirtation to get him on our side."

"What do you suggest?" Hope asked.

"I don't know," he said. "Some other present or something."

"Like what?" Hope asked.

"I can mix him a grim reaper and put it in a go cup," Nyx said.

"Do it," Hope said.

"We can stop by La Porte Mystique," Josie said. "Madam Elzora might have a present fit for a vampire."

"It's after midnight," I said. "Her botanica won't be open."

Hope glared at me and said, "It isn't far from here, and it won't hurt to stop by and see."

We left the Eden Club with Malik's go cup and a distinct chill in the air not caused by the lovely spring evening. Late-night pleasure seekers had begun roaming the streets of the Quarter, and to my surprise, La Porte Mystique was open for business.

The storefront glimmered faintly under the ghostly moonlight. Its sign, a battered wooden plaque painted with curling gold script framed by strings of multicolored beads and dried herbs, swung in the breeze. Flickering candlelight spilled through the frosted glass windows, casting shadows that seemed to dance to the rhythm of the night.

Inside the shop, there was a labyrinth of wonder and mysticism. Shelves groaned under the weight of exotic ingredients—jars of powders, bundles of dried plants, and vials of mysterious liquids. Fetishes and talismans hung from the low ceiling, swaying gently as if moved by unseen hands. The air was thick with incense, a heady mix of sandalwood, clove, and something ancient and metallic, like blood.

Madam Elzora, the shopkeeper, appeared from the back, a regal and unsettling figure. Her frame was draped in layers of colorful fabric, her neck adorned with bone-and-bead necklaces that clinked softly as she moved. Her eyes gleamed like polished onyx as they settled on us, her painted lips curling into a knowing smile.

'Well, well," she said like velvet and smoke. "The moon brings travelers seeking the unseen. What can I offer you this night?"

"We're here for a gift. For Malik," I said.

Madam Elzora's smile faltered for a fraction of a second, replaced by a look of curiosity tinged with wariness.

"Ah, Malik, the fanged one. Always a man of peculiar tastes. I have just what you need to win over a vampire's cold heart."

The old voodoo woman gestured to a locked cabinet and retrieved a small vial of viscous liquid.

"This," she said, holding the vial up so the candlelight caught its ruby hue, "is spiced blood. Rare. Delicate. A true vampire's delicacy."

"Is there a big demand for spiced blood in the French Quarter?" Eddie asked.

"You would be surprised," the old woman said with a smile.

Josie leaned in, intrigued. "What makes it so special?"

"The blood is infused with spices and herbs from the old world," Madam Elzora said, her voice dropping to a conspiratorial whisper. "It carries a heat that lingers on the tongue and dances in the soul. Even for one as ancient as Malik, it will evoke memories long forgotten."

"Where do you get your supply?" Hope asked.

"Imported from Italy," Madam Elzora said.

"Are there vampires in Italy?" Eddie asked.

Madam Elzora smiled again and said, "You'd be surprised."

Josie produced a wad of cash and slid it across the counter. "We'll take it," she said.

Madam Elzora tucked the vial into a silk pouch and handed it over. "Malik will appreciate this. But remember," she said, her tone dropping ominously. "It is never wise to disturb a vampire; you do it in your peril no matter what gifts you bear."

"We'll take your advice under advisement," Eddie said.

As we turned to leave, Calypso, the raven perched on a shelf near the door, cawed loudly, its beady eyes fixed on us.

"The magic surged, a force untamed,
And to the void, the house was claimed.
No more to stand on mortal land,
Lost forever, like time's slipping sand."

The bird's raspy and otherworldly voice sent a chill through the air. Hope clutched Josie's hand reassuringly, squeezing it when he paused at the door.

"Just a bird," Eddie said.

"One damn smart bird," I said, glancing back at Calypso as the raven fluttered its wings, its dark eyes gleaming.

Malik's Creole townhouse sat like a brooding sentinel at the corner of Governor Nichols and Dauphine, its weathered red exterior almost blending with the crimson hue of the setting moon. Black shutters hung unevenly as though they had grown weary with age. Unassuming yet foreboding, the tiny house exuded a palpable sense of isolation. Flickers of faint candlelight danced irregularly from within, casting warped shadows through grimy panes.

We approached cautiously, the air thick with the faint tang of iron and decay. I knocked, the sound dull and lifeless against the peeling door. From inside came a muffled groan and the slow creak of movement.

Moments later, the door swung open to reveal Malik, his pale face framed by messy curls. He wore a silk robe, worn at the seams but still elegant in a bygone way. Half-lidded with annoyance, his dark eyes swept over us with a disdainful glare.

"This," he begins, his voice low and gravelly, "had better be good."

The main room of Malik's home was a portrait of neglect and timelessness. Weathered, cracked, scarred furniture was scattered haphazardly around the dim space. Dust cloaked every surface, softening the edges like a shroud. The air smelled earthy and damp as if the walls themselves exhaled the scent of the grave. Unlit candles sat in tarnished holders at mismatched tables.

Hope stepped inside first, taking a long match from the table and striking it with precision. The sharp scent of sulfur briefly cut through the room's musk as she lit several candles.

Their warm glow cast Josie and her in a golden radiance that contrasted sharply with the gloom, flames sputtering as if struggling against the oppressive darkness. Both women moved with deliberate grace in their alluring lace and satin attire, their skirts swishing softly as they approached Malik.

"Malik," Josie said, leaning in to kiss his forehead. "We've brought you something special."

Hope followed suit, brushing a kiss to his other temple. The vampire's perpetual scowl softened, his lips twitching in what could almost be mistaken for a smile.

Josie retrieved the silk pouch from her clutch and produced the vial of spiced blood.

"From us to you," she said, holding it out to him like an offering.

Malik took the vial, his bony fingers brushing against hers as he did. He uncorked it, sniffing deeply. His eyes closed for a moment, and when they opened again, there was a faint glimmer of satisfaction.

"You've done well," he said, his voice smoother now, though still tinged with his signature sarcasm. "I suppose this warrants a few moments of my precious time. How can I be of service?"

Eddie and I exchanged a look, the unspoken relief palpable. We settled around the room, perched cautiously on chairs that creaked ominously under our weight. Still clutching the vial, Malik sighed, sank into an armchair, his robe pooling around him like spilled ink, and fixed us with a penetrating stare.

"We're here with hat in hand because we believe you have answers to questions nagging us," I said.

"What questions?" Malik asked.

"Like, what do you know about brain transferal?"

Malik laughed. "I know nothing about brain transferal. What made you think I would?"

"We have reason to believe it has something to do with the disappearance of Eddie's niece," I said. "Eliza is in the disappearing house."

"How do you know?" Malik asked.

"Eddie spoke with her," I said.

"Is she a prisoner?" he asked.

"Not exactly," Eddie said. "She refused to come with me."

"I have no clue what your niece is doing in the disappearing house, nor do I know anything about brain transferal," Malik said. "You must have another reason for questioning me."

"Before coming here, we visited La Grotte de la Vérité. When we queried the pool, your image appeared," I said.

"I'm sorry," Malik said.

Malik's gaze turned to Hope when she said, "Does someone you know want Eliza's brain?"

"Maybe," he said.

"The woman in the dark veils?" Hope asked.

"So, you've come for a history lesson..." Malik began, his voice low and rich with the weight of old secrets.

I smiled and said, "I always liked history class."

Chapter 27

The candles flickered, and the room grew colder as if the shadows leaned in to listen. Malik frowned when a motorcycle on the street outside the window backfired after its driver had gunned the engine.

"Damn rice burners," he said. "They ought to be banned from the French Quarter."

Malik laughed when Eddie said, "Tell us how you really feel."

Malik didn't laugh. "My story is long," he said.

"We have all night," I said. "At least what's left of it."

Malik opened his shirt and showed us the image tattooed there. It was a drop of blood, red still vibrant, against a background of scrollwork like you might see on the back of a dollar bill.

"This image was tattooed on my chest in France over three hundred years ago."

"Whoa!" Eddie said.

"It's called the Crimson Sigil and represents that I'm an original member of Ordre du Sang," Malik said. "Thirteen of us; twelve disciples and one more."

Eddie and I exchanged a glance. "What's Ordre du Sang?" Josie asked.

"Order of the Blood," I said. "Hope and I know about it. Maybe you'd better explain to Josie and Eddie."

Malik uncorked the vial of spiced blood and drank it. After a pleased sigh, he nodded and leaned back into his chair.

"It began during the reign of Louis XIV, the most powerful leader the world has ever known—the Sun King. He ruled France for over seventy-two years, though he had his fingers in things of interest worldwide."

Malik nodded when Josie said, "Wasn't he the one who built the Palace of Versailles?"

"Louis's interests were diverse: architecture, mathematics, and medicine. He was also an avid student of the dark sciences: magic, necromancy, and the occult. He was quite literally the most brilliant thinker I've ever known."

"So, the Order of the Blood originated with Louis XIV?" Eddie said.

"Louis created the order though he was never a member," Malik said. "The original thirteen were all vampires. There are many members around the world to this day. Most aren't literal vampires, the thirst for blood having morphed into their never-ending quest for power."

"You are no longer part of the power elite?" Eddie asked.

"Of the original thirteen members of Ordre du Sang, only three remain. Myself and two others. One of them a woman."

Malik nodded again when I said, "Anyone we may have heard of?"

"Athénaïs de Montespan," he said.

"Who is that, and why was she the only woman to become an order member?" Hope asked.

"Louis was a short man and physically unattractive," Malik said. "It didn't stop him from having several wives, numerous mistresses, and more casual affairs than you would believe. His dick was physically short, though psychologically the longest any human ever possessed."

"Because?" Josie asked.

"Power is a commanding magnet. Men and women desired a piece of Louis's soul." Malik laughed. "Though he was loose with his sexual favors, his soul was something he never shared."

Hope glanced at me and said, "Sounds familiar."

Ignoring her comment, I said, "Tell us more about the Sun King."

Malik was happy to comply with my request. "Though Louis had many relationships, he only loved one person," he said.

"Athénaïs de Montespan?" Hope said.

"Louis's favorite mistress," Malik said. "Athénaïs was exquisitely beautiful and inordinately intelligent. There was also no sexual act she hadn't tried. Her morals made those of an alley cat seem like a saint's. She would fuck a mangy dog without compunction if it advanced her position in life."

Hearing the world's oldest vampire use the eff word stunned me. From the expressions on the faces of Hope, Josie, and Eddie, I could see they were equally shocked.

"I'm confused," Josie said. "What was Louis XIV's interest in vampires about?"

"Even with all his power and wealth, Louis desired immortality more than anything. His scientists searched the world for answers to his questions," Malik said. "When they brought a vampire to France from eastern Europe, he had his answer."

"Seems we're missing something," Eddie said. "How did Louis turn you into a vampire?"

"A particular virus mutates normal cells, and the physical changes result in vampirism," Malik said.

"Bullshit!" Eddie said.

"People in the 17th century weren't stupid," Malik said. "Country folk knew that the bite of a rabid dog caused catastrophic changes in anyone bitten."

"You're telling us a virus causes vampirism?" Eddie said.

"And werewolves," Malik said.

"If that's true, why don't today's doctors know about this virus?"

Malik snickered. "There are many things modern doctors don't know or perhaps keep shrouded in secrecy for financial reasons."

"Why does everything you can't quite explain always become a conspiracy theory?" Eddie asked.

"Because sometimes it is," Malik said.

"Shut the hell up, Eddie, and let Malik tell his story," Hope said.

Eddie threw up his hands in despair and surrender. Affected by Eddie's outburst, Malik's friendly demeanor had disappeared. I noticed, and so did everyone else. Hope handed him the go cup.

"Nyx sent you a grim reaper. Your story is so compelling that I forgot to give it to you."

Malik opened the Styrofoam lid and sipped the sugary concoction.

After glaring at Eddie, Malik said, "Thank you, Hope."

"I'm sorry," Eddie said. "Please continue your story, and I won't interrupt you with more dumb questions."

"Not all questions are dumb," Malik said. "The thirteen of us became vampires during a gruesome ceremony performed by Etienne du Clairvaux, Louis's court magician."

"Why didn't Louis XIV become a vampire," I said.

"Vampirism poses complications," Malik said. "Louis was looking for another avenue to immortality when his favorite grandson and family contracted measles. Le Petit Dauphine was one of the original thirteen vampires."

"Louis XIV's grandson was a vampire?" Eddie asked.

"He was a close friend, and I volunteered to take the journey with him," Malik said.

"You said three of you are still alive. Who is the other man?" I asked.

My jaw dropped when he said, "My nemesis, Lucien D'Arcy."

We sat in the dimly lit study, shadows flickering on the walls as the only light came from the fire crackling in the hearth. Malik exited his chair and stood by the fireplace, his tall figure casting an imposing silhouette. His usually impassive face was heavy with emotion, his dark eyes glinting.

"You should know the truth," he said, his deep voice cutting through the tension. "You've stumbled into something much older—and far more dangerous—than you realize."

Hope shifted nervously on the couch, her hands clutching the edge of the cushions. Eddie leaned forward, his ever-present smirk absent for once. Josie, her arms crossed, narrowed her eyes.

"We weren't supposed to be here," Malik continued. "Any of us. Over three hundred years ago, Louis XIV sought to wield power over France and life and death. He had alchemists, mystics, and scholars at his disposal, men who dabbled in things they shouldn't have. Their experiments succeeded. They found a way to create us—

241

creatures bound to darkness but blessed with immortality and power beyond imagination."

Josie cut in. "Why New Orleans, then? Why send you here?"

Malik's lips pressed into a grim line. "We were too dangerous. Too hungry. Too unpredictable. Athénaïs de Montespan was the king's favorite. His obsession. When she fell ill with a wasting disease no physician could cure, Louis commanded the alchemists to save her. They turned her into what we are. But something went wrong—she didn't heal as she should have. Instead, her transformation was flawed. She gained immortality, yes, but her body continued to age, albeit slowly. And with every passing decade, her pain deepened."

"And what's Lucien's role in all this?"

Malik's expression darkened. "Lucien D'Arcy was the Duc de Saint-Laurent, a man of wealth and station. He was also a fool for love. Athénaïs, for all her beauty and power, was no saint. There were many of her lovers, and Lucien was among them. When Louis sought to save her, Lucien begged to join her—to share her eternity. He was transformed, willingly, out of devotion. But when Athénaïs's body began to betray her, Lucien vowed to find a way to restore her youth. Even now, centuries later, he searches for a suitable vessel to house her mind. A younger body still full of life. He believes he's found it in someone here."

Eddie raised an eyebrow. "And by 'someone,' I'm guessing you mean Eliza?"

Malik nodded, his gaze flicking briefly toward Hope. "Lucien calls Athénaïs his veiled queen, though I see her as a ghost of the past. His devotion borders on madness. He believes transferring her consciousness into a new host will save her and perfect her. Athénaïs is resigned, weary, though she clings to the anticipation that he is right."

"And Louis?" I asked. "What happened to him?"

Malik smiled faintly, bitterly. "The Sun King? He grew tired of us. After Athénaïs, he forbade the creation of more vampires. But we were his secret weapon, his expendable pawns. At least, he originally thought. He hid our existence from the world, and when we became too much of a liability, he sent us away. With the Casket Girls, we were packed onto ships and sent to the colonies. New Orleans became our prison—and, eventually, our home."

Hope's voice was barely above a whisper. "So...you've been here ever since?"

"Yes," Malik said, his voice heavy with centuries of pain. "Waiting. Hiding. And now, thanks to Lucien, I'm again at risk of losing it all."

The room fell silent, the weight of his words pressing down on us. The fire crackled softly, its glow dancing on our uneasy faces.

"I have more questions," I said. "What about Giselle, Marceline, and Rene?"

"They are Nocturnes," Malik said.

"What's their story?" I asked.

"Lucien's creations. Night people who've become more than nightly French Quarter fixtures," Malik said.

"I saw my grandfather's image in The Grotto of Truth. He told me that he is a Nocturne and begged me to join them."

"There is much more to this story," Malik said.

"Please tell me," I said.

"Not now," he said. "Dawn approaches, and I must retire before the sunlight through the window sends me to my final resting place."

Malik disappeared through a door. Hope followed him as he climbed into his ancient coffin and closed it atop him. We joined her when she motioned us.

"He has a coffin?" Josie asked.

"The original vessel in which the Casket Girls transported him to New Orleans centuries ago," I said.

Josie glanced around and said, "What now?"'

"My vote is for breakfast at Bertram's," Hope said.

When Josie and Eddie smiled and nodded their ascent, I said, "Let's do it."

"Great," Hope said. "I'm calling Nyx to join us."

As we stepped out of Malik's cottage, the French Quarter stirred like a restless sleeper. Dawn was a slow bloom on the eastern horizon, the sky awash in muted lavender and pale gold hues. A gossamer mist clung to the cobblestones, coiling around wrought-iron balconies and curling into the alleys like a ghost reluctant to depart. The air was damp and thick with the scent of rain-soaked magnolias and the faint brine of the nearby Mississippi.

The streets were eerily quiet, the chaos of the Quarter's nightlife evaporating like spilled whiskey in the heat of day. Gas lamps flickered, their amber light casting wavering shadows. The rhythmic clop of a lone carriage horse echoed down Royal Street, mingling with the soft shuffle of our footsteps as we walked through the dissipating fog.

A drunken reveler slumped in a doorway stirred as we passed, muttering something incoherent before retreating further into the shadows. A window creaked open somewhere above, and a bleary-eyed figure tossed a bucket of water onto the street, scattering a trio of feral cats.

244

Night People

When we turned onto Bourbon Street, the scent of stale beer lingered, mingling with the faint aroma of fresh beignets from a distant café. Bertram's bar was just ahead, its neon sign still dark but a soft glow emanating from within. We reached it as the first rays of sunlight broke through the canopy of iron and Spanish moss, gilding the tops of the buildings and painting the street in fleeting shades of rose and amber.

Chapter 28

Except for the Cajun bartender and his dog, Lady, we found Bertram's empty. He did a doubletake and whistled when he saw Hope and Josie's racy outfits.

"Wowee!" he said. "Party time! You getting back or just going out?"

"We were hoping you'd cook us some breakfast," I said.

"Depends," he said.

I glanced around the empty bar and said, "On what?"

"On telling me all about this party you just came from," he said.

"It's kind of secret," Eddie said.

"The McDonald's on Canal is open. You can get Egg McMuffins," Bertram said.

"Don't be that way," Eddie said.

"I'm starving," Hope said. "Tell him where we've been, or I will."

Bertram rubbed his hands together and said, "That's what I like to hear. I'm firing up the grill soon as I dispense drinks. If anyone's thirsty, that is."

Everyone was soon sipping cocktails, Bertram's grill heating as he began preparing ingredients. I was sitting at a barstool on the end.

When Nyx entered the bar and saw me, she stood beside Hope instead of sitting by me. I got up and traded places with Eddie so that she could sit. Bertram noticed and glared at me. Wonderful aromas coming from the grill soon lightened everyone's mood.

The contrast between Malik's shadowy lair and the warm embrace of Bertram's bar was as stark as night and day. Inside, the glow of low-hanging lights reflected off the bar, their golden hues casting a welcoming radiance over the room. The scent of strong coffee and frying bacon filled the air, mingling with the sweet aroma of maple syrup. Lady padded over to greet us with a wag of her tail, her soft fur a comforting presence.

Bertram soon served steaming mugs of chicory coffee and plates piled high with eggs, grits, and buttery toast. The clink of forks against plates and the soft murmur of conversation began to replace the lingering heaviness from our visit to Malik.

"Now," he said. "Where you been?"

"Malik's," I said.

Bertram backed up a step and said, "You mean his house? You got a death wish?"

Eddie grinned and said, "More like an undead wish."

"Funny," Bertram said. "No more scotch for you."

"Don't be that way," Eddie said. "Wyatt took us to a truth fountain in the alternate French Quarter, where we saw Malik's image when we asked about Eliza."

By now, Bertram's arms were crossed. He glanced at me and said, "Uh-huh!"

"Eddie isn't joking," Hope said.

She grinned when he said, "Is that why you and Josie are dressed like a pair of vampire harlots."

247

"No one uses that word anymore," Hope said.

"Well, tell that to my Mama. She liked it, and so do I."

"Your mama knew about vampires?" Eddie asked. Bertram reached across the bar and pulled Eddie's scotch away from him. "I'm sorry. I was joking, not casting aspersions on your mother."

"You can kiss my aspersions," Bertram said.

"I said I'm sorry," Eddie said.

Bertram pushed the scotch back across the bar. "Okay, then. Tell me about your visit to Malik and keep my mama out of it."

Hope, Josie, and I were struggling to keep straight faces. Nyx's expression remained dejected.

"In anticipation of Malik being pissed at us showing up unannounced, we took him a grim reaper go cup and a vial of spiced blood," Eddie said.

"Uh-huh!" Bertram said. "How did that work out."

"Better than expected," Eddie said. "Malik liked Josie and Hope's outfits."

"I'll bet he did," Bertram said. "Hope he wasn't expecting more than a look."

"Once we got in the door, Malik was a perfect gentleman," Hope said.

"Good thing, considering those tiny little skirts you girls are wearing. What does the inside of a vampire's house look like?"

"Early graveyard," Eddie said. "Smelled like the inside of a crypt. Bottom line is he told us what we went there to hear."

"Which was?" Bertram said.

"Why do the Nocturnes have Eliza," Eddie said.

Eddie's smile disappeared, and he slugged his scotch.

"Another?" Bertram said.

Eddie got off the stool, reached in his pocket, and tossed a hundred-dollar bill on the bar.

"I'm out of here," he said.

"Where are you going?" I asked.

"I still have friends at the DOJ. I'm going to visit them and find out the latest on the investigation of Lucien D'Arcy," he said.

Eddie waved when he walked out the door, and I said, "Good luck."

Hope and Josie got up to follow him. "We're going to my place and get some sleep," Hope said. "You coming, Sis?"

Nyx shook her head and said, "I'm going to my apartment after I drink another cup of Bertram's coffee.

"I owe you some money," Hope said. "Drop by the bar tonight, and I'll pay you."

"Will do," Nyx said. When Bertram brought his coffee pot to refill Nyx's mug, she said, "Your coffee is the best I've ever drank but maybe you can add some liquor to it and make it better."

"I'll do you one better, pretty baby," he said. Bertram began mixing a drink and soon presented Nyx with it. "This one's got a kick and a little flair—just like you."

After a sip, she smiled and gave him a thumbs up.

"Wonderful!" she said. "What is it?"

"Specialty of the house," he said. I call it Café Brûlot à la Bertram."

"Can I have the recipe?"

She smiled again when he said, "If I do, I'll have to kill you."

"Please," she said.

"It's got brandy, orange liqueur, sugar, cloves, orange peel, and a stick of cinnamon. If you want the exact recipe, you'll have to wait until my cookbook comes out."

"When will that be?" she asked.

"Ain't decided yet," he said. "I got customers coming in. Need anything else just holler and I'll come a running."

Nyx and I were suddenly alone at the bar and still sitting two stools apart. When I glanced at her, she looked the other way.

"I'm sorry," I said.

She looked at me and said, "For what?"

"For leading you to believe our dalliance was more than what it really was," I said.

"I came on to you," she said. "Not the other way around. That's not why I'm mad at you."

"Then why are you mad?"

"Because you lied to me."

"How is that?" I asked.

"You told me that Josie isn't your girlfriend."

"No lie. She isn't my girlfriend," I said.

"She thinks she is," Nyx said.

"No, she doesn't."

"She told Hope that you made love to her."

"That doesn't make her my girlfriend. I'm a French Quarter private investigator and not a Baptist deacon."

When she didn't respond to my reply, I moved onto the stool beside her and clutched her hand.

"I don't want you to think I'm easy," she said.

"This isn't high school. We aren't going steady," I said. "Besides, I thought you liked my cat."

"What does she have to do with anything?" Nyx asked.

"She likes you, and she's a good judge of character," I said.

"Does her owner like me?" Nyx asked.

"Cats don't have owners, nor do I," I said. "Doesn't stop me from liking you a lot, though."

Nyx looked at me with a smile. "Are you going to your room?"

"I was thinking about it," I said.

"My little apartment is depressing. Can I go with you?"

"Nothing I'd love better, as long as you realize we're not in a permanent relationship."

"I know that," she said.

"I don't need a roommate."

"I don't take up much space," she said.

She grinned when I said, "You probably have enough shoes and clothes to take up every inch of my closet."

"I can get rid of lots of things," she said.

"Famous last words," I said. "I'm going to bed. Go to your own apartment because I'm not ready for a permanent relationship."

She grinned again, stuck her tongue in my ear, and blew her warm breath. "Tell you the truth," she said. "Neither am I."

It was still dark when I awoke to a sound I recognized, though I couldn't quite put my finger on what it was. When my eyes focused, I saw Nyx. She was mopping my floor in the nude. She jumped when I spoke.

"What are you doing?" I asked.

"I fed and watered Buttercup, washed your dishes, and now I'm mopping the floor," she said.

"It doesn't need mopping," I said.

She smiled and said, "It's all right. I'm done. How does it look?"

Nyx had done more than wash the dishes and mop the floor. Everything was spotless, and all my clutter was stowed away.

"I had a wife once," I said. "It didn't work out."

"I wouldn't marry you if you asked me," she said.

"Good, because I'm not," I said. "What time is it?"

"Almost midnight," she said. "I have to go to the Eden Club and collect my wages."

"I'll go with you," I said. "You can't walk the streets of the French Quarter after dark alone."

"I'm fine," she said. "I can take care of myself."

I got out of bed and started dressing. "You'll be safer if I tag along," I said.

"Suit yourself," she said.

The French Quarter was alive with its midnight symphony—an intoxicating blend of jazz pouring from open doorways, the rhythmic clatter of horse hooves on cobblestones, and the occasional burst of raucous laughter from Bourbon Street revelers. Gas lamps flickered, casting long shadows that danced across the uneven brick walls and wrought iron balconies, where trailing vines swayed gently in the humid breeze.

I walked with an easy stride beside Nyx, scanning the dark corners and alcoves like a predator sizing up the night. She moved with feline grace, her heels clicking softly against the pavement, her dark hair shimmering under the streetlights like a veil of secrets.

We turned onto Royal Street, quieter now except for the faint strains of a lone saxophonist playing a mournful tune near the old cathedral. The smell of jasmine mingled with the earthy scent of damp stone, and the Quarter felt like it held its breath, teetering on the edge of magic and menace.

As we approached the Eden Club, its neon sign buzzed faintly, bathing the sidewalk in a soft red glow. Nyx glanced at me, her lips curving into a smile that hinted at mischief.

"I'm not coming up," I said.

"Afraid Josie will know what we were doing?" Nyx asked.

"Nothing to do with Josie or Hope," I said. "I have other plans."

"What other plans?"

"After Midnight, to ask Marceline a few questions. When I finish there, I'm going to Musik Azul to speak with Rene."

"Wait on me, and I'll come with you," she said.

"Eliza's disappearance isn't the only thing on my mind, and it's best if I go on my own," I said.

"What other things?" Nyx asked.

"I'd rather not say right now," I said.

"I promise I won't say a word, and it'll only take a minute upstairs to collect my wages," Nyx said.

"I'll be back when I finish," I said. "Wait for me."

"I'll be here," she said.

Chapter 29

Eddie stepped out of his Miata onto Poydras Street, greeted by the chaotic symphony of downtown New Orleans. The morning air was thick with humidity, already clinging to his shirt, and carried the aroma of chicory coffee and fresh beignets wafting from a café down the block.

Horns blared from cabs, and construction workers hollered over the buzz of jackhammers. Above it all, the towering high-rises stood as guardians of the Crescent City's secrets, their glass windows glinting in the sunlight.

Eddie reached to tighten his tie, an unconscious habit, before remembering he was dressed in khakis and a Hawaiian shirt. Feeling a bit self-conscious about his less-than-business-like attire, he strode toward the granite-faced federal building, a grim relic of the 1970s with its blocky design.

Inside, the air-conditioning blasted a cold wave stark against the warmth outside. Eddie's loafers echoed on the polished floors, the antiseptic scent of disinfectant mingling with the faint whiff of burnt coffee from the break room.

As he passed through security, the uniformed guard gave him a curt nod but didn't bother with pleasantries. This was no longer Eddie's turf, and both he and the guard knew it.

The offices on the twelfth floor hadn't changed much since Eddie's tenure. Beige walls, buzzing fluorescent lights, and a faint yellowing of the corners where smoke once curled from forbidden cigarettes gave the space a slightly worn feel. Desks were piled with case files and papers, and whiteboards cluttered with notes standing as battle plans for ongoing investigations.

A few staffers glanced up from their computers as Eddie entered but quickly averted their eyes. Some whispered to their neighbors, their smiles thin and knowing. Eddie kept his head high, though his pulse ticked faster. He could feel the invisible wall of judgment—he was the guy who'd tanked his career for love or foolishness, depending on who you asked.

At the far end of the room, Dan Clancy spotted him. A stocky man with thinning hair and sleeves perpetually rolled to his elbows, Dan rose from his desk with a quick wave, cutting through the tension.

"Eddie," he said, his tone friendlier than most but still guarded. "Let's grab a coffee."

Dan Clancy wore his years at the DOJ like a well-worn suit—practical, unremarkable, and a little frayed around the edges. In his early fifties, with a stocky build that spoke more to long nights at a desk than time at the gym, Dan had the tired eyes of someone who'd seen too much but never quite enough to climb the ladder.

"How you doing, Dan?" Eddie asked with a smile.

"Same old bullshit!" Dan said.

Eddie followed his old friend out the door and down the hall. Dan's thinning hair was always combed neatly, though it never stayed in place, and his face bore the ruddy complexion of a man who enjoyed his whiskey neat and his coffee black. A perpetual crease in his forehead hinted at his frustration with a career that had stalled in middle management, a place he had come to accept, if not embrace.

The break room was utilitarian, with chipped counters and humming vending machines. Dan reached into his pocket for a few quarters and punched in a code for a pack of peanut M&Ms and two cups of coffee in paper cups. After placing the two cups on a break table, he motioned for Eddie to join him.

"You're looking good, Eddie. I've always wanted to wear an outfit like yours to the office."

Dan smiled when Eddie said, "Get fired, and anything's possible."

"You know you're about as welcome as a turd in a punchbowl," Dan said. "What are you doing here?"

"My niece Eliza went missing, and I have reason to believe Lucien D'Arcy is somehow involved."

"Shit!" Dan said. "I remember Eliza from the summer she worked here as an intern. What a trooper she was! Everyone loved her. How can I help?"

"Tell me what you know about D'Arcy," Eddie said.

"That's classified," Dan said.

"I know it is," Eddie said. "Can you help me?"

Dan got off the bench and said, "Wait here. If you need more coffee, the code hasn't changed."

Despite his resignation to mediocrity, Dan had a sharp mind and a talent for seeing patterns others overlooked. He was reliable to a fault, the kind of guy who knew every office shortcut and could recite DOJ policy like scripture, though his cynicism added a biting edge to his otherwise dry humor. Beneath the gruff exterior was a hint of warmth—a man who might not have ambition left for himself but still had a soft spot for people like Eddie, trying to claw their way back from a bad hand.

Dan returned shortly with a folder under his arm. His eyes darted toward the hallway, making sure no one lingered nearby.

"So, you want to know about D'Arcy," he said. "Guy's as slippery as ever. Financials are all over the place—shell companies, offshore accounts, the works. But there's chatter about a new front. A property on the edge of the Quarter. It might be laundered through a boutique hotel or a restaurant. You know him better than anyone, Eddie. What do you think he's up to?"

Eddie unwrapped the candy, tossing a few in his mouth before replying. "D'Arcy doesn't gamble unless he can hedge his bets."

Dan chuckled. "True enough."

"What about NeuroGenesis Systems? Heard of it?"

"One of D'Arcy's shells acquired a while back. It's a private corporation, so we don't have a buttload of info on it. Its balance sheet was supposedly in the red when D'Arcy acquired it," Dan said.

"Why would he want a failing company?"

"Don't know. Must fit into his plan somehow, or he wouldn't have," Dan said.

"Do you know anyone who could tell me more about the company?" Eddie asked.

Dan fanned through the file. "Dr. Ian Lavoie, a computer science professor at UNO. He worked at NGS for a while."

"What do you know about him?" Eddie asked.

257

"We interviewed him. He was less than cooperative and didn't give us much," Dan said.

"Mind if I have a look through the file?" Eddie asked.

"Why not?" Dan said. "If someone enters the breakroom, shove it under the table."

"Will do," Eddie said.

Dan sipped his coffee as Eddie thumbed through the thick file. Eddie stopped when he came to a glossy color photo.

"Is this a picture of D'Arcy?" Eddie asked.

Dan nodded. "The only one we have. The man is amazingly secretive." Eddie stared at the photo. "What?" Dan said.

"This isn't how I imagined him," Eddie said. "He looks so young, and I always envisioned him with dark hair and eyes, not blond hair and blue eyes. Sure it's him"

"It's him," Dan said. "What else?"

"I'm curious. Where did D'Arcy come from? What's his backstory?"

"Who the fuck knows?" Dan said. "It's as if he appeared from the ether, with no birth certificate or high school or college records. Hell, Eddie, we don't even know where he was born."

Dan's eyes flashed when Eddie said, "What about a DNA report?"

"We don't have one but we've collected enough of his personal items that we could if we wanted," Dan said. "I'll file a request when I return to work."

"Will you keep me in the loop?" Eddie asked.

"Eliza was my personal assistant for a while," Dan said. "There's nothing I'd love better than to help her while nailing that bastard D'Arcy at the same time."

Eddie handed the folder back to Dan, then reached across the table and shook his hand.

"Thanks, Dan. I owe you."

Dan nodded. "Just watch your step, okay? Some of the folks here still think you're a liability."

Eddie popped another candy into his mouth and said, "Thanks for the heads-up. Don't worry about me. I've learned to live in the crosshairs."

Dan shook his head, a mix of admiration and concern. "Yeah, but I hope you've learned to duck this time."

The sun gleamed high over Poydras Street as Eddie slid into the driver's seat of his blue Miata convertible, its leather seats warm under the touch of his hand. The engine purred to life, and he eased into the traffic, the city buzzing around him like a living thing. He pulled the sunglasses from his shirt pocket and donned them, the polarized lenses cutting the glare of the mid-morning sun.

Above the rising hum of the city, the sky was a brilliant blue, unmarred by clouds. Eddie's mood lightened, at least for the moment, as the Miata roared down the wide streets toward Lake Pontchartrain.

The drive to the University of New Orleans campus was smooth. The wind rushed past him, carrying the scent of brackish water and a hint of flowers from the nearby gardens.

When the Miata pulled into the parking lot near the Department of Computer Sciences, Eddie stepped out, smoothed the wrinkles from his shirt, and scanned the buildings. Dr. Ian Lavoie's office was in an unassuming brick structure with wide glass windows reflecting the shimmering lake beyond.

Eddie found himself in a corridor that smelled faintly of books and coffee. Students and professors milled about, their murmured conversations echoing off the linoleum floors. He followed the brass placards until he reached a door marked: Dr. Ian Lavoie, Professor of Computer Science.

Eddie knocked.

"Come in!" a voice called, cheerful and resonant.

The office was crammed but orderly—bookshelves stuffed with tomes on computing, framed diplomas lining the walls, and a desk littered with open notebooks and a coffee mug emblazoned with the university's crest.

A large window overlooked the lake, its surface sparkling in the sunlight. Dr. Lavoie sat behind his desk, a man with salt-and-pepper hair, wire-rimmed glasses perched on a sharp nose, and the wiry build of someone who spent more time pacing than sitting.

"I'm Eddie Toledo. Can I have a few minutes of your valuable time?"

"Mr. Toledo," Lavoie said warmly, rising to shake Eddie's hand. "How can I help you?"

Eddie wasted no time. "I've been looking into a company called NeuroGenesis Systems. A client of mine seems to think they're into something shady."

Lavoie chuckled, folding his arms. "NeuroGenesis, huh? What a coincidence—you're the second person this week to ask me about them. Wyatt Thomas was here a few days ago with the same question."

Eddie raised a brow. "Wyatt?"

Lavoie nodded. "Sharp guy. Asked all the right questions. And now here you are."

Eddie leaned forward, lowering his voice. "What can you tell me about them?"

Lavoie's jovial demeanor faltered. He leaned back in his chair, suddenly wary, his fingers tapping a restless rhythm on the desk. "I can tell you that digging too deep into them—or the people they work with—might be hazardous to your health."

"You mean Lucien D'Arcy," Eddie said bluntly.

Lavoie froze, his eyes narrowing. "I didn't say that."

"You didn't have to."

The professor sighed heavily, rubbing his temples. "Look, Eddie, I'm a professor, not a crusader. I'm happy to answer questions about computer science, but this? This is dangerous territory."

Eddie wasn't deterred. "I need whatever you've got. Please, Dr. Lavoie."

For a moment, Lavoie hesitated, his gaze darting toward the door as if expecting someone to barge in. Then, with a resigned huff, he stood and moved to a metal file cabinet in the corner of the room. The drawer screeched open, and Lavoie rifled through the folders until he extracted a thin manila file. He handed it to Eddie without meeting his eyes.

"You can have it," Lavoie said curtly.

"What is it?" Eddie asked, flipping the file open.

"A dossier on a man named Victor Marigny," Lavoie said. "Take it and go, Mr. Toledo. And I don't ever want to see your face again."

Eddie blinked, surprised by the sudden hostility. "Dr. Lavoie—"

Lavoie cut him off, his face pale and his expression tight with fear.

"This conversation never happened. Get out before you drag me any deeper into this."

Eddie hesitated for a moment, then tucked the file under his arm and turned to leave. Exiting the office, he couldn't shake the feeling that whatever was in that dossier had just painted a target on his back.

Chapter 30

Nyx watched me disappear before opening the Eden Club door and going inside. After Midnight wasn't far, the chaos of Bourbon Street echoing in the distance as I reached it.

The door to the eclectic bar creaked open, spilling a sliver of soft amber light onto the slick cobblestones before closing behind me with a muffled thud. The bar was dim, a hazy refuge from the electric chaos of the French Quarter.

A low murmur of conversation mingled with Billie Holiday's haunting wail from the old jukebox in the corner. Smoke hung in the air, curling like phantom tendrils around the Art Deco sconces flickering along the walls.

I slid onto a cracked leather stool at the end of the polished mahogany bar. Behind the bar, Marceline looked up from wiping a tumbler, her sharp eyes catching mine like a cat spotting prey. Her dark hair was pinned up, loose curls framing her angular face, and crimson lips curled into a knowing smile.

"I've been expecting you," she said, carefully setting the glass down. "Thirsty?"

I tilted my gaze slightly. "Depends on what you're pouring," I said.

"House whiskey," she said.

"I'm an alcoholic. Soda and lime will work."

Marceline's laugh was a quiet thing, rich and laced with amusement. She reached for a bottle of whiskey, her bracelets jangling softly, and poured a generous two fingers without asking. After setting the glass before me and leaning on the bar, her sharp gaze cut through the shadows.

"Everyone cheats sometimes," she said. "Open your mouth." Marceline stuck her finger, pale and slender as porcelain, into the glass of whiskey. She grinned when I licked the drop of whiskey off her finger. "You like it, don't you?"

I smiled and said, "I'd like it even better if you dip something else in the glass."

Marceline's grin was wicked as she pulled down her already low-cut blouse and showed me her incredible breasts. With the practiced movement of a strip tease artist, she lifted the glass of whiskey and immersed one of her nipples in the alcoholic liquid.

"This will sweeten the whiskey for you," she said.

It had been a while since I'd imbibed hard liquor, and the cheap house whiskey burned as it went down my throat, affecting me almost immediately.

"I've never tasted anything so sweet," I said.

"It only gets sweeter," she said, slowly pulling up her blouse.

"I can imagine," I said.

"Doesn't have to be your imagination," she said.

"Love it! There's something else I'd like you to share."

"Careful," she said. "You know how this place is—everyone's got a secret, and nobody likes sharing."

"What was in that whiskey?" I asked. "My head is growing larger."

"I was hoping another part of your body was affected," she said.

"That too," I said.

Marceline grinned as she refilled my tumbler with the cheap whiskey. The air inside After Midnight was thick, steeped in velvet and shadow. Music swirled like smoke—soft, slow jazz laced with an untraceable melancholy. The bar gleamed, reflecting the low glow of red and blue lights scattered like dying embers.

I sat at the edge of it, beads of condensation running down like tears on the glass of whiskey. I'd been here before, but tonight felt different. Off. It wasn't just the music or the strange way the lights seemed to flicker at the corner of my vision. It was her. Marceline.

She leaned against the far end of the bar like she'd been sculpted there. Her raven-black curls framed a face that was both timeless and otherworldly, her dark eyes reflecting no light at all. She murmured, her voice too soft to be heard clearly, yet I could feel it threading into my ears and mind—a siren song that seemed to hum beneath my skin.

"Shouldn't have drunk the whiskey," I mumbled, shaking my head as though to clear it.

"It's not the drink," Marceline said.

I jolted, realizing she was beside me now, though I hadn't seen her move. Her hand rested lightly on my inner thigh, her touch sending a shiver spiraling through me. She seemed almost angelic, though her smile was anything but innocent.

"I shouldn't be here," I said, trying to rally my senses.

Think, damn it. But the fog in my head grew thicker, more cloying, as though I was walking a tightrope between waking and some sinister dream.

"We go where we are needed," Marceline whispered, leaning in closer.

Her breath carried the faint scent of roses and earth—something sweet, something dark. My vision blurred. The lights pulsed and stretched, and somewhere in the haze, I felt the presence of someone else.

"You're late," a voice said from my other side.

I turned. Rene.

The man wasn't as I remembered, this time thin and pale, almost spectral in his tailored black suit. Silver hair framed sharp features—a face carved in marble but animated by eyes that didn't belong to a man. I locked onto them involuntarily. Those eyes were gray, but not just gray—swirling, liquid, endless. They seemed to pull at something deep within me, reaching for my soul.

My tongue felt heavy in my mouth when I said, "Late?"

"To the truth," Rene said. His voice had a silky cadence, like a hypnotist's metronome. "You are here to learn about your famous grandfather, right? Charles Wyatt Thomas..."

I flinched at the name, blinking as though to steady myself. "What do you know about him?" I asked.

Marceline giggled softly, her lips inches from my ear. "Everything," she said.

Her hand touched my privates, the sensation feeling like a bolt of electricity. I gasped, trying to catch my breath. Rene's words returned me to reality—at least some semblance of it.

"We can tell you," he said, the hypnotic rhythm of his words impossible to resist. "But not here."

"Where, then?" I asked.

He paused. "St. Louis No. 1 Cemetery. That is where the answers lie."

I shook my head again, trying to escape the hallucinatory current sweeping over me. This isn't real, some part of my brain insisted. I need to get up. I need to leave.

But when I saw the reflection of my Moon's Eye earring on the surface of the bar flashing red, pulsing like a heartbeat, the sight both alarmed and calmed me. Marceline's hand trailed up to my neck, her nails grazing my skin like she could feel the pulse there.

"No need to be afraid," she said. "We mean you no harm. The truth is a gift... one only we can give."

"And it waits for you," Rene said. "Among the tombs."

I opened my mouth to argue but couldn't find the words. Rene's eyes were on me again, and I felt myself slipping deeper into the fog—a fog scented with roses, steeped in silky whispers and invisible hands pulling me toward the inevitable.

My instincts screamed, "Move! Run!"

But my legs felt detached. The truth was, part of me wanted to go. The curiosity burned in my chest, mingling with something darker—an intoxicating allure Marceline had woven into me like a spell.

"The cemetery?" I said.

Rene smiled. "Yes. Come with us."

Somewhere in the haze of movement, I realized I was standing. Marceline slipped her arm through mine like we were old lovers on a midnight stroll. Rene stepped beside us, his presence a silent specter guiding the way. The music from After Midnight grew fainter with each step, though I could still hear it thrumming in my blood.

As we pushed through the club's heavy doors into the night, the mist rolling through the French Quarter seemed to swallow us whole. The Moon's Eye earring pulsed once more—a warning, a protest—before fading to black.

St. Louis No. 1 awaited.

The iron gates of St. Louis Cemetery No. 1 groaned on rusted hinges as Rene pushed them open, the sound echoing like a dirge in the still night. An unearthly glow hung like a supernatural mist, ephemeral lights casting eerie shadows along the cemetery's crumbling walls. My breath quickened as Rene led Marceline and me deeper into the maze of tombs.

The path ahead was narrow, hemmed by towering tombs streaked with moss and time's relentless decay. Marble angels and weeping saints loomed overhead, their faces shadowed and streaked with blackened tears where rain had carved paths through centuries of grime.

The air was thick and cloying, heavy with the mingling scents of damp earth and decayed flowers left long ago by grieving hands. Our shoes crunched on broken shells scattered across the path, the sound unnervingly loud in the oppressive silence. Above, the moon hung low and full, bathing the cemetery in the pale light, but it did little to chase away the deeper shadows clinging to every corner.

Supernatural fireflies hovered in the air like ghostly embers, the light dancing between the crypts, pulsing in an unsteady rhythm, casting wavering halos on the crumbling tombstones as if guiding our way to something ancient and inevitable.

Rene moved ahead, silent and surefooted, his dark silhouette blending with the shadows. Marceline glided beside me, her presence both comforting and unnerving, her movements unnaturally fluid as though she were weightless.

The deeper we went, the more the cemetery changed. The tombs grew grander, their facades adorned with intricate carvings of vines and cherubs now cracked and worn. The air grew colder, the chill biting my bare skin, our breath visible in misty puffs.

Ahead, a crypt came into view, towering above the others like a king among paupers. Its marble surface gleamed under the moonlight, untouched by the decay that plagued its neighbors. A sculpted angel perched atop its roof, its wings spread wide in eternal vigilance. But its gaze had no solace—it stared down at me as if it had waited longer than forever for me to appear.

My steps faltered as realization hit me like a blow to the chest. The name carved into the crypt's face, the angel's familiar form—it was my family's resting place. The weight of unseen eyes pressed down on me, and the whispers of the past seemed to rise from the earth itself, wrapping around my ankles like phantom chains.

"Come," Rene said, his voice cutting through the stillness.

I couldn't move and stood frozen, my stomach knotting as I stared at the crypt, my brain screaming for me to turn and run. The fireflies swirled around me, their light flickering like mocking laughter. I couldn't look away from the angel's gaze, its stone eyes seeming to bore into the deepest recesses of my soul.

Marceline's hand found mine, her touch calm and firm. "We're here," she said, her voice soothing and dangerous all at once.

The crypt loomed closer with every step, its dark maw of an entrance waiting like the gates of some forgotten underworld.

The angel atop the family crypt felt alive, its marble wings outstretched in silent benediction. I froze as a chill coursed down my spine, recognition searing like a hot blade.

My heart thundered. This is where my parents lay, where my grandparents lay. Where memories of my family's secrets and unspoken tragedies lingered like a curse. Something primal clawed at my chest—a desperate urge to flee, to rip myself free from this moment.

"No," I said, stepping back, my boots scraping against the loose gravel. "I don't want to be here."

Marceline turned, her face luminous, her eyes glinting with something ancient and predatory. She shed her clothing in an instant, her skin aglow with a golden hue that shimmered unnaturally in the dim light.

I had seen beauty before, had held it, desired it. But this—this was otherworldly. Marceline's perfection wasn't human. She had no blemishes, freckles, or wrinkles, only flawless skin that seemed to pulse faintly, as though alive with a rhythm all its own.

"I have to get out of here," I said.

"Don't go," Marceline said, her voice honeyed and commanding. She pressed herself against me, her fingers tracing my shoulders, her touch burning and numbing in equal measure, and I felt my strength leave me as my body slackened against her will. "There is much for you to learn."

Before I could summon the strength to resist, a plume of acrid smoke erupted from Rene. The air twisted and churned, and when the haze dissipated, Rene was gone. In his place stood a tall figure draped in black velvet robes, his elegant fingers gripping a chalice that seemed alive. Dark liquid swirled and rippled within it as if reacting to a hidden force.

My voice broke as fear coursed through me like ice water. "Who are you?"

The man's piercing eyes locked onto mine, and an unsettling smile spread across his lips.

"I am Etienne du Clairvaux," the man said, his voice silky and laced with menace. "The Sun King's magician. And tonight, you will join us."

I attempted to pull away, but Marceline's arms were unyielding. She whispered soothingly in my ear, her words hypnotic. Before I could resist further, her golden hands slipped the shirt from my shoulders, the fabric falling to the ground as though cast off by invisible hands.

"This will only hurt for a short while," Etienne said, stepping forward with deliberate grace. In his free hand, a gleaming iron needle glowed faintly with crimson light, its tip pulsating with ominous energy.

"I don't want to be one of you," I said.

Etienne chuckled, a sound devoid of mirth. "It is not about what you want. It is about what you are destined to become."

A sudden wail, cold and mournful, pierced the stillness. The air grew heavy, and my breath fogged as the temperature plummeted. The figure materializing from the shadows caused my blood to run colder than the grave. A translucent specter floated toward me, its eyes hollow yet piercing, its mouth a gaping void of silent screams.

"Charles Wyatt Thomas," I said.

It was my grandfather—the man whose stern gaze haunted old photographs, now standing before me. The specter leaned closer, and I felt the icy tendrils of death wrapped around his neck, each breath heavier than the last. Cold fingers brushed my ear as the ghost whispered, its voice a death knell.

"There is no escape, Wyatt. You belong to the blood."

The words were a shackle, binding my very soul. The needle's crimson glow intensified as Etienne raised it high, and Marceline's lips brushed my ear, her fangs appearing.

"Embrace the darkness," she said.

A scream rose in my throat, though never escaped, swallowed by the oppressive air and the inexorable pull of the crypt's unholy ritual of which I'd become an integral part.

Chapter 31

The night hung heavy and oppressive over St. Louis No. 1 Cemetery, the air thick with the coppery scent of searing flesh and the faint aroma of decayed flowers.

I sat on the crumbling stone pathway, my back pressed against the cool marble of the family crypt, my chest wracked with pain. Despite a spring chill in the air, sweat dribbled down my bare chest, mingling with the blood trickling from the intricate lines of the Crimson Sigil as Etienne du Clairvaux worked the ink into my flesh.

Etienne's long fingers moved with precision, holding the crude needle-like tool with the reverence of an artist. Each stab felt like fire igniting beneath my skin, the sigil's lines glowing with an unholy crimson hue. I couldn't help but groan, my jaw clenched in pain, powerless to resist the sinister ceremony.

Marceline awaited, her alabaster skin luminous under the pale light of the crescent moon. Standing utterly naked, her body seemed a paradox of grace and danger, her dark eyes fixed on me with ravenous anticipation. When her lips parted, they revealed long canines. As she leaned against a cracked tombstone, her lithe body quivered with the look of a hungry predator.

Perched atop the family crypt, my grandfather, the ghostly figure of Charles Wyatt Thomas, sat with one knee drawn up, his translucent form casting an eerie blue glow against the shadows. His eyes were hollow, his expression an enigmatic mask of judgment and pity as he watched the scene below unfold. A faint breeze seemed to whisper his unspoken warnings into my ear.

When Etienne finished using the sigil, he leaned back, his hand still clutching the tool, his face carved with satisfaction. The sigil burned like a brand, pulsing faintly as if alive. Marceline pushed off the tombstone, her movements feline and predatory. Her fingers grazed my jaw as she knelt beside me, her lips curling into a smile both seductive and savage.

"It is time for you to become one of us," she said.

Marceline straddled me, her fangs bared, her mouth descending toward my neck. Before the bite came, the world erupted in a flash of fire and thunder.

A powerful explosion shattered the quiet, shaking the ancient cemetery. Flames bloomed in the distance, casting the graves in flickering light. The deafening roar drowned out even my cry of shock, and the concussive force sent Etienne sprawling backward and Marceline tumbling to the ground, her alabaster form momentarily splayed like a fallen goddess.

Nyx emerged from the swirling shadows, grasping my arm and jarring me free of my stupor. She pulled me to my feet, her grip firm and unrelenting.

"We have to go. Now," she said, her voice sharp with urgency.

I stumbled to my feet and let her guide me. The world around me was a disorienting blur of gravestones, firelight, and Marceline's enraged shrieks. The ghostly figure of Charles Wyatt Thomas turned his spectral gaze toward us, his ominous form fading into the shadows as Nyx and I quickly fled the chaotic plume of smoke trapped in the damp air above the graveyard.

Behind us, Marceline's scream pierced the night—a sound of fury, hunger, and thwarted desire. The cemetery seemed to awaken fully with its ancient dead and restless spirits. The oppressive stillness was shattered by chaos as we exited the graveyard amid the clang of the heavy iron gate.

When my hearing returned, I asked, "What the hell caused that explosion?"

"Percussion grenade," she said. "I never leave home without one."

"Where the hell did you get a percussion grenade?" I asked.

Nyx shook her head and said, "Army surplus."

I had to grin despite the burning pain wracking my chest, sore muscles, and ringing ears.

"Most women carry a can of pepper spray in their purses," I said.

"I'm not most women," she said. "Where to?"

"My apartment," I said. "I lost my shirt in the cemetery and then the "Eden Club. Eddie's meeting us there. He called earlier and said he has news."

"Let's go straight to the Eden Club," Nyx said. "Hope has waiter's smocks, and if you wait in the alley, I'll get you one."

"Sounds like a plan," I said.

Eddie was waiting with Hope and Josie when we finally made it upstairs. Malik was also at the bar and nodded when he saw us.

"What's with the waiter's smock?" Eddie asked. "Part-time job you haven't told us about?"

"Left my shirt in the cemetery, and I'm borrowing a smock to wear until I can return to my apartment," I said.

"Want to tell us what you were doing in the cemetery this time of night?" Eddie asked.

"You said you have new information about Lucien D'Arcy. Tell us what you have, and then I'll explain how I lost my shirt."

Hope was behind the bar and said, "Can't wait to hear that one."

"What you got?" I asked.

"I visited the DOJ offices this morning and received less than a warm reception," Eddie said. "A friend took me to the breakroom and filled me in about what was happening with the Lucien D'Arcy case."

"And?"

"He let me look at a dossier that featured a rare picture of D'Arcy. I was surprised, to say the least, when I saw it."

"Because?" I asked.

"He looked nothing like the D'Arcy we saw the night we visited the disappearing house. He was younger and had blond hair and blue eyes."

"Not D'Arcy," Malik said.

"You think he's a stand-in?" I asked.

"Makes sense," Eddie said. "D'Arcy controls numerous interlinked corporations. Lucien's a vampire, for Christ's sake, and can't venture out during the day when companies do most of their business."

"If this person posing as D'Arcy isn't a vampire, how did the Nocturnes recruit him?" Josie asked.

"Good question," Eddie said.

"What's the answer?" I asked.

"D'Arcy didn't recruit him. He is D'Arcy."

I smiled and said, "Excuse me!"

"My connection at the DOJ gave me a contact that might shed light on the subject. A UNO professor named Dr. Lavoie."

"I talked with Lavoie," I said.

"He told me you did. He gave me something he didn't mention to you," Eddie said. "A dossier on a man named Victor Marigny."

"We're listening," I said.

"Victor Marigny was born and raised in Baton Rouge, Louisiana, the only child of a middle-class family. A quiet and unassuming man, he lived an unremarkable life."

When Eddie paused a moment too long for a sip of scotch, I said, "Go on."

"Marigny worked as an IT specialist at a regional bank, where his days were spent in a windowless office debugging systems and processing cybersecurity audits. Reserved by nature and plagued with social anxiety, he had no close friends, no spouse, and only distant ties to his aging parents, who had retired to Florida."

"The perfect nobody," I said.

"Exactly," Eddie said. "Victor's lack of connections made him an ideal target for D'Arcy and NGS. His life was predictable, and his absence barely rippled the lives of those around him."

"How did anyone ever find this guy?" Hope asked.

"NGS identified him through their secret partnerships with tech companies that provided covert access to personal data. His solitary lifestyle and regular visits to a mental health clinic for mild depression flagged him as a viable candidate for their experiments."

"Is this going where I think it is?" Josie asked.

"If you're thinking brain transferal, then the answer is yes," Eddie said.

"How did they pull off his disappearance?" I asked.

"One evening, he left work and never returned. To the world, it appeared as though he had chosen to vanish. His car was found abandoned at a rest stop along I-10, its doors unlocked and keys still in the ignition. A hastily written note left on the passenger seat hinted at a decision to "start over," leading authorities to classify it as a voluntary disappearance. Given Victor's unassuming nature and lack of close relationships, the investigation into his disappearance quickly fizzled out."

"But that's not what actually happened to him," I said.

"He was abducted by operatives working for NGS. Under the guise of a wellness program for individuals struggling with depression, he was lured to a secluded facility near the Atchafalaya Basin. Once inside, he became a subject in NGS's clandestine memory-replacement project."

"Then what?" Josie asked.

"NGS has perfected a radical neurobiological procedure, blending advanced neuroscience and computer technology. Victor's brain was erased and replaced by a copy of Lucien's. For all practical purposes, Victor is Lucien," Eddie said.

"And he plans to do the same with Eliza and replace her wiped brain with Athénaïs's," I said.

"In Marigny's case, the programming has subtle flaws—small inconsistencies and suppressed fragments of his original self that sometimes bubble to the surface. According to the dossier, NGS is trying to work out the bugs," Eddie said. "We must get Eliza out of the disappearing house before they succeed."

"What about Lavoie?" I asked.

"Complicit as hell," Eddie said. "Thank goodness he is."

277

"Amen to that," I said.

Everyone grew silent as we digested Eddie's ominous report. Our spirits, especially Eddie's, livened when Hope began dispensing more drinks."

After a long pull of his refreshed scotch, he said, "Now, tell us how you lost your shirt in the cemetery.

Hope and Josie gasped when I unbuttoned the smock and showed them my new tattoo.

"The Crimson Sigil," Malik said. "Are you one of us now?"

"If Nyx hadn't saved me, I would be."

Josie's hand went to her mouth, and she said, "What happened?"

"I visited After Midnight to question Marceline about something personal," I said.

"You want to share it with us?" Hope asked.

"My grandfather," I said. "Rene took me to the Grotto of Truth, where my grandfather's image appeared. He wanted me to become a Nocturne."

"Your grandfather was a Nocturne?" Josie asked.

"I don't know. That's why I went to After Midnight," I said. "I wanted to find out."

"Wyatt's granddad was a very powerful man," Eddie said. "He was Governor of Louisiana when he was assassinated."

"I didn't know that," Josie said.

"He died long before I was born," I said.

Everyone's gaze turned to Malik when he said, "Wyatt's grandfather was the reincarnation of Louis XIV."

"Are you making this up?" Hope asked.

"Louis couldn't achieve immortality, though he found a way to make it to the colonies and reassert his vast power," Malik said. "An assassin's bullet ended his dream."

278

Malik shook his head when I asked, "Was my grandfather a vampire?"

"He was running the Nocturnes when he was assassinated. Some say Lucien D'Arcy was responsible," Malik said.

"Charles Wyatt Thomas was in line to become President of the United States," Eddie said. "The most powerful man in the world. His assassination is beginning to make sense."

"Who tattooed you with the Crimson Sigil?" Malik asked.

"Marceline lured me to the St. Louis No. 1 Cemetery," I said. "Rene accompanied her. When we reached the cemetery, he became Etienne du Clairvaux, Louis XIV's court magician."

"Rene wasn't one of the original thirteen," Malik said. "How did he get to New Orleans?"

"Not so much how as why," I said.

"Sounds as if he and Marceline have designs on overthrowing D'Arcy," Eddie said.

"Who cares about all of the intrigue?" Josie said. "We need to rescue Eliza before D'Arcy wipes her brain and replaces her thoughts and memories with those of the Veiled Queen."

"Yes, but how?" Hope asked.

"I'll return to the disappearing house and bring her out forcefully if I have to," I said.

"The house recognizes you," Malik said. "You'll never get inside again unless Lucien wants you there. None of us can get inside."

"I can," Nyx said. "No one there recognizes me."

"Forget it, Sis," Hope said. "I won't allow it."

"Your sister is right," Malik said. "Without someone to show you where to go, you'd never make it out alive."

"I have to try," Nyx said.

"Maybe there's another way," Malik said.

"What other way?" Eddie asked.

"Rene and Marceline," he said.

"They tried to kill me," I said.

"No, they didn't. Their plan was for you to become the leader of the Nocturnes. That means they wish to depose Lucien. They are his enemy, and you know what they say."

"They're our friends," Eddie said.

"Exactly," Malik said. Another grim reaper, please."

Hope smiled and said, "This one's on the house, big guy."

After sipping the grim reaper, Malik said, "Nyx and I are going to Musik Azul and speak with Rene."

"We'll all go," Hope said.

Malik shook his head and showed her his palm. "Too many cooks spoil the pot," he said. "Nyx is the only person who needs to accompany me."

When they were gone, Hope said, "What was I thinking? I just let my little sister walk out of here with a vampire."

Chapter 32

When Nyx and Malik left the Eden Club, the night air in the French Quarter was thick with lingering mist, carrying the faint scent of magnolias and the salt of the nearby Mississippi River. The streets were quiet, though not entirely asleep.

An occasional figure shuffled by on the sidewalk, a street cleaner humming along the cobblestones, and a lone saxophonist playing a poignant melody beneath the flickering glow of a gas lamp. Red and blue neon lights cast a haunting light over the wrought iron balconies and shuttered windows as the ground fog rose around Malik and Nyx's ankles.

When Nyx shivered and folded her arms tightly around her chest, Malik asked, "Are you frightened?"

"Just a chill," she said. "I forgot my light jacket."

"Take mine," Malik said, draping his heavy coat over her shoulders.

"Thank you," she said.

"You are brave even to consider breaching the disappearing house," Malik said.

"I've never felt so secure in my entire life," she said.

"You owe no allegiance to Eddie Toledo. Why are you doing it?"

"You're right; I don't, though neither do you. I could ask you the same question."

"Wyatt is a direct descendent of the Sun King. I still owe allegiance to Louis XIV."

"Bullshit!" Nyx said. "He took everything you own and gave you nothing in return. As powerful as he was, he was just a man. You owe him nothing."

"Loyalty is a holy burden," Malik said.

"A chosen burden," Nyx said. "Toss it from your shoulders and leave it behind."

"Maybe so. Still, I don't think you understand what you're getting yourself into," he said, his deep voice almost swallowed by the darkness.

Nyx didn't look at him but smiled, her gaze fixed on the horizon where the Quarter gives way to the rest of the city.

"I understand that you are a person with special integrity who has allowed others to take advantage of you," she said.

Malik ignored her admonition, pretending he hadn't heard it. "I can only do so much to protect you," he said.

Nyx smiled and touched his big hand. "I'm a grown woman, not a maiden in distress."

"I realized as much when Wyatt told us how you rescued him. Forgive me for being condescending."

"You're just worried about me. My mother raised Hope and me, and we never had a father. You feel like a father to me."

Nyx's comment left Malik speechless, and they lapsed into a comfortable silence. In the muted stillness, their bond strengthened like the first fragile spring bloom, delicate but undeniable. Malik, who had walked these streets for centuries, felt an odd sense of unfamiliarity—not with the Quarter but with himself. He liked the feeling.

Nyx, her blond hair catching the flickering neon, walked with a confidence that seemed entirely her own and something she drew from him. Malik didn't feel like a predator or a shadow for the first time in years. Beside her, he felt like a man.

As Musik Azul came into view, its dim neon sign flickering faintly against the retreating night, Malik slowed.

"Are you sure about this?" he asked.

Nyx met his gaze, her eyes piercing in clarity, and said, "I've never been more certain of anything."

Inside Musik Azul, a sultry haze of cigarette smoke mingled with the blue-tinged lighting, bathing the club in an otherworldly glow. The air was heavy with the mingled scents of aged whiskey and leather and the faint perfume of frangipani drifting from the vents.

It was an intimate yet grand space, the low ceiling hung with scattered crystal pendants that glowed like shards of moonlight. Mismatched chairs and small round tables encircled the stage, each holding flickering candles that cast wavering shadows across the room. Nyx had been there once with Hope. Tonight, with Malik, it felt different.

The small stage, framed by velvet curtains so dark they almost appeared black, drew the audience like a wistful magnet. The spotlight was fixed on Rene, his lean figure clad in a crisp white shirt, open at the throat, and dark trousers. Profound and arresting, his voice filled the room with a timeless melody as his fingers glided over the piano keys.

Rene's voice filling the room was like stepping into a hidden part of New Orleans that tourists only dreamed of. Something about that kind of music felt like magic in a place as dark and timeless as Musik Azul, pulling everyone into a shared moment. Nyx was entranced, tucked into a candlelit corner, letting that song wash over her and Malik.

Rene's audience, a collection of bohemians, immortals, and shadowy figures, was equally moved and swayed by the music. They seemed out of place in the human world, their eyes half-closed and entranced, like Nyx.

Malik and Nyx sat at a table near the back, their presence captivating despite their subdued demeanor. Tall and broad-shouldered, Malik leaned back in his chair, his dark eyes tracking Rene's every move with a simmering intensity. The lithe and ethereal Nyx leaned close to him, her sharp features softened by the candlelight, her sleek black dress hinting at danger, and her ash blonde hair cascading over her shoulders like liquid starlight.

"He's so fucking good!" she said. "I could listen all night to his singing."

"Never knew he could sing," Malik said.

"You know him?" Nyx asked.

"Someone from centuries past."

Nyx heard something in his voice and said, "Is he a friend?"

"I thought he was. Now, I'm not so sure," he said.

As Rene's song ended and applause rippled through the room, Malik rose with a predator's grace. Rene stepped down from the stage, catching sight of him, and his expression froze for a moment before shifting into a wry smile as he approached their table.

"Hello, old friend," Rene said, his voice smooth, laced with a teasing warmth.

The room fell still as Malik moved with an unhurried elegance. His backhand slap sounded sharp and shocking, cutting through the ambient murmurs like a blade. Rene tumbled backward, his chair clattering to the floor as gasps rippled through the crowd. The club bouncer hurried from somewhere in the back.

For a beat, silence reigned. Rene, sprawled on the ground, didn't rise immediately. Instead, he tilted his head, smiling faintly even as blood trickled from the corner of his mouth. He wiped it away with a thumb, his voice low and amused.

"What was that for?"

Malik loomed over him, his voice like thunder barely restrained.

"That burning needle you used on me some three hundred years ago. I still haven't forgotten the pain."

The Nordic-looking bouncer with big arms highlighted by colorful tattoos moved toward Malik. Rene stopped him.

"It's okay, Hans," he said. "Malik's an old friend."

"You sure?" Hans said.

"I'm fine," Rene said. "Return to what you were doing."

Hans, the simian bouncer, nodded and disappeared into the club's darkness. The room's tension was palpable, the audience frozen in a tableau of curiosity and apprehension. That changed when the music began playing again. Rene rose slowly, dusting himself off with an elegance that belied the moment's violence. His gaze flickered to Nyx.

"Still carrying grudges, I see. But you've brought fascinating company."

Malik gestured for Rene to sit, and he returned to the table just as Marceline appeared, her arrival like a breath of electric air. Marceline was tall, her silhouette striking against the smoky backdrop, and dressed in a midnight-blue gown that clung to her like a second skin. Her raven-black hair was pinned up, revealing a neck adorned with a delicate string of pearls. She glanced at Nyx, and her smile curled into something almost predatory.

"Who is this enchanting creature?" she said, her voice smooth and pure, her eyes lingering on Nyx's neck.

Nyx met her gaze, unflinching, her lips quirking in a faint smile that revealed no fear.

"I'm Nyx," she said. "Associate bartender at the Eden Club."

Marceline grasped her hand, kissed it, and said, "Charmed. Who is this handsome gentleman with you?"

"Malik the magnificent," Nyx said.

Marceline measured one of Malik's upper arms with her hands and said, "That, I can see."

Malik cut through the tension with his commanding voice.

"I need a favor," he said.

Rene rubbed his swollen lip and said, "Not exactly how I ask for favors. What do you need?"

"For you to escort Nyx into the disappearing house to rescue Eliza."

Rene laughed. "Lucien is the King of the Nocturnes."

"But not your king," Malik said.

"I'm still loyal to the Sun King," Rene said. "Doesn't matter because Lucien would drive a stake through my heart, cut off my head, and leave my body to disintegrate in the hot sun on Canal Street."

"Louis missed his chance for immortality when he decided against becoming a vampire," Malik said. "Now, he is dead."

"Though not gone. He wants Wyatt to assume the mantle," Rene said.

"Never going to happen," Nyx said. "Wyatt is his own man and not another person's wild ambitions."

Rene looked at Nyx and said, "It was you who threw the explosive device, wasn't it?"

Nyx nodded and said, "It was me."

"You have balls, girl," Marceline said.

"Nyx has volunteered to enter the disappearing house and extract Eliza. She's willing to attempt the impossible alone, though that is suicidal. Help her, I beseech you," Malik said.

"What do you want us to do?" Rene asked.

"Accompany her into the house and then watch her back while she negotiates with Eliza," Malik said.

"Eliza is the victim of brainwashing," Rene said. "She won't leave the house willingly."

"Then I'll knock her ass out and drag her out by the hair," Nyx said.

Marceline grinned and said, "I like this girl."

"Despite your bravado, you won't escape the house alive," Rene said. "What's your plan?"

"Set a fire once Eliza is corralled, and the disappearing house will dispel you. We'll hide Eliza and deprogram her."

"Lucien will never let it stand," Rene said.

"I have a plan to thwart Lucien," Malik said.

"Please explain," Rene said.

"I'll do better than that," Malik said. "If we successfully extract Eliza from the disappearing house, I will demonstrate for you."

"What about Marceline and me?" Rene asked.

"You've blown your future with Lucien. When he learns you betrayed him, your immortality will cease to exist," Malik said.

"You didn't answer my question," Rene said.

"All I know is it's better to die' fighting than groveling. What's your answer?"

A daring plan," Marceline said. "And quite dangerous. I like it."

Rene leaned back in his chair, still nursing the sting of Malik's strike but now grinning in earnest.

"You always did have a talent for the dramatic, Malik. Count me in."

"If my pretty girl here has the balls to enter the disappearing house alone, she deserves my assistance. I'm in," Marceline said.

"Thank you," Malik said. "Thank both of you. I'm curious. Why are you a vampire, and how did you get to New Orleans?"

"It was Louis's idea," Rene said. "He never ceased searching for answers. He sensed the New World was the place to be and sent me here as his emissary. He intended to join me. As the reincarnation of Charles Wyatt Thomas, he almost succeeded."

"Whose magic accomplished that feat?" Malik asked.

"Haitian voodoo," Rene said. "Louis's voodoo man infected me with the virus."

"I didn't realize Louis was into voodoo, though I don't doubt it," Malik said. "There was little he didn't know about."

"He had compassion for the slaves, and it was he who passed the Code Noir decree in 1685 that governed the treatment of slaves in the French colonies."

Malik nodded and said, "Louis was a Renaissance man."

"Your plan is foolhardy, though I'm all for trying it. Let's order champagne and drink a toast to our alliance," Rene said.

Rene and Marceline grinned when Malik said, "Can we add a little blood to the bottle?"

As they touched flutes and drank a toast, the muted jazz of the next performer began, and the atmosphere of Musik Azul returned to its peculiar blend of glamour and menace. The deal was struck, but in the flickering shadows of the club, it felt as though the actual game was only beginning.

Chapter 33

An unsettling quiet cloaked the French Quarter, along with a darkness that seemed deeper than night. Gas lamps, casting trembling shadows that danced like restless spirits, flickered amid the cobbled streets.

The air was thick and humid, carrying the faint scent of an approaching storm. Somewhere in the distance, the mournful wail of a saxophone rose and fell, only to be swallowed by the suffocating silence.

The disappearing house stood at the end of the alley, a derelict structure that seemed to breathe a life of its own. Its shutters flapped lazily though no wind stirred. The door creaked open as Nyx, Rene, and Marceline approached, revealing an interior steeped in an unnatural gloom.

They stepped inside, the floorboards groaning beneath their weight as if the house was protesting their presence. They hadn't come unarmed, Rene carrying Excalibur, the regal sword Malik had lent him.

The air was heavy and tinged with the acrid smell of decay. Candles burned in sconces along the walls, their flames unnaturally still, casting shadows that didn't match the room's angles. Strange shapes flitted at the edges of their vision—

figures cloaked in shadow that disappeared when they turned to look.

A long hallway that seemed to stretch endlessly lay before them. A low murmur filled the air, and incomprehensible whispers grew louder with every step. A heavy mirror hung on one wall, its surface rippling like water. Their reflections stared back at them with twisted grins and eyes black as voids. Nyx averted her gaze, remembering how visiting a carnival crazy house had once affected her senses.

The hallway opened into a parlor, where three figures played cards at a rickety table. Wide-brimmed hats obscured their faces, but their movements were jerky and mechanical. The players' hands were skeletal, their fingers clicking unnaturally as they shuffled cards. They crept past, careful not to disturb the scene.

Ahead was a narrow staircase spiraling upward. The steps felt like they were shifting, softening, as if the house was alive and moving slowly like the measured breaths of a sleeping beast. Nyx glanced over the railing and saw the darkness below roil like ink in water.

The air was colder at the top of the stairs, charged with an energy that prickled their skin. Rene pointed to a door at the end of the corridor, its frame splintered and warped as if something had forced its way inside.

"That's where they keep the girl. Marceline and I will guard the stairs," he said.

When Nyx hesitated, Marceline said, "Go get her."

Nyx gripped the doorknob, its touch icy cold, the door's creak screaming against the otherwise oppressive silence, and opened it. Gloom cloaked the room, its atmosphere thick with dread. A dim bulb hanging from the ceiling cast a feeble orange glow that barely illuminated the space.

Peeling paper covered the walls, its floral patterns distorted and curling. The scent of mildew and something far fouler permeated the air. A broken mirror leaned against one wall, its shattered fragments catching the light and refracting it into jagged patterns on the warped floorboards.

A rusted iron bedframe stood in the center of the room, its mattress sunken and covered in threadbare sheets. Eliza sat on the bed, her back hunched, her hands clutching her knees as she stared blankly ahead. She looked up when Nyx spoke.

"Eliza?"

Eliza's eyes were dulled, her skin pale and sallow, as though drained of life. Her vivid red hair hung in wild tangles around her face. Her white nightgown looked like a relic from another time, its edges frayed and stained.

At the sound of her name, Eliza flinched and looked up. Her eyes widened briefly, but the moment was fleeting, and her expression hardened into something distant and unreadable. When she spoke, her voice was hoarse, as if affected by numbing drugs.

"Who are you?"

"I'm Nyx. I've come to take you home."

When Nyx reached out, Eliza recoiled, shrinking back against the wall.

"Don't touch me," she said.

"I won't hurt you, I promise," Nyx said. "Why are there marks on your face?"

Eliza shook her head, tears appearing in the corners of her eyes.

"Please don't hit me again," she said.

Eliza recoiled when Nyx tried to touch her face. "I would never hit you. I'm not one of them. Your Uncle Eddie sent me."

A light in Eliza's eyes flickered and died at the mention of Eddie, and her words garbled when she spoke.

"You hurt me, and I don't believe you anymore," she said.

"Not me," Nyx said. "This is the first time we've met."

When Eliza whimpered, and her tears began to flow profusely, Nyx wrapped her arms around her and started rocking her like a baby.

"You're going to kill me, aren't you?" Eliza said.

"No one's going to kill you," Nyx said. "I'm here to save you. Please, trust me."

"I don't want to be here anymore," Eliza said.

From the bruises on Eliza's arms, face, and legs, Nyx could see she'd been the recipient of numerous beatings, not to mention the mental abuse she must have endured.

Eliza shook her head when Nyx said, "Can you walk?"

"They told me not to get off the bed for any reason," she said.

Nyx stood, took Eliza's hand, and pulled her to her feet. Unsteady, she wobbled, and Nyx feared she was about to faint. Nyx eased her back on the bed.

"I need help. Wait here," she said.

Eliza's tears increased. She extended her hand and said, "Please don't leave me."

Nyx could see Rene and Marceline through the open door and called to them.

"Marceline, I need help."

Marceline hurried into the room, shaking her head when she saw Eliza.

"You poor girl," she said. "What have they done to you?"

"She's coming with us, but I can't get her alone."

"Wimp!" Marceline said. "Give me your arm, baby. We're busting you out of here."

Without waiting for Nyx, she put her shoulder beneath Eliza's arm, lifted her off the bed, and took her to the top of the stairs.

A loud creak echoed from the hallway, and Nyx's stomach tightened.

"Brace yourselves," Rene said. "They're coming for us."

Lucien D'Arcy stood in the shadows of the parlor, his tall frame outlined by the flickering light of the dying candles. His icy gaze turned toward the spiraling staircase.

With a flick of his wrist, he summoned the Obsidian Vanguard. The air around him shimmered and darkened, and a squadron of nightmarish figures emerged from the shadows. The Vanguard were clad in obsidian-black armor, their forms impossibly sleek yet jagged, as though chiseled from volcanic glass. Their hollow eyes glowed faintly red as they awaited Lucien's orders.

"Don't kill the redhead. We need her," he said. "Take the others to the torture chamber. Before I finish with them, they'll be begging for a hasty death."

They saluted and moved away, their movements eerily silent as they advanced toward the staircase. Rene crouched at the top of the stairs, breathing steadily despite his heart pounding. In his hand was one of Nyx's percussion grenades, its metal casing glinting faintly in the dim light. Nyx shook her head.

"We're screwed," she said. "That damn thing won't do anything except scatter them for a moment."

"Have faith, dear girl," Rene said. "When the bomb detonates, the smoke and noise will cause the house to expel it. It'll take the Guard with it, and they can't survive long outside the house."

"My fingers are crossed," Nyx said. "Hope you're right."

Rene smiled and said, "Me too."

Marceline crouched beside him, her jaw set with grim determination.

"Brace yourself," she said. "Here they fucking come!"

"I got this," Rene said, his voice calm.

He waited until the first Vanguard reached the foot of the stairs. Then, with a practiced motion, he pulled the pin and tossed the grenade.

The explosion was deafening, the blast shaking the entire house, sending shards of wood and stone flying everywhere. A massive plume of smoke erupted, swirling chaotically, filling the area around the staircase.

The house reacted instantly, the walls shuddering as though alive, their surfaces rippling like water. A section of the floor yawned open, forming a gaping maw that sucked the smoke out of the house with a sound like a shuddering gasp.

The Vanguard, caught in the blast, was flung into the opening by the force of the explosion. They clawed at the air, their movements desperate but futile. As each flew through the threshold, their obsidian forms began to crack and splinter, their glowing eyes flickering like dying embers.

The moment they left the confines of the house, they disintegrated into clouds of black ash, their inhuman shrieks echoing faintly before being swallowed by the night.

Rene's eyes narrowed as the last of the Vanguard vanished. The house trembled again, the gaping hole closing with a low groan, leaving no trace of the breach.

Marceline exhaled and said, "Hell, yeah!"

From below, Lucien's voice cut through the smoky air like a razor. "Fools! You think you can escape me?"

The house seemed to respond to its master's fury, its walls creaking and warping. The temperature plummeted as an icy wind swept through the corridors. Rene tightened his grip on Excalibur, his sharp eyes scanning the shadows.

"Stay sharp," he said.

Time was slipping away, the tension in the house palpable. Nyx froze, her jaw tightening. She could hear the rhythmic pounding from below—the unmistakable sound of boots and armor. Lucien had summoned more of his forces. The house groaned, the walls seeming to warp and shift as though the building was preparing for battle.

"We got this," Marceline said.

Rene broke off a portion of the wooden banister and tossed it to Nyx.

"Hope you don't need to use it, but if you do..."

He grinned when Nyx said, "Let's kick ass!"

Rene's head snapped toward the staircase, his expression grim. "We've got company."

The house had roared to life. The walls trembled violently, and the air grew thick with malevolent energy. Shadows coalesced and surged upward as D'Arcy's forces began their ascent. Vampires in elegant yet grotesque attire, their eyes glowing with hunger, moved with unnatural speed. Behind them, the remaining Obsidian Vanguard marched relentlessly, their armored forms glinting in the eerie light.

Marceline uttered a curse and then said, "That's a lot of teeth and claws."

Nyx tightened her grip on Eliza, her muscles screaming from the effort. Rene grinned, his calm demeanor belying the chaos.

"We need to move before they reach the stairs. Now!" he said.

The sound of Lucien's forces grew louder, a cacophony of hissing, growling, and the metallic clang of boots against wood. The angry hoard began advancing up the stairs.

"Retreat to the room where they were keeping Eliza," Rene said.

"Then what?" Nyx asked.

"We're about to find out."

"Toss me the sword," Marceline said. "I'll hold them off."

Marceline snatched Excalibur from the air when Rene smiled and tossed it to her. She swung the sword, the mighty blade slicing through the unnatural forms, vampires and Vanguard alike. Nyx gritted her teeth, her focus on carrying Eliza through the chaos.

Lucien's icy laughter rang out from below, chilling them. "You can't escape," he said above the din and confusion. "This house is mine. You're mine."

The house seemed to laugh with him, its walls groaning and twisting as if to swallow them whole.

When they reached the room, Rene opened the door, pulled the plug on his last grenade, and tossed it inside. The explosion shook the walls, and smoke billowed into the hall when he opened the door.

Marceline remained faced off against the Vanguard and vampires storming the stairs. After pushing Nyx and Eliza into the smoke, Rene rushed to the stairs and grabbed Marceline's arm.

She was still slashing with the sword as he dragged her to the smoking room and then shut it after them.

The building groaned in protest, its structure twisting and shuddering as if alive. The walls rippled, bulging outward. When a gaping hole appeared, the smoke rushed out along with the intruders as the house expelled them with a thunderous roar.

Nyx, Rene, Marceline, and Eliza were hurled through the open hole, landing in a heap on the cobblestones of the deserted French Quarter street. The cool air was a shocking contrast to the oppressive heat inside the house.

Nyx glanced at the sky, seeing it was almost dawn.

"We don't have much time," she said as Josie's black Range Rover screeched to a halt nearby.

Josie leaped out, her hair wild, her eyes scanning the group.

"Get in! Now!" she said.

Eddie, Hope, Wyatt, and Malik flanked her, their faces pale with worry. They quickly helped the explosion-shaken crew into the vehicle and then piled in as the first rays of dawn began to paint the sky with streaks of gold and pink.

Josie jammed the accelerator to the floorboard, the powerful SUV's tires squealing as it sped away from the disappearing house. Malik gripped the armrest as the vehicle roared through the Quarter's empty streets.

Seeing the anxiety in his eyes, Nyx touched his arm and said, "It's okay."

She laughed when he said, "These damned monster contraptions are instruments of the devil," he said.

They reached Malik's safe house in minutes, hurrying inside and sealing the heavy black-out curtains against the rising sun. The room was silent save for their ragged breaths, the tension thick enough to cut.

"I need a drink," Eddie said.

"You'll have to get it somewhere else," Malik said.

"We're safe, you two," Josie said.

Eddie and Eliza embraced, and Hope had Nyx in a similar posture.

"You scared the shit out of me, Sis," she said.

"You're cracking my ribs," Nyx said.

"The dawn is upon us, and no one can leave the disappearing house until darkness falls. When it does, Lucien will have his revenge," Rene said.

"The disappearing house was the only home I've ever known," Marceline said.

"My house isn't big, though you're welcome to stay with me forever," Malik said.

Marceline kissed him and said, "Does this mean we're married?"

"Why not? Assuming any of us survive Lucien's wrath," Malik said. "Maybe one of us will come up with a plan."

"I don't know about a plan, but this earring is calling to me," I said.

"What is it saying," Malik said.

"It keeps reminding me what the raven told us the times we visited Madam Elzora," I said.

"None of the verses made any sense," Josie said.

"They do when you put them together," I said.

"Can you quote it for us?" Josie asked.

"Beneath the shroud of night's embrace,
A house appeared in a fleeting place.
Its walls aglow, a beacon bright,
A marvel born of shadow and light.

By unseen will, it came and went,
Its fleeting presence a tale well-spent.
But skies grew dark, and fate took hold,
A spell was cast, both fierce and bold.
The magic surged, a force untamed,
And to the void, the house was claimed.
No more to stand on mortal land,
Lost forever, like slipping sand."

"What does it mean?" Eddie said.
"Let's go to Bertram's. You can get your drink,
and I'll tell you," I said.

Chapter 34

The French Quarter stirred as the city awoke, blissfully unaware of the darkness still brewing in the Quarter. As we left Malik's house, parking Josie's Range Rover near Bertram's, a drizzling mist hung in the air. With Eliza in tow, there was no gloom in our group as we entered the bar. When Bertram saw Eliza, he hurried from behind the bar and hugged her.

"Baby, what in the hell happened to you?"

Eliza was still sobbing and had yet to speak since Nyx, Rene, and Marceline had rescued her.

"I forgot you knew Eliza from the summer she worked as an intern for the DOJ," Eddie said.

"Hell yes, I know her," Bertram said. "Take her to my guest bathroom. Get her cleaned up and dress her in some clean clothes. I'll have breakfast ready when you get back."

Hope, Nyx, and Josie hustled Eliza through the door to Bertram's suite of rooms behind the bar as Bertram poured Eddie a scotch and me a lemonade. Hope soon returned to the bar.

"Eliza's a mess," she said. "We need some drinks."

"Coming right up," Bertram said. "She going to be okay?"

"We cleaned and dressed her wounds, washed away the grime, and dressed her in the comfort of clean clothes. I believe she's going to survive."

"Good deal," Bertram said.

When they returned to the bar, Eliza looked more than presentable. She was glowing. Her flaming red hair was braided, and she wore a denim miniskirt and yellow gingham blouse. Her tears were gone, and she had a smile on her face.

"Now that's the Eliza I remember," Bertram said.

"Something smells wonderful," Hope said. "What's cooking?"

"Andouille Sausage and shrimp etouffée omelets," he said. "Fluffy and golden, stuffed with savory and spicy fillings, topped with freshly chopped scallions, and my world-famous cheese grits, creamy and rich, served in bowls with a dollop of melted butter and a hint of garlic."

"Bertram, you are so awesome. Why the hell aren't you married?" Hope asked.

"I got Miss Lady and don't need a wife," he said. "Besides, except for Wyatt, none of you galoots have ever been married."

"Picky, picky," Hope said. "I'm digging in."

No one spoke as we ate breakfast. A few customers had begun filling the bar, Bertram busy taking orders and mixing drinks.

When we'd finished eating, Eddie said, "Now tell us what the poem means."

"You nailed it the last time we visited La Porte Mystique," I said.

"I did? I don't remember, so tell me," he said.

"Calypso's poem is a prophecy and tells us how to get rid of the disappearing house," I said.

"How so?" Eddie said.

"Magic," I said. "Madam Elzora's magic."

Hope sat her fork on the empty plate and said, "How's magic going to rid us of the disappearing house?"

"New Orleans, especially the Quarter, is a hub connecting planes of reality. Rene showed me as much. His In-Between is a parallel version of the French Quarter that can only be accessed by magic."

"What's the In-Between?" Eliza asked.

"A place where the past, the present, and the could-have-been all bleed together," I said. "Only a special few even know it exists."

"How is Madam Elzora going to help?" Josie asked.

"By casting a spell for us," I said.

"You think she has the power to affect reality?" Hope asked.

"Why not?" I said. "Mathematicians can send a spacecraft to the Moon by programing an algorithm. Change the algorithm, and the spaceship will go to Mars," I said.

"What's your point?" Eddie asked.

"Hell, I can barely spell algorithm, much less know how to use one. The point is that someone does, and someone, namely Madam Elzora, knows how to use magic to achieve a purpose."

"It won't hurt to try," Eddie said.

"Nothing except my pocketbook," Josie said.

"Madam Elzora doesn't want your money," I said. "Just your most treasured possessions."

"Hey," Nyx said. "That's what makes the world go round."

"I'm game," Eddie said. "Can someone please stay with Eliza?"

"Sis and I will keep her company," Hope said. "Go knock yourself out."

Eddie clutched Eliza's hand. "Will you be okay?"

Eliza hugged him and said, "Thanks to you, Uncle Eddie, I'm good to go. Can I borrow your phone?"

Eddie handed her his cell phone and said, "Hot date?"

She smiled and said, "I'm calling Mom."

When we left Bertram's, steady rain replaced the drizzling mist. I returned inside to borrow an umbrella, and we huddled beneath it as we walked to La Porte Mystique. The gloomy weather had dampened the number of tourists exploring the Quarter. When we reached the botanica, we found it devoid of customers.

The bell above the botanica's door jingled as Eddie, Josie, and I entered La Porte Mystique. The air was heavy with the earthy scent of dried herbs and burning incense, mingling with the faint metallic tang of magic. Shelves lined with jars of mysterious powders and roots loomed over them, and vibrant voodoo dolls and talismans seemed to watch our every move.

Behind the counter, Madam Elzora emerged from the shadows. She was imposing, her dark eyes sharp and knowing, her skin like weathered mahogany. A brightly patterned scarf wrapped her head, and gold bracelets clinked softly on her wrists.

"Happy to see you again. Need an elixir or potion, or do you need the Madam to cast a dark spell for you?"

"More of the latter, Madam Elzora," I said.

She smiled, rubbed her hands together, and said, "I'm here to help. What sort of spell?"

"Maybe not a spell as much as magic," I said.

"Of course," she said. "White magic or the darker variety?"

She grinned when I said, "The magic we need is very black."

"Tell me," she said.

"There's a house in the Quarter—one that disappears and reappears—"

"Ah, the disappearing house," Elzora said, her voice gravelly but resonant. "The spirits whisper about it. What do you want me to do about this house?"

"Burn it to the ground," Eddie said.

Madam Elzora shook her head and said, "I can't do that."

Eddie looked at me and said, "Told you so."

"I don't have the power to destroy the disappearing house, though I can use my magic to shift its location to another place and time."

She nodded when Josie said, "Make it leave for good?"

"My magic isn't free," the old woman said.

Josie's hand reflexively brushed the gold ring on her middle finger. The same ring Eddie had given her long ago. Elzora's eyes flicked to it, narrowing.

"That ring," she said, her voice suddenly sharp. "It has history. Power. If you want me to help you, I will accept your ring as payment for my services."

Josie stiffened, her jaw tightening. She hesitated, glancing at Eddie, whose face betrayed no emotion. With a resigned sigh, she slipped the ring from her finger and placed it in Elzora's waiting palm. She glanced at Eddie with a wry grin.

"You can stop whining now about me not returning your ring," she said.

"I never said a word," he said.

Madam Elzora said nothing, only turning the ring over in her gnarled fingers. Then, with a sharp nod, she flipped the sign on the door to "Closed" and beckoned us to follow her through the black curtain behind the counter. It led us into a place even stranger than Madam Elzora's shop.

The room beyond was dark and otherworldly, a shrine bathed in flickering candlelight and creeping shadows. Vivid altar cloths draped the walls, and statuettes of saints and spirits stood guard. A painted vevé glistened on the floor, and the air seemed to hum with unseen energy.

Elzora motioned for us to sit and said, "My nephew Marcel will assist."

There were no chairs, and we sat on a colorful rug. Marcel, a young man with a wild Afro, appeared from the shadows, carrying a drum. His bare chest gleamed with sweat as he began to beat a hypnotic rhythm. Josie clutched my hand and squeezed as Elzora's voice rose in a low chant, her words indecipherable but resonant, vibrating deep in her chest.

The tempo of Marcel's drumming quickened, the candles flickering wildly, and shadows beginning to dance across the walls. Elzora moved with a frenetic energy, her chanting rising to a crescendo.

"Shadows rise, and secrets waken,
Veils of night by whispers shaken.
Through the mists, reveal the guise,
A house unseen by mortal eyes.
By moonlit thread and spirit's vow,
Show what's hidden, here and now!"

The wavering outline of the disappearing house appeared in the candlelight, ghostly and translucent. Josie gasped, clutching my arm as the image grew more distinct, hovering like a mirage.

"Echoes call where time stands still,

Through cursed ground and spirit's will.
Walls of shadow, windows bare,
Return to light from empty air.
Bound by power, sealed by fate,
Reveal thy truth—illuminate!"

Otherworldly spirits began filling the dark room, lacing through the shadows, lowering the temperature by twenty degrees. I could feel Josie's shivers as she huddled close, clutching my arm. The translucent spirits morphed into vampires with bloody fangs and demons breathing fire.

"By blood and flame, by shadows flight,
I banish fear, invoke the light.
Through cursed veil, let vision break,
Truths arise for all at stake.
Bound no longer, spirits yield,
Reveal the house—the past unsealed!"

Marcel's drumming, by now almost earsplitting, crescendoed. The spirits and demons sputtered and disappeared, replaced by the flickering vision of the disappearing house.

Madam Elzora's voice echoed off the walls. "Spirits of time and place, take what does not belong!"

When a clap of thunder shook the botanica, the candles flickered and died, leaving us in total darkness except for the shimmering image of the disappearing house floating around the room, over our heads. Then, with a deafening crack, the image of the disappearing house imploded, dissolving into a puff of gray smoke.

Josie leaned closer to me, squeezing my arm as the acrid scent of burning sulfur filled the room and the sound of a sinking ship bubbling below the ocean's ominous surface. The noise and chaos suddenly ceased, and the candles filled the room with flickering light.

Without a word, Marcel picked up his drum and disappeared through the black curtain. It wasn't yet over for Madam Elzora.

The air hung heavy, charged with the weight of unseen eyes as Madam Elzora lowered her hands, her voice trembling with both reverence and exhaustion. The flickering candles on the voodoo shrine before us cast jagged shadows against the walls, dancing wildly as if the spirits themselves were moving among them.

Madam Elzora bowed her head, her voice a low murmur. "Loas and saints, forgive my trespass. Accept my humble offering as a token of my repentance and devotion."

Reaching into the folds of her dress, she retrieved Josie's ring. The simple gold band caught the light, its surface gleaming as though imbued with its own otherworldly energy. Turning to the shrine, Madam Elzora held the ring aloft, her hands trembling slightly, before placing it on a velvet cloth embroidered with mystical symbols.

For a breathless moment, nothing happened. The room felt suspended in time, the very air unmoving. Then, a resonant hum began to fill the room, emanating from the shrine itself. The candles flared bright, their flames stretching upward unnaturally before dimming as a curl of smoke rose from the ring.

With a sharp pop, the ring vanished, leaving a puff of gray smoke that spiraled upward before dissipating. Josie gasped, clutching my arm tighter as her eyes widened in disbelief. Eddie's hand instinctively moved to his chest as though trying to steady the rapid pounding of his heart.

"What just happened?" Josie asked.

Madam Elzora turned to face us, her expression serene but solemn. "The spirits have accepted the offering. Their blessings and forgiveness are ours. The deed is done."

As the room fell silent, the lingering scent of smoke and incense mingled with the cold air, and the shadows seemed to retreat, leaving us to stare at the shrine in a mixture of wonder and unease.

Exhausted, Madam Elzora slumped against the altar, her breathing labored.

My ears rang as we sat in stunned silence, the realization washing over us like a tide. Josie opened her mouth to speak, but Elzora raised a hand, silencing her.

As we left the botanica, the air outside seemed lighter, the world brighter. Just as we were about to step away, Calypso, the raven perched near the doorway, cawed ominously.

"Beware, what is gone may still leave its mark."

The bird's eyes glittered with an intelligence that sent a chill up my spine.

It was pouring rain, a late April thunderstorm gripping the French Quarter as we huddled beneath Bertram's umbrella, Eddie and Josie's moods elevated. They both soon noticed that mine was still melancholy.

"What's the matter?" Josie asked.

"You saved Eliza's life, and I couldn't be happier," Eddie said. "With the disappearing house gone for good, everything looks rosy. Why are you so gloomy?"

"My grandfather's ghost," I said. "I need to deal with it and don't know where to go from here."

"Eddie and I were discussing your problem and may have a solution," Josie said.

"You do?"

"There's a woman in Chalmette," Eddie said. "She and her husband are partners in the dog training facility on the island, and they visit often."

"And?"

"She's a traiteur, a Cajun witch. She and Odette, my hotel manager, banished the ghosts in the Oyster Island lighthouse and the Majestic Hotel that I own."

"Can they do the same for my grandfather's ghost?" I asked.

"I'll call them when we get to Bertram's," Eddie said.

"I need a drink," Josie said.

Eddie nodded and said, "I need an entire bottle.

They laughed when I said, "What I need is a long nap."

Chapter 35

I was more tired than I thought, and my nap lasted longer than anticipated. When I awoke and went downstairs, I did so to the applause of a group of friends and a few people I didn't recognize congregated at the bar. Eddie was smiling and applauding the loudest.

"We've been waiting for you and were betting whether or not you'd come downstairs tonight," he said. "I have someone I want you to meet."

Two attractive women flanked Eddie. Both had dark eyes, though one was blond and the other a brunette.

"I'm Wyatt Thomas," I said.

"These two lovely ladies are Odette Mouton and Paula Boutet. Odette is the manager of the Majestic Hotel. I'd be lost without her. Paula and her husband, Jimmy, are partners in the island's dog training facility. She's also a traiteur."

"Pleased to meet you," I said, shaking their hands. "Eddie tells me you banished the ghosts in the island's lighthouse and hotel."

"Paula's a ghost whisperer," Odette said. "She convinces them to cross over peacefully."

Paula smiled and said, "We needed help with the Majestic ghosts. "They weren't exactly benevolent."

"Paula and Odette are going to convince your grandfather to cross over," Eddie said.

"Whoa!" I said. "If you can accomplish that, I'll forever be in your debt."

Paula stood two inches taller than Odette. They were both attractive, although Odette was a stunner. When Bertram appeared from the back, both women embraced him.

"You know these two attractive ladies?" I asked.

"Yessir, I do. I've known Paula and her hubby, Jimmy, for years. I only met Miss Odette when I visited Eddie's Island for the first time. Don't matter none 'cause I feel like I've known her forever."

"Bertram's a sweetheart. He's helped out at the hotel bar and restaurant several times now," Odette said.

"Paula's a traiteur," Bertram said. "A very special person."

"With special talents," Odette said.

"I prefer to call myself a sensitive," Paula said. "Ghosts and spirits are everywhere, though not everyone can see them. I can, and sometimes it's overwhelming."

"I'll bet," I said.

Odette and Paula were drinking martinis, and their moods were ebullient. Eliza was sitting at a table with Hope, Nyx, and Josie. Bertram had provided their table with a bucket of unpeeled shrimp, and they looked like they were enjoying themselves while working through them. Newspaper covered the table, where the crew was putting the husked shells.

"Where do you find newspaper anymore," I asked. "I thought they were all out of business."

"It ain't easy," Bertram said. "If it keeps going like it is, I'll soon have to use butcher paper instead of newspaper when I do a shrimp boil."

"Let's hope it never gets to that," I said.

"I'm taking Paula over to Bourbon to show her the club where I used to work," Odette said. "We'll be back in an hour or so."

"We'll be here," Eddie said.

When Odette and Paula were gone, I said, "Odette worked in the French Quarter?"

"Put herself through college by working as a stripper," Eddie said.

"I can see how," I said. "She's gorgeous."

"My business wouldn't last a week without her, so don't get any ideas," Eddie said.

"Just looking," I said.

"Make sure that's all you do," he said.

"I hear you," I said.

"I've invited the crew for a complimentary stay at the Majestic," Eddie said. "Nyx and Hope are taking me up on it."

"Who is going to watch the Eden Club?" I asked.

"Hope has a manager, and Rene, Marceline, and Malik are going to help," Eddie said.

"That'll be a hoot," I said. "I'd like to be there when one of the weekend warriors invites Marceline to exchange blood."

"Me too," Eddie said.

"What about Lucien?" I asked.

"The vampire is gone," Eddie said.

"But not his brain," I said. "What about Victor Marigny?"

"The person with Lucien's brain is human and won't find it easy to elude justice. Whatever, it's no longer my problem."

"You aren't worried about NGS?" I asked.

313

"When I turn over Lavoie's secret file to the Justice Department, they'll soon be sucking air," Eddie said. "What about you? Take a week off and enjoy a vacation on me. I owe you one, and you deserve it."

"I don't know," I said.

"Come on," Eddie said. "Loosen that tight ass of yours and take a break. The island's wonderful."

"Maybe," I said.

I was alone for a moment, and Nyx joined me. "Got a minute?" she said.

"You know I do," I said. "What's up?"

"Hope and I are taking a holiday on Oyster Island," she said.

"Eddie told me. After everything you've been through, you deserve it." I squeezed her hand and said, "Eliza wouldn't be free if it weren't for you. You're a hero in my book."

"I never told you, but I was engaged to be married."

"Oh?" I said.

"James Edward called me last week. We talked."

"And," I said.

"We're going to try and make another go of it. He's meeting me on Oyster Island. After a week, I should know if he loves me."

"I'm happy for you," I said.

"I was hoping you'd talk me out of it," she said.

"My apartment's small, but why don't you move your stuff over?"

"Do you love me?" she said. When I hesitated, she said, "You don't. I see that."

"I'm not asking you to marry me, just to live with me," I said.

Nyx smiled and kissed me. "It was fun, Wyatt Thomas. Your apartment's way too small for the two of us."

Nyx's rejection was like a slap in the face. I was still smarting when Josie joined me.

"What's the matter?" she asked. "You look stressed."

"Not enough sleep lately," I said.

"That's not it. Everything's working out for you. Why do you seem so glum?"

"I haven't been dumpster diving with a beautiful woman lately," I said.

"That was fun," she said. "Did Eddie tell you Nyx and Hope are spending a week on Oyster Island?"

"He told me," I said.

"You're between cases. Why don't you join us?" she said.

"Nyx told me her former fiancée is joining her," I said. "It might get awkward."

"Forget Nyx," she said. "Hope and I will be all the women you need. Will you think about it?"

"Of course," I said.

Josie kissed me and said, "We're leaving now. Join us if you get the chance."

Josie, Hope, and Nyx waved as they disappeared out the front door. Eddie and Eliza soon followed. Bertram handed me a lemonade.

"Now what?" he asked.

"I just went from having too many girlfriends to having none at all," I said.

"A blow to your ego?" he asked.

"A little bit," I said.

"What about Odette?"

"Eddie told me to keep my hands off of her," I said.

I laughed when he said, "Since when have you ever listened to Eddie?"

I didn't have time to answer, Odette and Paula walking in the door, returning from where they had been.

"The time is right," Paula said. "First, I need to visit the ladies room."

I was left alone with Odette. Standing close enough to her to touch, I could see how attractive she was.

"Paula's intense," I said.

"She's more than a traiteur; she's a witch," Odette said.

"Is that a bad thing?" I asked.

"Paula would kill me if she knew I had told you."

"Because?" I said.

"She doesn't trust men. Says they're all chauvinists."

"Even her husband?" I asked.

Odette giggled. "In all the years she and Jimmy have been married, he's never once seen her naked in the full light."

"That seems unusual," I said. "Why is that?"

"She has a witch's tit and doesn't want Jimmy to know she's a witch," Odette said.

"What's a witch's tit?" I asked.

Odette lifted her tee shirt, baring her chest. She pointed to a bump beneath her left breast.

"A witch's tit is an extra nipple that every witch has. I have one, and for years, I thought it was a mole."

She grinned when I said, "I'm sorry, what did you say?"

"I was a titty dancer at a strip club not far from here. Men liked looking at my titties, and I got used to them seeing me naked. Sorry."

I smiled and said, "Guilty as charged."

"That's not all," Odette said. "Paula has one blue eye and one dark one. She wears a contact to make people think both of her eyes are the same color."

Odette nodded when I said, "Is that a mark of being a witch?"

"She's paranoid about people knowing," she said.

"Because?" I asked.

Odette grinned and said, "Guess she doesn't want to be burned at the stake."

Paula returned as Odette was pulling up her tee shirt.

"Odette and I are going to the cemetery. Can you give us directions to your family crypt?"

"The cemetery isn't safe at night," I said.

"Maybe not, but it's the best time to perform the crossing ceremony," Paula said.

"Then I'll go with you," I said.

Paula nodded and said, "Let's go."

The night was heavy with the scent of damp earth and night-blooming jasmine as Paula, Odette, and I crossed the French Quarter to the St. Louis No. 1 Cemetery. A gossamer mist curled around our ankles, snaking through the wrought-iron entrance gate.

"This gate is locked at night, but I have a key," I said.

"How did you rate that?" Odette asked.

"I didn't," I said. "I acquired it by midnight acquisition."

"You stole it?" Paula asked.

She smiled when I said, "Borrowed it."

The heavy iron gate clanked when we entered the cemetery, and I shut it behind us. The ground fog followed us, spreading across the graves like an ethereal tide. Overhead, puffy clouds all but cloaked the moon, which hung low and full.

The light was fractured by the sprawling branches of ancient live oaks draped with Spanish moss. The live oaks loomed like silent sentinels, their silhouettes swaying gently in the cool breeze, which carried the faintest whispers of voices—real or imagined.

Paula clutched a string of prayer beads and a brass lantern, its flickering glow casting restless shadows that danced along the rows of weathered tombstones.

"How much further?" she asked.

"Not far," I said. "Just up the path."

The pathway was narrow and uneven, choked with weeds and broken branches. Our footsteps crunched softly against the gravel, echoing louder than they should have in the cemetery's profound silence. The crypts on either side seemed to press closer, their cracked facades weeping streaks of mildew and time.

Marble angels with chipped wings and headless saints stood as mournful guardians, their hollow eyes following us as we moved deeper into the maze of tombs. Paula paused, her head tilting as if listening to something only she could hear.

"The spirits are restless tonight," she said. "Too many lost souls, too many stories unfinished."

Odette shifted uncomfortably. "Let's hope none of them are looking for company."

As we approached the family crypt, the air seemed to thicken. The once-subtle breeze disappeared entirely, replaced by an oppressive stillness that pressed against our chests.

The lantern's glow grew dim, its light barely reaching the ornate and rusting iron door of the crypt, which had the name Thomas carved into its arch. A pair of stone urns flanked the entrance, overflowing with wild vines that looked more dead than active. Paula raised her hand, her breath visible in the sudden chill that swept over them.

"Here," she said, her voice a whisper. "Are you ready?"

"Yes," I said.

"We need you for one thing only. When Odette and I are ready, you must call for your grandfather. When he appears, you must disappear into the shadows. Got it?"

I nodded and said, "Got it."

"If I need you, I'll call. Do as I say, and don't try to interfere," she said.

She smiled when I said, "I'm hip."

I backed into the shadows as Odette and Paula began removing their clothes. They started to dance in a way that was at once both sensuous and surreal. There was no music, no drumming, though the limbs on the trees surrounding the crypt seemed to move with them, as did the puffy clouds floating overhead.

When they stopped dancing, Paula reached into her backpack and removed two black garments, tossing one set to Odette. Odette and Paula pulled the black dresses over their heads. When Paula lit the black candle in her hand, we immediately heard an earsplitting shriek that echoed through the cemetery. Paula faced the crypt and raised her arms.

"I've lit the spirit candle. Its smoke will help you cross over."

Odette and Paula stepped back when a snarling demon appeared in a puff of smoke.

"Who summons me?" the demon said.

The smoke from the candle wafted sideways as if controlled by a supernatural force. Paula moved closer to the demon.

"You are no demon," Paula said. "You are Charles Wyatt Thomas."

I stood mortified in the shadows as the demon began to transform into the ghost of my grandfather. When it had fully transformed, it let out a blood-curdling wail.

"Who are you?" he asked.

"Kindred spirit here to help you cross," Paula said.

"I can't cross over," the ghost said.

"Yes, you can," Paula said. "You have a consecrated grave with your name on it. You were laid to rest in a Christian ceremony. You are no longer part of this world. Cross over now and experience eternal peace."

"I can't," the ghost said.

"Why not?" Paula said.

"I didn't accomplish my goals, and only one person can do that for me now."

I stepped out of the shadows when Paula called me. The spirit's stare burned into my soul.

"Grandpa, it's Wyatt," I said.

"I have plans for you," the ghost said.

"Lucien was responsible for killing you," I said. "We banished him. He and his evil are gone."

Paula reached down and scooped up a handful of dirt. "No one lives forever. This is hallowed ground. It's time to cross over, and this sacred soil will hasten your departure."

Thunder clapped, and the lantern flickered as Paula tossed the dirt at the spirit. An explosion occurred when the dirt struck my grandfather's spirit, raising a tornado of forceful wind that blew us to the ground. When the motion ceased, my grandfather's spirit was gone. Paula and Odette helped me to my feet.

"It's done," Paula said. "He's crossed, God bless his soul."

Epilog

Things don't always go as planned. I had helped Eddie rescue his niece Eliza, and now they were going to Oyster Island. Lucien D'Arcy, thanks to Madam Elzora, had been banished to a new plane of reality. Lastly, my grandfather's ghost had crossed over, his soul forever free. I should have been happy; I wasn't, and Bertram noticed.

"I seen that look before," he said.

"What look?"

"Like a puppy that just realized he was alone in a big house with no one to play with."

"I'm a grown man, not a puppy. I'm fine."

"You know what they say; there's plenty of fish in the sea. You'll find another woman," he said.

"Hell, Bertram, I wouldn't know a good woman if she kicked me in the ass."

"That's a fact," he said.

"You don't have to agree with me."

"Maybe your problem is that earring," he said.

"If that's what you think, maybe you should see my new tattoo."

Bertram shook his head and said, "You going hippie on me?"

"There are no more hippies anymore," I said.

I unbuttoned my shirt when he said, "Show me this new tattoo." He stared and said, "What the hell is it?"

"The Crimson Sigil," I said. "I'm probably the only person on earth with one of these who's not a vampire."

Bertram shook his head in disbelief. "Go upstairs and get some sleep. You'll feel better tomorrow."

"You kidding? I've had enough sleep for a week. It might be a while before I hit the sack again," I said.

The storm outside had turned the French Quarter into a wailing symphony of wind and rain. Thunder rumbled low and ominous, vibrating through the floorboards of Bertram's bar. Inside, my mood was as heavy as the weather.

"Cheer up," Bertram said. "The weather's affecting you. It'll get better."

The door swung open, letting in a gust of wet wind and a flash of lightning. A striking woman strode in, her silhouette framed dramatically against the storm outside. She wore a sleek coat that shimmered in the dim light, and her shoulder-length blond hair fell in damp waves that only seemed to enhance her allure. Her piercing blue eyes swept the room before landing on Bertram and me.

Ever the host, Bertram set down his towel and leaned casually on the bar.

"What're you drinking, pretty lady?" he asked, his grin as warm as his drawl.

She tilted her head, her sapphire earrings catching the light as she smiled.

"Surprise me."

Bertram nodded knowingly and began mixing something with flair, but his gaze flicked toward me.

"So, what brings a beautiful woman like you to New Orleans on a night like this?" he asked, sliding a colorful cocktail across the bar.

She took the drink, swirled it once, and sipped before answering.

"Looking for Wyatt Thomas," she said, her voice smooth but firm, the kind that didn't waver under pressure. Then she added, "Have you seen him?"

Bertram chuckled, leaning closer to me with a wink, and said, "He's sitting right beside you."

The storm outside raged on, but something had shifted in the room. The heavy air had lightened, and my thoughts changed from melancholy to curiosity.

The striking woman smiled, shook my hand, and said, "I'm Delta. Delta Becht, Eddie Toledo's law partner."

"Happy to meet you, Delta. The Cajun bartender here is the illustrious Bertram Picou."

She glanced at Bertram and said, "This cocktail is wonderful. What is it?"

"Tequila sunrise," he said.

"Love it," she said. "Eddie told me you were the best mixologist in New Orleans."

"He would know," Bertram said.

"I was coming here to meet him when he called and told me he was returning to the island."

"Then why didn't you turn around?" I asked.

"Because we have a problem on the island, and Eddie said you could help. I was almost here and decided to ask you in person."

"I just helped pull his chestnuts out of the fire," I said. "Now, what's he got himself into?"

She smiled, her gaze locking with mine. "A voodoo woman has moved into an abandoned mansion on Oyster Island. Strange things have begun since she did."

323

"Voodoo?" I said.

"It's bad, Wyatt. Eddie and I need you," she said. "Will you come to the island and help us?"

Bertram whistled softly, already knowing my answer. Feeling better than I had all day, I smiled and nodded, the storm brewing outside suddenly feeling more like a prelude than an ending.

"Delta," I said. "I wouldn't miss it for the world."

End

Book Notes

In *Night People*, I brought back one of the original *French Quarter Mystery* characters in Eddie Toledo. Eddie first appeared in Book 2, *City of Spirits*. His absence resulted when I spun off the *Oyster Bay Mystery Series*. Eddie acquired the Prohibition Era Majestic Hotel and Casino from mob boss Frankie Castellano.

Several characters from the original series, most notably Bertram Picou and J.P. Saucier, have crossed over and appeared in the island series. However, until now, no Oyster Bay Mystery Series characters have appeared in a French Quarter Mystery Series book. At least until *Night People*.

I hope you enjoyed reading *Night People* and that you enjoyed the characters from both series. I hope you'll read all my *French Quarter Mystery Series* books featuring moody private detective Wyatt Thomas.

You might also like my *Paranormal Cowboy Series*, which features Buck McDivit, my modern-day cowboy detective who likes horses, cowgirls, and Australian sheepdogs. Hopefully, you're already a fan of the *Oyster Bay Mystery Series*, set on a Louisiana island near New Orleans. In *Oyster Bay Mambo*, Wyatt visits the island to help Eddie with a problem involving a mysterious Haitian voodoo woman.

Thanks for being a fan. My stories would be little more than morning fog wafting across a forgotten lawn without beautiful readers like you. Thank you.

About the Author

Eric Wilder is an American author known for his gripping mystery novels set in New Orleans. He was born and raised in Louisiana, where he discovered his love for storytelling at a young age. After completing his education, Wilder spent several years in the oil and gas industry before pursuing a career as a writer.

Wilder's breakthrough came with the publication of Big Easy, which introduced readers to his signature blend of suspense, action, and local color. The book instantly succeeded, drawing critical acclaim and a devoted following. Wilder followed up with a collection of thrillers set in the heart of New Orleans.

Wilder's writing is characterized by his deep knowledge of the city and its unique culture and his skillful use of suspense and plot twists to keep readers on the edge of their seats. His books have been praised for their authenticity, vivid descriptions, and compelling characters.

Today, Eric Wilder is a respected author with a loyal fan base and a reputation for delivering top-notch thrillers that transport readers to the heart of New Orleans.

Wilder is the author of twenty novels, several cookbooks, many short stories, and Murder

Etouffee, a book that defies classification. His series features characters who often find themselves involved in the paranormal.

Eric Wilder lives in Oklahoma near historic Route 66 with his wife, Marilyn and their two dogs, Moe and Buddy.

www.ingramcontent.com/pod-product-compliance
Lightning Source LLC
Chambersburg PA
CBHW011431240626
47153CB00011B/2929